TOUGH TARGET

TOUGH TARGET

a Novel by

LEE BROWN

First Printing, 2016

ISBN 978-1-944256-00-5

2E Publishing
P.O. Box 5
Floyd, NM 88118
www.2epublishing.com

Ordering Information:

Individual or quantity sales. Special discounts are available on quantity purchases of more than five copies. For details, contact the publisher via the info above.

Printed in the United States of America

First Edition

1   2   3   4   5   6   7   8   9   20   19   18   17   16

To my Mom, for teaching me how to read.

To my Dad, for teaching me what to read.

"And he saith unto them, Follow me, and I will make you fishers of men."

- Matthew 4:19

BOOK 1
Bait

1

New Mexico

CASS ELKINS took a deep breath and waited for the signal. The scenario was simple. Eighteen hostiles, two hostages, and she was the one-man rescue team.

The strategy was straight forward. Get in, shoot the bad guys, don't shoot the hostages, and definitely don't miss.

Easy enough. The trick was being fast. She figured twenty seconds. That's what it would take.

There were three loaded magazines on her left hip and on her right was a Desert Eagle. Eight plus one rounds of magnum force. Cocked, locked, and ready to rock.

The competition had more rounds, more reliable guns and a heck of a lot less recoil. She had accuracy and knockdown power, but that didn't do a bit of good this close in. A tight smile made it to her lips. A challenge.

After a few long seconds, she got the go ahead. She threw open the door, pulled the gun, and ran inside. As soon as it was up, and before both feet had touched the ground past the threshold, she was pulling the trigger. She put two rounds into the foreheads of the nearest targets, each pair of bullets sent downrange with no more than a quarter-second between. Rounding a corner, she ducked low and fired four more shots. Four targets hit in half as many seconds and two of them were now flat on the ground. All visible threats cleared, she made her way down a hall towards another door. Moving fast, she shoved in a new magazine. A small window gave her shots at four more hostiles. She emptied another magazine into them before reloading and making it to the end of the corridor.

Out of the hall now, she faced five targets. She put a bullet into the first one and the others started moving before she got another shot off. Undaunted, she used the rest of that magazine, missing only twice, and dispatched the troublesome targets, knocking them all to the ground. At last she reached the room where the hostages were being held. The three remaining bad guys were taking cover behind their captives. One of them had only part of his head showing. Cass put in her last magazine, concentrated on her trigger finger, and fired six times. The man on the left got two in the head, the right guy got two in the heart and the one on the middle took a round between the eyes. Cass growled at herself when she saw that the last bullet had hit one of the hostages in the head. Too much trigger finger.

"If you are finished, unload and show clear."

2

New Mexico

CASS BARELY HEARD THE COMMAND, but she fol-
lowed it quickly. She ejected the magazine, racked the slide to
throw the round out of the chamber, and locked it back so the
range official could verify that the firearm was now clear and
unloaded.

"Ok, slide down, hammer down, and holster."

She dropped the slide, pulled the trigger, and without looking, slid the gun into the holster.

"Range is clear." Esteban looked at the shot timer. "One-
eight point eight-one. Not bad, but I've seen you do better."

"I guess I'm a little off today." Cass shrugged in the direction of the unlucky hostage.

Stephen walked around the wooden barricade to the first
target and started calling off shots. He went to each of the ten
paper targets and yelled, "Two alpha," at each stop. Both hits
in the A-zone, the top scoring area. She winced when he got to
the hostage setup and changed his pattern. "Alpha..." he paused,
searching, then finished with a surprised tone, "Alpha, mike,

and a no-shoot. Looks like one of the prisoners ain't making it home."

When he had finished marking the score sheet, he brought it over for her to initial. "Nineteen A's, one miss, all steel, and one no-shoot. Looks like your brother's gonna beat you today, kid."

"No shame in that, I reckon." Cass initialed the score. "I'll get 'im next time."

She moseyed back over to where the rest of the shooters were waiting and watching. Her younger brother was grinning from ear to ear, just waiting to rub in his victory.

"Hey sis! Nice shootin." Heath Elkins gave her an affectionate elbow.

She smiled at him and returned the gesture. Despite her mistakes, the score was very respectable. She could shoot. Nobody cared to argue that.

"How's Shorty doin'?" Cass's little sister, Glenn, was shooting on a different squad.

"Shootin' steel and takin' names," he said. "As usual."

"Always said she was the meanest of all of us."

Heath took a long swig of soda and asked, "So, you wanna find somethin' to eat later? I'm hungry."

"Sure. Where?"

"How 'bout El Rancho? Spicy Fajitas are the special tonight. Your favorite."

"Sounds like a plan. Meet you there at eight?"

"You bet." He turned away. "I'll let the munchkin know so she won't get mad at us."

Cass replied absently and retreated into her thoughts. She was enjoying herself. Spending time with her family...shooting stuff. Life was pretty good. Hard to argue with it.

But she always tried.

3

New Mexico

STOMACH FULL OF FAJITAS, Cass followed her family out of the restaurant into the night. She nodded to her sister who was holding the door. "Thanks."

"You're welcome." Glenn's reply was equal parts genuine and sarcastic.

Once outside, the Elkins family stood around Cass's motorcycle and refused to shiver in the evening chill.

"You're welcome to spend the night here." Cass's mother put her hands in her pockets. "It'll be cold on that motorcyle."

Cass smiled and nodded. "I'll be fine. Thanks."

"You sure?"

"Yeah, if I don't' get back tonight, I won't get anything done tomorrow. You know."

Her mother nodded. "Okay, if that's what you want to do, be sure and call me when you get there."

"I will." Cass hugged each member of her family, before stepping back and throwing her leg over her motorcycle. She reached into one of the saddlebags for a scarf and a pair of clear goggles. "I'll see ya'll later. Love ya." She walked the motorcycle back and waved once to her family before she pulled out onto the street. She waited until she was out past the last stoplight before she kicked into high gear.

It was ninety-seven miles from El Rancho to the Two-E Ranch, but after the first twenty, there was no traffic, just long stretches of almost straight highway. Two-lanes, barely, but plenty good for her two wheels to drive more than a little faster than the posted limit.

She enjoyed driving at night, especially alone. The cold air was refreshing and the moon was bright enough to illuminate everything just enough to see, but not enough to distract. It certainly made the miles of dry grass look less depressing. Only the burned patches where fires had charred the ground to black stayed the same. In the moonlight, it was even blacker.

Cass concentrated on the cool air and the road.

A little less than two hours later, she pulled off the highway onto a dirt road and stopped to get the gate. She pulled the key out of her pocket, opened the padlock, and removed the chain. She walked the bike through and closed and locked the gate behind her. The cycle threw the dry dirt up in a thick cloud in the still, early morning air. She was almost home.

Ten more minutes of winding trails called roads and she pulled the bike into her barn and killed it. She pulled her gun case out of the saddle bag and closed the barn before walking up to the house.

Situated in a small draw on the edge of a mesa, the simple ranch house was hidden from three angles and towards the west it faced the sheer drop-off into the valley. It had been built by someone who was reasonably paranoid. Cass approved. The house's covered porch wrapped all the way around and as she stepped up on the deck, three dogs rounded the corner and started fighting for her attention. They were not quite mutt, but not really anything pure either. One was definitely cowdog, one was mostly sheep-dog, and the third was absolutely worthless. They pushed up against her legs, wagging tails and barking. She slapped her thigh with her free hand and the cowdog, Millie, lightly jumped up and leaned on Cass's leg, the dog's head just the perfect height for Cass's hand. Cass rubbed it until the sheep-dog, Bear, pushed the other dog aside with his big head and took his share of head-rubbing. The third one, Tripper, lived up to her name and planted herself on Cass's feet until Cass rolled her over and started scratching her belly with the toe of her boot.

Millie jumped on Bear's head, trying to get back in the game and Cass stepped over Tripper to the door. The dogs protested, wanting more attention, as always, but Cass left them and entered the house.

She navigated the dark hall with ease until she got to the kitchen. She flipped the light on and dropped the gun case on the table where it joined a pile of papers and a couple of empty coffee mugs. Despite the late--or early--hour, Cass was wide awake. She hated sleep and hated waiting for it even more. She tossed the grounds out of her coffee press over the porch railing and set a pan of water to boiling on the stove.

While the water heated, she turned on her computer and waited for it to boot up. She needed a new one, but until this one consistently started demonstrating the blue screen of death, she had better things to spend borrowed money on. Like feed.

And ammo.

Before the computer was ready, the water boiled and she poured it over the fresh grounds in the press. She grabbed a knife off the cabinet and stirred the black mixture before putting the lid on and letting it brew.

The computer was ready, and she opened the browser. The home page was news and she skimmed the headlines. There was nothing good, and very little even interesting. The inauguration was approaching and there were lots of details on who would be attending, who would not be there, and who the entertainment would be. She didn't care--about it, or for the man.

Cass's political view was simple. Less is more. She didn't care about all the social issues of the day or whether a particular behavior was good or bad or what. She just wanted the feds to stay out of it.

Short of murder, injury, and maybe theft, rules just made lawyers rich and people sheep. Things were different in different places and sweeping laws that cover the whole country didn't make much sense because of that.

This was why Cass didn't like to read the news. All it did was make her angry and tired. But she couldn't abide ignorance either. A paradox that she hadn't found a good answer to. The best she could figure out was to read something fun after, get her mind off reality a little.

She poured herself a large cup of coffee and sat it down on the table by her recliner, next to the book she'd started two days ago. She returned to the computer to shut it down, but stopped when she saw the email notification. The browser window had been hiding it.

She didn't want to check, but she had to. Just as she had dreaded, it was from the accountant. He was coming out for a visit. She stabbed the power button on the computer and clenched her teeth. He was the last person on earth that she wanted to see.

He was the man who would take the ranch away.

4

Virginia

The house was hard to see from the road, the trees in this part of Virginia being good and thick and green. Even when it came into view, it conjured images of quaint farmers from an earlier age or retirement for a wealthy former D.C. official.

Dirk Chandler, former vice-president of the United States, saw the home of one very sneaky man.

He had burned the note inviting him here. Already primed with something flammable, it disappeared in a bright puff of flame in his ashtray. The Cowboy had always been a little theatrical--but no one was about to tell him that.

Chandler followed the gravel drive around behind the house and parked the car. The note had been short, but 'back door' was underlined--and unlocked. It was dark inside the house and he had to wait for his eyes to adjust before closing the door and following the hall to the living room. Just like always, he turned on the floor lamp, poured himself a drink from the cabinet, sat down in an antebellum leather chair, and waited.

Seven minutes later, the Cowboy arrived. He came around Chandler's chair, quiet on the carpet, and sat down in the matching seat in the corner facing the door. His hands were empty, but Chandler would bet a good deal that there were at least two or three deadly weapons within easy reach, maybe more.

Paranoid did not do the man justice.

Of course, there was no doubt that plenty of people were very much out to get him. The Cowboy had never been short on enemies. He would tell you he collected them--and he most likely meant it.

"Good morning, Dirk." The Cowboy spoke with the clipped speech of an eastern education, but Chandler had heard him adopt different accents and dialects as it suited him. The few people who knew he existed just called him the Cowboy---and why they called him that was unknown as well. Probably had to do with some old code name. Spooks did love their code names.

"Yes it is. But I have appointments with two different Presidents this afternoon. Can we skip to business?" Chandler tried not to sound impatient, but he was a busy man.

The Cowboy, never in a hurry, took a sip from the ornately-engraved, silver flask he kept in his pocket. He screwed the cap on and returned it to its home inside his lapel. Then, he opened the tabletop humidor next to his chair and fiddled with something inside before pulling out a large cigar. Chandler couldn't make out the label in the dim light, but it was undoubtedly very good.

The Cowboy bit the end off the cigar and spit it into the darkness. "We have a problem."

"What? With the operation? Which one?"

"All of them. The guy you wouldn't run against has been busy putting his personal idiots in too many places. Most of my operators have ties to one acronym or another and as fast as they're leaking information, I won't have a secure operator left by the time he takes the oath."

"Is it really that bad?"

"Two of my best guys were compromised last week. Yesterday one was killed and I had to scrap the operation they were on. I can't have this. Off-the-radar is the name of the game. Without it, we can't play the game."

"What can we do?" Chandler said.

The Cowboy stuck the cigar in his mouth and struck a match on his watchband. He held it up and puffed until the end was glowing. He threw the match in the same direction as the cigar tip.

Chandler watched the flame go out in midair.

The man was insane, without a doubt. But completely useless otherwise. He waited, watching the man blow smoke thoughtfully into the room. The smell was excellent.

"You said you didn't have time." The Cowboy blew a mouthful straight at his guest and smiled. "No cigar. Too busy. Your words."

Chandler didn't take the bait. He really didn't have the time. If he waited long enough the Cowboy would return to the topic.

The smile faded and the Cowboy tapped a finger on the cigar. "Start over."

"What?"

"That's all we can do. Is start over."

"Are you serious? It took a decade to get where we are. There must be an alternative? Something less severe."

"Nothing without holes, Dirk. The only way to guarantee security is if I take everything outside. No more normal channels."

"How are you going to pull that off?"

"No more operators with any government connections. Civilians and crooks. People who see authority and run the other way."

Chandler frowned. "That sounds like a lot of trouble."

The Cowboy smiled, cigar wagging in his mouth. "That's the idea."

"I'll get my people on it. Get you a list of possibles right away."

"No. You can't do a thing without the government crapping all over it. The people I need would smell it a mile away, and probably get off a few shots. Besides, finding them won't be that hard, bringing them in will be the trick." He leaned back and rubbed his forehead, making circles of smoke curl above his red and grey hair. "You know ol' Simon. I've always admired him.

"Simon who? The American Idol guy?"

"Naw, Simon in the Bible. The fisher of men. That's what I like to think of myself as these days. And I'm finally going after the tricky ones. The ones that see their fellows fooled by the lures and just laugh; the kind that ain't tempted by nothing but the real thing. You know what I'm sayin'?" The Cowboy's accent had drifted into something much more in line with his moniker.

"Less so than usual. But I take it to mean you have a plan."

"Let me put it this way--stink bait ain't gonna catch the fishes I'm looking for. No, it'll take live bait, bleeding and scared, to reel 'em in all the way."

"I don't think I need to hear any more."

"Right. The less you know, the better. I was doing this sort of thing long before I met you. I haven't forgotten how it works."

Chandler scowled at the reference to the past. "I'd rather not go there. Just remember where your interest lies now."

With a sly smile, the Cowboy nodded. "I'm your man."

5

Virginia

THE COWBOY WATCHED the former Vice-President leave and head back to the concrete and steel of Washington. A good enough man. Smart, reasonable, and ruthless enough to be useful. He liked Chandler, but he was still a politician. That was something that could never be fully trusted--or forgiven.

Cigar between his teeth, the Cowboy grabbed the laptop leaning against the side of his chair and used his passcodes to remotely log on to his workstation in the basement. Dobbs had setup a secure LAN for the house and the Cowboy had taken to leaving laptops lying around so that computer access was never far away.

The computer connected and he opened up a spreadsheet he'd had for a very long time. It was a list of possibles, frequently updated. He was always adding new names and crossing out old ones. The sort of people on this particular list were prone to getting crossed-off. That was the nature of the thing. That was why they were on the list.

Outliers, action-takers, crazy people. They got called a lot of different, less than complementary things, but he called them possibles. That was what they were. Walking, talking, potential. Men and women who did not know the meaning of the word impossible. At the moment, he had the list sorted by skill. He narrowed it down a little more by filtering out anyone in the game or even close to it. He wasn't looking for the obvious. He was looking for the opposite.

There were still many prospects to consider. He had access to multitudes of sensitive information. Databases and lists from every government agency and a few even more rarified. His favorite was a heavily encrypted database and the internal list of names, rarely used, and very illegal. People of interest; civilians who, for one reason or another, were considered more of a threat than the average citizen. The fact that the government kept track of them despite being law-abiding citizens of a supposedly free country was a truth that was closely kept. Heads would roll if it was ever confirmed to be more than a myth. Ironically, the very names on the list would be the ones most likely to do the chopping, but only because the list existed in the first place. It was a self-fulfilling prophecy. The government was scared of its people and liked to spy on them, the people were scared of the government spying, and so the vicious circle goes, winding tighter and tighter until someday, it would snap. That day was still in the future, but the Cowboy had no doubt it would come. That was just the way of things.

Today, he had other concerns. Like finding people crazy enough to trust.

He already had a list, but it was still too long. He narrowed it down further by looking for certain traits combined in the same person. Independent development of the skills he needed was a rare characteristic among the populace, but there were always exceptions--and he was always on the lookout.

Humanity was infinite in its diversity, but never fair or random. People would like to believe that they are unique and that the odds of being special are even. But in truth, there were always more sheep. That was the biggest flaw in any theory of natural selection. Logic may favor the strong, but chance favors the weak. And as a wise man once said, "better to be lucky that smart, any day."

It required a bit of both to find those certain people, the ones that chance overlooked. But the Cowboy didn't need any more practice. He ended up with a single page of names.

He manually encoded the list twice before sending it as an encrypted e-mail. He picked up the secure telephone on his desk, dialed a number from memory, and waited for the altered voice that answered on the second ring.

"Yello. Can I help you?" The voice was distorted like it was yelling over a chasm.

The Cowboy had already laid the groundwork for his plan. He had the facilities, a decent bankroll, and a paranoia-level that could be respected. The first of his new crew--and the last of the old. The one man wily enough to keep himself safe despite the security leaks.

"Alan, you need some sunshine?"

"Not really, but I know that's not the answer you're looking for. I haven't recovered from the last time you asked that. What do you want?"

The Cowboy laughed. Dobbs was a true geek, most comfortable amid his lair of hardware, but he was reliable and had proved to be remarkably trustworthy. And when it suited him, he made a decent spook. "I'm going to send you a list of names. Run down all the info you can on each of them and get it back to me as quick as you can. Think you can handle it?"

"Yeah. Send it over."

"I already did."

"Sweet. I'll get on it."

"You do that. And Alan, you remember that plan I mentioned a while back?"

"The crazy one?"

"Yep."

"Sure, I remember--and I seem to recall an empty bottle too."

"Did you set up the stuff I asked?"

"Yeah, the money was good. I'll do silly things for money, you know that."

"Great. It's a go."

"You really mean it, don't you?"

"You got a problem?"

"No, man, I'll do it. But it'll still take some time, even with the preparations you had me do."

"Fine. Keep in touch."

"Can I name the op this time? How about..."

The Cowboy cut him off. "Rawhide."

"You're the boss." There was the pause of a comment restrained and replaced with a curt, "Later."

The Cowboy admired the length of the ash on his cigar and with a little peevish satisfaction, he knocked it off by forcefully flicking it over the ashtray. He entered his own thoughts and began filling in the outlines of his agenda with the details needed to bring in all the wily fishes that he wanted.

Kansas

THE TOWN WAS LIKE MANY OTHERS, the car was not. The town was small, remote, and possessed two not-very-busy stoplights. The car was expensive, European, and fast. Bobby Blade had driven through many such places in his black Lamborghini and despite the fact that he had just spent the night in this one, he had absolutely no idea where he was. Somewhere in Kansas, he was fairly sure. But the name of the town was not something he had cared to notice or remember. It didn't matter. It was probably something nice and simple, not like back east, where there were so many little towns that they apparently had to try and outdo all others by coming up with the most pretentious and unsuitable names. Suitable names were very important. That was why he'd changed his. Robert Bartleby, Jr. was not who he wanted to be or had ever been. It was too much like his father's and not even vaguely cool.

Bobby Blade, on the other hand, was very suitable.

The stoplight turned green and he left two dark marks on

the asphalt behind him. He kept relatively near the speed limit until he was well out in the country again. At that point, he shifted gears and despite the fact that he was already moving at a moderate pace, spun the tires once more. He made it past a hundred and twenty seven before he had to slow down for a corner. He went around and slammed on the brakes. Two cars, clearly belonging to the local sheriff's department, were blocking the road.

Bobby reacted fast, pulling a one-eighty just before he reached the roadblock. The deputies ducked the spray of gravel and Bobby laughed. He sped away and watched as they shook their fists and shouted after him. He went around the corner again and cursed out loud as he twisted the car sideways and then into the ditch. He hit reverse and the wheels spun, but the car went nowhere.

Bobby slapped his hands against the steering wheel and started giggling. He was stuck, some lucky backwoods sheriff was about to put him in jail, and his car was going to need a wash. But fun had been had by all. He opened the hatch and stepped out with his hands above his head and waved his license and registration for the officer to see.

Bobby nodded to the man as he approached, not wanting to speak first. He wore a tan uniform, a shiny pistol, and a white cowboy hat. But despite the expected appearance, Bobby decided that he had made the right move. He didn't want to get this man riled. The sheriff's eyes were hard and he didn't walk like he was scared. No, he reminded Bobby of his last Judo instructor, a former marine and a merciless sensei. No bluster, no aggression, just coiled confidence, ready and waiting. He took the proffered documentation and studied it for a few moments before speaking.

"Do you know how fast you were going, boy?" the sheriff

didn't quite drawl, his accent was too fast, but it was still distinctly what Bobby would call southern. Just not deep, a plainsman. Probably a long-time local, then.

"Not specifically, sir," Bobby lied, adopting a similar accent. He liked to keep track. Watching that speedo climb was sort of a suspenseful thrill. He didn't just like going fast, he liked knowing that he was going fast. "But, I'd imagine it was pretty fast."

The sheriff smiled. "Well, at least you're honest." He glanced back down at Bobby's license. "...Mr. Bartleby. But I can't let you off for being honest. Driving like that is dangerous and I cannot let it go unpunished. In my book, that means a little time in the jailhouse to ponder your sins."

"No offense, sir, but I didn't think speeding was an arrestable offence."

The sheriff smiled and pushed his sunglasses further up his nose. "What makes you so sure, Mr. Bartleby? Your license tells me that you don't spend a lot of time in this part of the world. You ain't in Detroit anymore, son."

Bobby knew he shouldn't correct the man, but he couldn't help himself. "I'm certain, sir. I like to read up on laws in my spare time. I knew I'd be passing through your fine state and I did my research accordingly."

"That may be, but I'm taking you in for reckless endangerment. Turn around and put your hands behind your head."

Bobby did as he asked and barely listened as the man recited the standard litany that all handcuffed persons got to hear. It wasn't new. The officer put him in the back seat of his patrol car, which was actually a full-size SUV, and gently closed the door.

The sheriff got in, started the car, and headed back towards that last town. Ignoring Bobby, he put his radio mike to his lips and said, "I'm bringing in the driver. Get Josh out here to bring that car in. Tell him not to go faster than he should or I'll throw him in too. And tell him to be careful. That's a nice car, don't mess it up."

When he was done, Bobby leaned forward and said, honestly, "Thanks for that, sir."

"There's no reason to see a fine machine suffer for the sins of the fool driving her. I've never seen a Lambo in person before and I doubt I will again. I ain't gonna let anything happen to her." He glanced back at Bobby through the screen. "But you won't be seeing her for a bit."

Bobby nodded and leaned back against the seat. He was tired. At least jail would be a change from sleeping in the car. He'd be out soon, and then back on the road.

"Sir, does the jail have wifi?"

The morning sun was halfway past noon when Bobby was forced awake by the sound of someone beating something against the bars of the holding cell. "What's that noise?" He rubbed his eyes until he could make out an unfamiliar man standing just outside his cell.

"Good afternoon, Mr. Blade."

Bobby smiled. "Yeah. That's my name. What's up?"

The man clutched his briefcase and put on a serious face. "I'm here to offer you a proposal on behalf of my employer, Tip Top Productions. How would you like to be a television star?"

1

New Mexico

"I'LL BE THERE in an hour. See you soon, Miss Elkins."

"Not if I see you first," Cass said, but Daniel J. Hearst, big-city accountant and professional pain-in-the-rear, had already ended the call. Too bad. But until he clearly demonstrated his evil, the rifle stayed in the corner. It was a pity that ignorance wasn't a sin--even if it was going to ruin her life.

Since squeezing the life out of the old telephone handset wasn't accomplishing anything, Cass hung it up, careful not to overly tangle the cord. At least he'd finally figured out how to dial the landline. He had difficulty grasping the idea that cell service was spotty at best on the Two-E and internet reliability was worse. "Dead-zone" described most of the ranch. Cass snorted at her own joke and bit down on her toothpick. Her jaw clamped down so hard that the pointy piece of wood snapped clean in two. Cass growled and spit before getting a fresh toothpick from the drawer next to the stove.

Turning the radio back on just in time for the commodities report, Cass turned the stove off and went about eating her overdone steak. Stupid accountant had ruined her breakfast too.

Cattle prices had hit bottom and were finally starting to go back up, he was right about that, but that only mattered if she had some to sell. Two years into the worst drought since the dust bowl, Cass had already liquidated half the breeding stock. She was down to the bare minimum of cows and the calves wouldn't be big enough to sell for another six months. She needed to convince Hearst to back off because those calves were the only income to look forward to this year. He didn't seem to understand that until the drought broke, success was defined as anything shy of bankrupt.

He held everything she had in his soft hands--and he didn't know the first thing about it.

Cass had been about to head out horseback and check fences and water. She left the bridle on the nail in the barn and turned to her dirt bike. Now, there was no time for a horse- -or fences. Cass kicked the starter and the two-stroke engine screamed to life beneath her, louder than the orange paint of the bike. The fences could wait, they always did, but the water couldn't. If she rode fast, there was time for a quick run to check that all the windmills were working right. There was plenty to go wrong on a ranch, any day, but running the cows out of wa- ter was the definition of bad news. Once in a lifetime was more than enough for Cass. She would put off anything but that.

She spun the bike around towards the door, leaving a thick, circular gash in the dirt floor, and screamed out into the already too warm sunshine.

Instead of heading north, towards the cattle guard and the road, she pointed the cycle south, away from the only gate in the small trap that fenced the cattle off of her headquarters. A few feet from the fence on either side, she'd pushed up a pile of dirt just a little taller than the five-wire fence.

Accelerating fast, she hit second gear, revved it up into the power band, and ran up the side of the dirtpile. She cleared the fence by more than enough and touched back down about halfway down the other makeshift ramp. Her face was locked into a grimace. She shifted quickly up to fifth, mechanical and cold, her mind on the phone call. As she gained speed, the tires started skimming, touching only the high points of the rough ground and making the ride relatively smooth.

Fresh air, breakneck speed, miles of space to run--it was a freedom that usually thrilled Cass. But the grimace was not broken. She was too mad to enjoy the ride.

8

New Mexico

WITH NOT MUCH TIME TO SPARE, she jumped the cycle back inside the fence around her house and slid it to a stop inside the barn, cutting another groove in the floor. The water was as good as it ever was and the gate was unlocked. She wasn't ready for D.J., but he was coming. She kicked the ground, uselessly stirring up more of the fine, dry dust.

Too quickly, the cloud of dirt settled, and she looked north towards the highway for a similar cloud that would herald an approaching vehicle. Seeing nothing, she walked around the side of the barn to the shed and checked the dogs' feed and water. The split-barrel they shared with the barn cats and a couple of skunks that Cass hadn't caught up with yet, was three-quarters full and the water tub was fine as well.

The dogs were already in their standard daytime position, napping on the porch. They didn't do much more than cock an ear at her as she stepped around and over them. The sun was well over the horizon and there was still no sign of Hearst. He was coming to give her bad news, did he have to be late as well? Of course he did. He didn't seem to care about inconvenience as long as it was someone else's.

She tried to call him, to see if he'd gotten lost, again. But no luck. He was either dead--one could hope--or just unreachable. Unfortunately, she couldn't blame him for bad cell service.

There was no way she wasn't going to be here when he arrived. She didn't trust him to be left alone in or around her home. She hardly trusted anybody to do that, even her friends. With no answer and no way of knowing how late he would be, she made coffee and sat down on the porch with the sun in her eyes and dogs at her feet.

The sun was well and up when Hearst finally pulled in, a good hour late. Still sitting on the porch, Cass didn't shush the three barking dogs at her feet. She sat her empty coffee mug down on the rail and stood, doing her best to not scowl. The dogs, for all their faults, were decent guards, and they too had taken notice of the visitor. They followed her down to the car, looking a lot meaner than they really were. With not a little petty satisfaction, she noticed that the ugly Cadillac, not more than a year old, was covered in a heavy layer of fine, red dust and the not-as-ugly accountant was eyeing her dogs a little nervously.

"Morning, D.J. Hope you didn't have your car washed lately." Cass put a hand out to hold the dogs back.

Hearst and his briefcase made it out of the car and even managed walking on the dirt instead of concrete.

"Yesterday, actually," he said, looking at the dusty film with obvious disgust. "The nearest town is Santa Rosa, right?"

"Yeah."

"Do they have a car wash?"

"Probably."

Lee Brown

"Well, where do you get yours washed?"

Cass shrugged. "I don't." There was no point in paying money for a wash when they'd be dirty again before she could get home.

"I see." He quickly surveyed the area and his gaze settled on the house. "Can we go inside and get to business?"

"Sure." Cass led him up the weathered steps, grabbing her coffee cup as she went.

In the kitchen, she cleaned off an extra chair, putting the stack of gun magazines on the floor. "Sorry 'bout the mess. I don't get much company. Especially on short notice."

"It's not a problem, I assume?"

There was no point in answering. "You like coffee?" Cass said instead, filling her own cup.

"No, thank you." Hearst started taking papers from his briefcase and laying them out on the table.

"Suit yourself." Cass sat down and waited for him to say something stupid. It didn't take long.

"You need to sell the cows."

Cass raised an eyebrow. "Do what now?"

"Cattle prices are higher than they've been in three years. I recommend selling the cows immediately and putting the profit towards your debt."

Cass drank some coffee to calm herself.

It didn't work.

She sat the mug down. The table rattled and more than a few drops of coffee stained the Accountant's papers. "That's not a good idea."

"I don't see how. You need the money and you'll be getting three times what you paid for them."

"D.J., without those cows, I ain't got nothing that'll turn a profit. In case you haven't noticed, this is a ranch. The way you make money, on a ranch, is by having cows. You don't sell the cows. You keep the cows, the cows have calves, and then when they're big enough to be weaned off their mamas, you sell the calves."

"You can restock when the conditions are better."

Cass rolled her eyes, just a little. "If you think cattle prices are high now, wait 'till people start trying to do just that. Breeding stock will be better than gold. The longer I can hold onto anything that'll have a calf, the more money I might make. Sellin' out now is just plain dumb. It ain't gonna happen."

"I see. Do what you will, but I cannot condone it. My advice has been given and noted. I am not responsible for your bad judgment. Unfortunately, my advisory position allows me to go no further."

"Until I get too far behind? Miss your next payment deadline? Then you can be as dumb as you want."

He pursed his lips, but didn't reply.

"You don't think I've got a chance, do you? You're just going through the motions, waiting. Then you can sell everything off in pieces, pay off the bank and never have to drive down a dirt road again."

"I have some other recommendations, if you will let me go over them."

Cass finished her coffee. "No, leave 'em on the table if you want. I'll have a good laugh later. I've got work to do now. You've said your piece and I've said mine. I'll let you know when I get some cash to put on the note. 'Till then, I'd appreciate it if you'd let me alone to run my ranch. 'Cause it's not yours yet."

"I'll be expecting a payment in four months." He stood and closed his case, leaving a couple of spreadsheets behind.

"It'll be six, D.J." Cass opened the door and pointed towards the distant highway. "First of November, just like the last two years. Talk to you then."

When he was long gone, Cass made another batch of coffee and sat down at the computer. She went over all the financials for the thousandth time and once again, she came up with the same conclusion. Unless the weather got a lot more water-inclined, real soon, there was no way she would ever get the money in time.

Her grandfather had left her the ranch, just like she'd always wanted, but it had come with one huge caveat. A debt. Because of some greedy former-family members, who Cass didn't talk to anymore, the estate had been unable to settle the debt and the lawyers had given Cass two options. Inherit the ranch and the debt and pay it off according to an accelerated schedule, as overseen by the wonderful Mr. Hearst. Or, sell the ranch to pay off the debt, and keep whatever cash is left over. Basically, Cass had to choose between a bunch of cash now or the ranch and no cash, maybe ever. But it wasn't about cash, it was about life, and living it the ways she'd always wanted.

She'd been in the cattle business in one form or another since she was six-years old. The ranch was what she'd always wanted and she had the skills to make it work. But skill and experience can't make it rain. She was losing the race, and there was nothing she could do. It hadn't rained in over eight months, half the cows were gone, and all there was to do was keep praying--or win the lottery, but since she never bought a ticket, that was unlikely.

Her brand, the Two-E, had been handed down since her great-great-grandfather and his twin brother had come into this country and settled. Two Elkins, that's what it stood for. Keeping her ranch was important. Without it, she didn't know what she'd do.

9

New Mexico

ANDREW JIMENEZ removed his sweat-stained hat, wiped his forehead and stared at the primary cause of his discomfort. The afternoon sun glared at him through the dusty haze that perpetually hung over the land. Though it was minutes away from sinking below the horizon, it continued to heat the dry desert plains. He unslung the canteen from his saddle horn and gulped two large mouthfuls of warm water, emptying the gallon jug.

A small smile came to his lips and he reined his mustang to a stop as he crested a tall ridge. The valley below him was some of the best land around. It had twice as much grass as the rest of the ranch and a shallow aquifer ran right through the middle, making water easy to get. But that was not what made him smile. A couple of miles into the valley, his home was visible. He imagined his three young children splashing about in the yard sprinklers and his beautiful wife looking on from the porch with a tired smile on her face. He longed to be there with them right now, but unlike in the city, work could not be scheduled. When it had to be done, it had to be done. Whether it took two hours or twelve, the day was over when the job was done. He briefly considered spurring his horse and riding straight and fast to the house right then, but quickly discarded that thought and reminded himself of the job at hand.

The night before, two cows and a calf had come up missing. They had apparently gotten out on the neighbors ranch because the O-Bar-Z foreman had called that morning to ask Andrew to unlock his outside gate and let one of the Bar-Z's hands trailer the strays back home. A good day. Missing cattle weren't always so easy to find.

After dinner and a short noontime nap, he had saddled his horse and headed out to check fences. He needed to find where the cattle had gotten out and fix it before any more of his stock decided to visit the O-Bar-Z. After six long, hot hours of riding, he had ridden nearly the entire border fence between his ranch and the next and found nothing that would have facilitated the escape of a full-grown cow.

Tired and confused, he had three more miles to ride before he could call it a day and head back to the house. As his horse trod steadily along, he squinted into the reddening sun, looking for a break in the barb wire.

He rode another mile before he found what he was looking for.

He cussed out loud when he saw the problem. It was not a natural hole in the fence like he was used to. The wind, or rain erosion was frequently the cause. Rather, much to his dismay, it was without a doubt, a manmade hole. The five rusty, barbed wires had been neatly cut right next to one of the cedar posts. The loose ends had then been rolled back out of the way. He stared angrily at what amounted to a truck-sized gap in his fence. Lucky only three head got out.

With a sigh he dismounted. He would be eating supper cold tonight. No two ways about it, this had to be fixed before he went home. Using nothing but a pair of fencing pliers and some baling wire, he jury-rigged the fence in a way that would make any adventurous cows think twice; even if it wouldn't withstand a serious attempt to escape. He would return in the morning and fix it permanently. While he worked, he eyed the multiple sets of tire tracks that had gone through the gap. Judging by the effects of the wind, they were close to a day old. Unconsciously, his hand brushed against the outline of the Ruger Vaquero in its holster on his hip.

Most likely, it had been nothing more than a bunch of local boys, looking to get into trouble or hunting out of season. But Andrew knew also, that it could have been more nefarious. Coyotes, smuggling illegals into the country, were known to come through these parts and rustlers were around too--though that seemed unlikely since he wasn't missing any cattle. He hated to admit it, but he wondered if it had something to do with O-Bar-Z. He couldn't prove anything, but had suspicions that less than legal activities occurred on his neighbor to the west. It was supposed to be owned by some big-shot millionaire from back east who only visited once or twice a year. The grand house, heated pool, lighted runway, and all the other extravagant features certainly supported that story. But it didn't explain the frequency of planes landing at night and taking off again before the next morning. His wife berated him for being so suspicious, but it never hurt to be careful. He'd rather be wrong than unprepared.

He was less than half a mile from the house when he heard the familiar whine of a small, low-flying airplane. He paused his horse a moment and watched as it flew over his house, directly lined up for a landing on the lighted tarmac of the O-Bar-Z. Though not uncommon, he still watched the plane as it flew. A good-sized hill lay between him and where he knew the Bar-Z's runway to be. Just before the plane went out of sight, he clucked to his steed and started on towards the house.

Even though he knew he could no longer see the plane, he looked back towards where it would be. All of the sudden, a huge fireball rent the sky over the hill. Moments later, the sound of the explosion caused his horse's ears to lay back. Spooked, the horse bolted towards the corrals near the house and Jimenez let him go. Whatever had caused the explosion, as long as it didn't start a grass fire, it was none of his business.

Supper was waiting.

10

New Mexico

CASS SAT AT A TALL BENCH, the disassembled Desert Eagle forty-four magnum on the wooden surface in front of her. She picked up the receiver and began scrubbing it with a solvent-soaked brush to remove the residue left over from her afternoon target practice. Due to the unique gas-powered bolt system, powder residue made quite a mess. But the effort to keep it clean was worth it. A well-treated Desert Eagle, in her opinion, was like nothing else. Eight rounds of pure joy. A freakishly large semi-automatic handgun chambered for one of the most powerful pistol cartridges in the world, and to Cass's way of thinking, the best cartridge. It was the gun Dirty Harry wished he had.

She had many guns. But there were more forty-fours in her safe than any other caliber.

She finished the receiver and moved on to the frame. She ran her fingers along where the pieces rubbed against each other every time the gun cycled. Thousands of rounds had resulted in a polished surface that didn't match the matte finish the gun had started with years ago. Elsewhere, the slightly textured nickel-plating was still intact. She liked to feel the way it changed from rough to smooth near the places where it caught and rubbed in a holster. The wear was part of the gun, something that separated it from the others; the ones that didn't get shot often enough or carried every day. That was the good kind of wear, the kind on the outside.

Inside, it was as perfect as she could keep it. Other than replacing the recoil springs once a year, this particular gun had served her well. She had acquired others, but they would never be her first or her favorite.

She cleaned it almost every night. It was her only offering to routine. Her days were never the same, and rarely peaceful. In contrast, cleaning guns was both peaceful and relaxing; almost a form of physical meditation. It cut out all the worry and lingering crap that the world piled on and it was one of the only things that cleared her mind enough to sleep. There was something reassuring about lying down with the smell of solvent and oil lingering--almost as comforting as the loaded forty-four within arm's reach.

She inspected each piece visually and with her hands, running a finger along every possible surface, checking for that which was invisible. As she found no burrs or other problems, she wiped each component down with a thin oil, and taking a clean rag, she buffed and dried everything, leaving a protective coat, but nothing that would be sticky enough to attract any grit.

She'd picked up a small syringe of lube and begun to oil the trigger mechanism when she was interrupted. The dogs were barking.

She wasn't expecting anybody. Few people outside her family even knew where she lived--and the damned accountant. But after last week, he'd be out of her hair for a while. He liked to remind her of the impending doom, but he liked driving out to the ranch even less--and she let her phone's battery run down and stay dead more than she ought to.

Besides, he would never come at night, he wasn't that dedicated.

He also didn't have a key. She unlocked the gate when she knew he was coming. Only her closest friends and family had a key. But even so, they always called ahead. That was common courtesy.

She tried to think if the gate had been unlocked for some reason. She hadn't been out that way in days, but it should have been locked. She'd made sure of it after Hearst left--and hadn't been back. It had to be someone with a key.

Or, if not.

She grabbed the nearest loaded gun, a Baby Eagle forty-five, and went to answer the door.

She was waiting when the knock came. Standing to the side, she opened the door to see a little man in a dark suit standing there, carrying a briefcase. Pale, lost, and wanting something. Not supposed to be on her front porch.

Cass stepped into the doorway and glared. "What do you want?"

"Allow me to introduce myself." The man looked up and smiled. "Alan Dobbs, Tip Top Productions. I would like a word with Cass Elkins."

"How did you find me?" Cass gave him a harder look. He was out of place and out of his mind. She decided to give him the benefit of the doubt, but not much more. The gun stayed ready at her side. She'd already picked a target before she opened the door.

He smiled. "Research. That's my job." He nodded. "It wasn't easy, if that makes you feel any better."

It did a little. Cass kept her attention focused, her mind racing, trying to figure out what was going on. "The gate was locked."

"No. It was open."

Cass had no reason to believe him. "No it wasn't."

"Are you certain?"

"Yes."

He relented, deflating. "I was given a key. I promised not to reveal my source. They thought it would be a good idea if I surprised you."

"That's never a good idea. Who sent you?"

"A friend who thought you needed the money."

"Money?" Cass didn't trust much the man was saying, but it was possible, and as much as she hated it, she needed cash. He seemed reasonable. No harm in hearing him out.

She stopped scowling, but didn't really smile. "Are you alone?" She looked out at the vehicle he'd brought. A pitiful excuse for a pickup, but she could see down into the bed from her height on the porch and into the seat. It looked empty.

He nodded, smiling, or trying to. The man's smile was betrayed by the way he looked nervously over his shoulder at the growling canines. "May I come in? I can assure you, you won't need that weapon." He held up his briefcase like it was a badge of office.

"I think I'll keep it." Cass decided that because of the way he held the case, a head shot would be better. "Come on in, but don't try anything. You're a long ways from civilization, mister."

She led him into the living room and pointed to a chair. "Have a seat."

He did as she said, sitting with the briefcase on his lap. "Aren't you going to sit down?"

"No thanks, I'll stand." Cass leaned against the doorframe, her presence a better barrier than the missing door. She didn't like doors inside her house. She tolerated walls as a place to hang awards and her collection of movie posters, but doors just got in the way.

"Okay."

Cass waited for him to explain himself for all of a few seconds. She crossed her arms, letting the gun rest casually on her shoulder, pointing up and towards the back of the house. She realized she was smiling.

The man pointed at it. "Shouldn't you keep that pointed down?"

Cass looked at the gun and raised her eyebrows. "There better not be anybody else out there to worry about." She spoke with the accent of the dry, flat part of the southwest. Hard, but drawn out, there was plenty of time to emphasize the words. "I'll reiterate. What do you want? You said a friend of mine sent you cause I need some money. I don't necessarily believe you, but I'm giving you the benefit of the doubt, 'cause I'm such a nice person. Give me the short version."

"I've been sent by my superiors to make you a proposition; a proposition that could make you a good deal of money. Will you hear it?"

Cass tilted her head back against the wall. Might as well. "Shoot, mister."

"Very good, I represent the production team of a new reality TV series, Tough Target. Our research team has selected you as a potential contestant for the show."

11

New Mexico

THAT WAS NOT WHAT CASS WAS EXPECTING. "Uh huh?" She drug out the gutteral question and filled it with skepticism. She leaned forward and let her hand drop to hang against the front of her leg, still holding the gun.

"Indeed. The primary theme we are looking for is the ever popular 'hometown hero.' You were involved in such a scenario."

Cass straightened, and careful to keep a relatively neutral face, raised her eyebrow. "Is that a fact?"

"I'm sure you remember the man that you killed? I've heard that people don't usually forget that sort of thing."

"Eh." She shrugged with her eyes. There wasn't a good reason she could think of to 'fess up to what had happened. Not to a stranger.

"Your identity was never released to the press and the full details of what happened are still unclear. However, with the proper resources, the information is available." He looked smug, confident. Maybe he did know. It actually made his story seem more likely. Most of the people who knew, also had keys to the gate, and were ornery enough to send him as a surprise. It was possible.

But no good reason to confess. Cass wasn't ashamed, and she'd been officially cleared of any wrongdoing. It was self-defense, and other-people-defense. But Cass didn't like to share personal information. If he knew, then he knew, but she wasn't gonna be the one to tell him. She put on a look of dawning comprehension. "Yeah, you're talkin' about that thing with the Russian slavers or something. Read about that. I met a couple of the girls they rescued."

The man sighed. "There is no reason for you to continue this charade. I've read the real reports and I know as much about what you did as is possible without witnessing it firsthand."

Cass didn't move. "Alright, mister. What did I do?" Be interesting to hear it from another direction.

"Are we really going to do this?"

Cass just looked at him.

"Fine. Two years ago, one Cass Elkins was kidnapped by a group of Russian-connected slave-traders. They had captured thirteen girls, and were on their way to ship them out of the country where they could be sold."

Cass interrupted, thoughtful. "I never did hear where they were headed."

"Shall I go on? Or do you want to tell the rest?"

Cass nodded, still keeping her face pretty straight. "You keep right on, mister."

"Right. The report states that the kidnappers stopped to overnight. Sometime during the night, you overpowered the guards, escaped, and then proceeded to capture all but one of the remaining perpetrators."

"What about the one?"

"The leader of the gang was found shot through the head with a thirty-eight caliber bullet. All evidence points to you as the shooter."

"Well, that right there proves your story wrong, mister. I don't shoot anything small as a thirty-eight. "

"Your admission is irrelevant. Our facts are confirmed. We know what you did and that is why we want you to be part of our program. Are you interested?" Dobbs was leaning forward, squeezing the handle of his briefcase.

"I'm listening. You were telling me about money." Cass took a seat on a stool, rested the gun on her knee. She didn't know what all the man wanted, but there wasn't much harm in hearing him out. He was the most interesting thing she'd had to put up with lately. Beat the heck out of sleeping.

"If you accept, we would fly you to our first filming site in Virginia. There, you will be asked to participate in several competency exams in order to confirm your abilities and secure a place on the contestant roster. Is that agreeable?"

Cass nodded. "So, the money, I have to win it?"

"Yes. The grand prize is one million dollars.

"Minus taxes." Cass frowned. She figured to clear about half then. It wouldn't be enough to settle everything, but it'd do to keep the lawyers and that damn accountant, Hearst, off her back for a while. Bound to be easier than making it rain.

"I suppose."

"Right. What'll I have to do to win?"

"You have to qualify first."

"Answer the question."

"I'm afraid that is classified and I am not at liberty to say."

Cass was considering the offer. Might as well start the act. She didn't watch reality shows, but they were impossible to completely avoid. She knew enough. She knew that outrageous was the secret. She could do that. "Well now, given the fact you traipsed all the way out here to talk to me, I reckon ya'll want me pretty bad. So, you can just sit there until you answer. If not, well, let's just say that I don't take too kindly to trespassers. I'm afraid this is private property and I am at liberty to shoot." A lopsided smile crossed her face and she gestured, palm up with her left hand. Her right still relaxed, holding the gun across her knee. "Now, won't you reconsider?"

"Um, don't do anything rash. I could lose my job if I tell you anything."

"You could lose more than that, mister." She had to admit that she was beginning to have a little fun. Messing with people was always a laugh.

"Well, when you put it that way. Could I at least call the producer and ask him?"

"You do that."

Dobbs pulled out a phone and speed-dialed someone. "Hello, sir. Yes I believe she is willing. However, she wants to know more about what will be required. No sir, I tried that and she, um, threatened me. Yes sir, she did. Yes sir, hold on a moment."

"Well?" Cass raised an eyebrow.

"He wants to speak to you." Dobbs handed her the phone.

Cass took the phone from him and answered. "Howdy."

"Good evening Miss Elkins. You appear to have made quite an impression on Mr. Dobbs. He seems to think that you have a rather blunt affectation."

"I've found that it gets better results." She glanced at the pale man. "Entertainin' too."

"Don't be too hard on him. I sent him because I trust him. Leaks are unacceptable in this business."

"That's fine. What I'd like to know is what I'd be gettin'

into.

"I see. I don't normally do this, but I'd really like to have you. I can't tell you over the phone. I can't let anything leak out ahead of time. We'll have to meet in person. "

"Alright. I hate talking on the phone, anyway. When and where?"

"Dobbs is scheduled to fly back here tomorrow. Can you accompany him?"

Cass had made a decision and a calculation. If they really wanted her, she'd see them out, but as bad as things were, she couldn't drop everything and leave. "Not for nothing. I've got work I need to do and I can't afford to hire somebody else to do it. I lack about two and a half million of having thirty-seven cents. There's no time or money for a vacation. Why don't you come on down here?"

"That's not possible right now. However, I can pay you to come here for the interview. How much will you need to be away for a week?"

Cass added up a few numbers and tacked a little on the top. "Ten-thousand."

"That's fine. Dobbs will get it to you in the morning. I'll be looking forward to meeting you."

"Hold your horses, mister. I ain't goin' nowhere until I give it some thought. I'll let you know."

The line went dead and she handed the phone back to Dobbs. A few moments later, it chimed a text alert. Dobbs paled when he read it, but nodded to Cass. He stood and placed a business card on the table. "Here is my contact information. We leave at ten tomorrow morning."

"That'll work. Now, how 'bout you skedaddle." Cass let him out, called the dogs off, and followed behind him all the way to the gate. When she couldn't see his light anymore, she locked the gate and went back to the house.

She finished lubing and assembling her Eagle, but it was all by rote. Relaxation was not to be found. She racked the slide back and forth a few times to work the grease in and wiped it all down again with a clean cloth.

Grabbing a loaded magazine, she slammed it in, racked the chamber full and went out on the front porch. She stepped over the sleeping dogs and breathed the cool, dusty air until her eyes adjusted and she could see the fifty-yard target. The last step of cleaning was always a test-fire. She extended her right arm, found the sights, and pulled the trigger. She fired the first four slow and the rest fast, but they all hit the eight-inch plate.

Steel still ringing, she pulled the earplugs out, hung them on the nail by the door and went back inside, the dogs cocking their heads at her. With a loaded magazine and a busy mind, Cass Elkins took her Eagle and went to bed.

12

New Mexico

THE NEAREST AIRPORT WASN'T CLOSE and wasn't very big. Cass looked at her brother. "This is silly."

He nodded, smiling. "It'll be fun. You'll win." He put the pickup in park. "Then we'll all sit around drinking coffee and laughing about it."

Cass let out an almost imperceptible breath and opened the door to step out. "Alright, let's get this done."

Heath waited while she retrieved her luggage from the back and followed her as she started across the tarmac.

"It's almost noon." Dobbs was sitting in a folding chair under the wing of a Cessna One-Eighty-Two.

"Uh huh," Cass squinted as she walked across the tarmac, her brother a step behind. There was no one else around. "I suppose. Thought you were gone already."

"I was, but the producer called and gave orders not to take off without you on board. He likes you very much."

"Huh. You sure I'm that special?"

Dobbs shrugged. "I'm not in charge."

"I get half a mil, right?"

"The grand prize is one million, yes."

"That's what I said. Taxes."

"Yes, Miss Elkins."

"Well, I just got done not hittin' my accountant. Make it twenty for the week and I'm in."

Heath snorted quietly.

Dobbs gave him a short glance. "That is acceptable." He folded the chair and stowed it along with Cass's luggage. "Is this all you need?" He picked up the small suitcase and nodded to the oddly shaped hard-shell case that was Cass's hat box.

"That and the money."

He smiled and reached into the cockpit for a white envelope. "Here it is."

Cass took the envelope and handed it to her brother. He opened it and flipped through it, counting. "Twenty."

Cass raised her eyebrow. "How'd you know that'd be the number?"

Dobbs shrugged, smiling slightly. "The producer had a hunch."

Cass nodded. "Okay then." She turned to her brother, her face as solemn as it ever got. "Take care. Tell Shorty not to teach my dogs any weird tricks."

He grinned and offered a hug. "Show 'em how it's done."

Cass accepted the terse embrace and then punched him in the arm. "Later."

He turned and walked away and she joined Dobbs in the cockpit. She turned to him and with a straight face said, "Do you know how to fly this thing?"

He shrugged, and started pushing buttons. "I'm an ace on the flight simulator."

13

Massachusetts

CASS ELKINS STEPPED OFF the plane and wrinkled her nose at the unmistakable odor of a city. The smell of too many people crammed together like cattle. More like sheep, really. Cattle had more spirit. She took a shallow, but significant breath and tried to relax.

The sun was dimmer than she was used to, but it was bright enough to make the man standing on the tarmac squint and shade his eyes with his hand. He was wearing a light tan suit that contrasted his skin, dress shoes, and no hat. Cass always found it strange how people would rather burn their face and shade their eyes than wear a decent hat. Go figure.

Cass was just wearing a ball cap from the feed store her cousin owned. It did a fine job of keeping the sun out of her eyes. She turned back to the plane and retrieved her bags.

Dobbs gingerly offered his hand. "Good luck, Cass."

Cass shook his hand. "You not coming?"

He shook his head and looked down. "No, I'll see you later." He cocked his head towards the hatless man leaning on the car. "That's Wallace. He will take you to your hotel and everywhere." He ducked his head and said again, "Good luck."

Cass picked up her bags and headed towards the parked car. The man was leaning against the side of the non-descript vehicle and Cass couldn't help but notice the bulge under his right shoulder. It wasn't printing enough to make out the model, but it was plenty obvious. A semi-automatic, judging by the proportions and the flatness of the bulge, but anything else was just a guess.

"Looking for me, mister?" Cass tipped her hat.

The man looked at her for several seconds. "Are you Elkins?"

"I reckon so. Didn't see anybody else get off the plane. I thought ya'll were expecting me."

"Yes. Ah, I'm Justin Wallace. I'm here to drive you to your hotel."

Cass nodded, detecting something he didn't say. "I understand. I wouldn't expect me either."

Wallace just pointed to a car. "This way." He pointed towards the trunk.

Cass nodded with the edge of her cap. She picked up her suitcase and her hat box and walked to the rear of the late-model, European wannabe car. Silver, dull, and not nearly as fast as it liked to think.

Wallace opened the trunk and awkwardly let her load the bags.

Cass let him close the trunk.

Wallace didn't say much until they were out of the airport.

"So, you think you can win Tough Target?" he didn't look away from the road, and Cass was glad of that. The traffic was more than she'd want to mess with.

"Sure." Cass kept her eyes outside. She wanted to see everything. Big cities were nerve-wracking, but they were also interesting.

"What makes you think that?"

Cass shrugged. "I have to."

"And that matters? What if you're not the best?"

"It's all that matters."

"That's an interesting view."

"I guess it might be," Cass said. "But that's just how I do things. Always have."

"You may very well have what it takes, then. We'll just have to see."

"Guess so." Cass turned her attention to Wallace and the deft ease with which he navigated the multi-lane traffic. She hated driving in Albuquerque, much less someplace like this, but she paid close attention to how he was doing it. She might not like it, but she wanted to be decent at it if she had to.

He seemed done with conversation and she was fine with that. She had to be ready. There would only be one good chance to impress and secure her spot on the show. She had to make it. Reality television wasn't the real world. She had to make herself into a character; an outrageous, entertaining character. That's what they'd want.

By the time Wallace pulled up in front of the hotel, Cass had a plan, the kind of plan she needed--an outrageous one.

Wallace insisted on carrying her bags and he checked into the room. "Here's your room. You can get settled and then I'll pick you up later for dinner. He handed her the key and she took it and then picked up her luggage before he could.

"When do I get to meet the guy in charge?" Cass started walking towards the elevators.

"He's very busy, but I'll let you know as soon as possible. Tomorrow, I expect. My number is on the paper I gave you. Be ready for my call."

Cass nodded and stopped in front of the elevator. Before she could put down her suitcase, Wallace pressed the call button and turned to her, his face inscrutable.

"Would you like me to escort you to your room?"

Cass shook her head. "I'll be fine. But you can do what you want."

He nodded, but his face didn't change. "You should be relatively secure here, but D.C. is a dangerous place, especially for a nice young lady by herself."

Cass just looked at him. "I appreciate your concern, Mr. Wallace, but I can take care of myself. If some unsuspecting lowlife mistakes me for a nice young girl, he'll find out that even though I may be young and I might be a girl, I ain't all that nice."

"Miss Elkins, I still don't think it would be wise for you to go around by yourself."

Cass shrugged as the elevator doors opened and she stepped inside. Wallace followed and pressed the button for her floor. Cass sat the suitcase down and enjoyed the ride.

They reached Cass's floor and Wallace offered to carry the suitcase. Cass, unsurprised, decided to let him. She glanced at the slip of paper with her room number on it and then at the plaques on the wall in front of her. The room was to the left. She started walking and Wallace followed.

Her room was around a corner and down the end of a short hallway, very isolated. She was okay with that, but she was also aware of it. There was no one else in sight, but something was prickling her neck hairs. The door to the stairwell, just past the door to her room, drew her attention. She kept an eye on it as she approached. There was something. She looked up at a security camera at the end of the hall. It was pointing directly at her door. Not scanning and not in a position to see the rest of the hall. She looked back the way she'd come to see if there was another camera, making up for the blind spots, but there was nothing but an empty hall.

She pulled her key out and played along. "I've got it from here, Wallace. You can go on."

He nodded. "I'll be back soon. Don't go anywhere."

"I'll be fine."

"I really must insist that you stay here. You don't need to wander off."

Cass figured he meant well, or was under orders, or something else reasonable, but she didn't have the luxury of being reasonable. She had a plan. The camera was watching. She put down her hat box and turned around to face Wallace.

She crossed her arms, but not tight, not tangled. "So, you're gonna protect me then? What makes you think you can do better?" She nodded to the bulge location, but kept her eyes on his." Are you referring to the gun under your coat? What is it, a Glock, a Sig? A forty-five, a nine mill?" Cass stepped closer until she stood within arm's reach. He probably didn't deserve this, but he hadn't won her over either. She had a reason to get a reaction out of him, a good reason. This was a TV show, right? They were looking for entertainment. Might as well enjoy it. Besides, it had been a long day.

She put on an innocent look. "How long you been at this gig?"

Wallace looked indignant and he quickly answered. "Long enough. Why do you ask?"

"I see. How come you just let me kill you?"

"Kill me?" he said, looking more curious than scared. Yep, definitely a setup.

"I've been standing close enough to you to kill you half a

dozen different ways since we started talking."

"Should I be worried?"

"I don't know. You tell me."

"I am still better armed. I have a gun and you don't."

Cass laughed. "Not a problem at this distance. Unless you can draw as fast as my brother--and I sincerely doubt that you can."

"Why exactly are you telling me this?"

"'Cause I want to play. All you have to do is touch it. Just see how fast you can put your hand on it. Nothing dangerous. Just a friendly dare." Cass looked around. There was nobody in sight. But that didn't mean they were alone. It just meant that anybody watching was no bystander. "Come on. Don't worry about anybody seeing. They won't see nothing. Come on. You afraid of a girl? Tell you what, if you're fast enough, I'll take your advice."

"Is that so?"

"Sure, but if I win, you quit telling me what I can and can't do. Deal?"

"Very well. Ready?"

"Whenever you are. You go first."

Cass stood still, arms relaxed, waiting for Wallace to make his move. Calm on the outside, but less so on the inside. She was buzzing with anticipation, primed, ready for him to make the move. "I'm waiting."

Wallace tensed and his right arm pulled his jacket back to expose his Glock while his left hand reached for the gun. At least that was what he tried to do. Even though his right arm moved first, as soon as he moved, Cass grabbed his left arm with her right. She'd seen the gun, and his watch. She already knew what was going to happen. She already had the plan. As he registered what had happened to his plan, her left hand hardened into an arc and accelerated towards his exposed throat. She stopped it a hairsbreadth away, and held it there frozen, just as he was, waiting for his mind to catch up with what had happened.

She watched his eyes. For just a moment, while her hand neared his throat and before he had time to consider, there was a flash of panic. That was okay. Somebody once told her that the difference between fear and respect was small enough that one was a good substitute for the other. It disappeared and was replaced by something both smug and curious.

He broke the gaze and eyed the hand which had stopped a fraction of an inch from crushing his throat. "You win."

Cass released him. She realized that she was smiling.

He took a step back and straightened his suit, his own wry grin appearing. "That was interesting."

"Just keep telling yourself that, if it makes you feel better, bub. Now get along, I've got bigger fish to fry."

Cass turned towards the stairwell to see a wiry man with close-cropped, reddish hair, wearing stylishly cut denim jeans, an Allman Brothers t-shirt and a well-worn leather jacket, step out of the shadows and begin clapping slowly.

Cass cocked her head. About time.

"Not bad. Not bad. You're even better in person, Miss Elkins. I can also see why Mr. Dobbs thought you a bit blunt. Do you test everyone you meet this way?"

Cass shrugged. "Only when I've got an audience. That's what I'm here for, right? To entertain? That's what TV's about."

"You knew I was here? I'm impressed. I must be losing my touch."

"I don't know about that, mister." Cass didn't really know how she knew that he was close, but she'd been right. "Maybe I've been on my lonesome too long. I notice people."

"Curious," said the man, who Cass decided had to be the

producer. "Let's go someplace more private and we'll discuss the details. Are you hungry?"

"Always." Cass slapped her stomach, her mind jumping ahead to food. She really was hungry.

"Excellent. We'll have dinner. Wallace will pick you up in an hour."

Cass watched critically as the man casually walked out of the room. His outward appearance had been unassuming in every way, but to her eye, his walk gave him away. Confident, relaxed, balanced, smooth, a predator amongst the unsuspecting prey. Like a mountain lion, only smarter.

Curious to you too.

14

Massachusetts

CASS TOOK HER LUGGAGE and locked the door behind her. She wasn't afraid of much, but she didn't want to be bothered. There was plenty on her mind and she hadn't relaxed all day.

She sent a quick text home saying that she'd arrived and then sat down and tried to drink a glass of water. It tasted funny, so she tried the bottled water. It tasted less funny, so she stuck with it. She had no idea where they were eating, so she decided to put on some nice clothes, just in case.

She opened up the suitcase and laid out her best pair of wranglers, a dark red, button up shirt with a simple, classy black yoke, and her black leather vest and blazer. She ironed the wranglers and the shirt. She put her boots back on. They weren't the best, but they'd do. Not like anybody in this part of the world was gonna know the difference. Same with the belt. It was in decent shape, still mostly black, and the buckle was old anyway; a team-roping trophy from before she was born. A pair of silver-stud earrings and a necklace she'd made herself from a piece of black leather lace and a perfectly expanded, Winchester Silver-Tip bullet that had been through both the barrel of her Desert Eagle and a rattlesnake's head.

She checked the time and there was plenty of it left. Wallace had sent a text that said he'd meet her in the lobby. She still had fifteen minutes. She opened up the misshapen box and put on her good black hat. Now she was dressed up.

Making sure her knives were all out of sight and secure, and her room key was in her pocket, she closed the door and went to find him. He was sitting in a chair in the lobby, his back to the elevators. There was another chair, with its back to his. Just to see what he would do, Cass slowly made her way across the floor and quietly seated herself in the other chair. He didn't seem to notice. She was sitting there, still trying not to laugh, when his phone rang.

He answered and spoke into the mouthpiece. "Yes. I'm headed up to get her now. We'll be there in fifteen minutes."

Wallace closed the phone and returned it to its place. He stood and started towards the elevator. He didn't notice Cass. "Pardon me," she said, standing. He saw who it was and sighed. "You. What are you doing?"

Cass just stood there, arms crossed, grinning. "Waiting on you. "

"You've just been sitting there behind me this whole time? Why?"

"I was a little early, didn't see any reason to bother you just yet. I figured you'd notice me soon enough. Anyway, where were we? I think you were about to come and get me or something like that. Right?"

"That's correct. Are you ready to go to dinner, Miss Elkins?"

"Well, I already ate dinner. I usually eat supper around this time. But seeing as how I'm pretty sure that what you call dinner is what I call supper and considering how hungry I am, I reckon I'm ready to go eat." She gestured toward the entrance. "Lead the way."

They arrived at the appointed restaurant fifteen minutes later. Cass got out of the car and nodded to Wallace. "You got your weaknesses, but I gotta tell ya that I'm impressed you're able to drive in this mess. I wouldn't be much good in all this traffic. There's no way I would've made it in fifteen minutes, least not without a big cow-catcher and an absence of conscience."

He shrugged.

Cass said nothing and went inside.

It was a fancy restaurant. Cass was no stranger to fine food, but she'd never been anywhere quite as upscale--outside of Las Vegas. But that didn't really count. She walked in, looking for the man from the hotel. The maitre'de stopped her as soon as she entered. Good thing she'd decided to dress up.

"May I help you?" He stepped in front of her and looked everywhere but her eyes. "Do you have a reservation?"

"I don't know, mister. I'm supposed to meet a feller here for supper, err, that's dinner to you yankees. Anyway, the evening meal. I guess I'll just go on in and see where he's sitting."

"I'm afraid that's not possible." The tuxedo attired man puffed up, but he was too skinny to be a penguin. "I can't let you go in there."

She looked past the man and crossed her arms. "Why not, mister?"

"There is a dress code here. You can't wear casual attire," said the man as if it was the most obvious thing in the world.

"What are you talking about?" Cass pretended to take offense. "This is the best pair of britches I own. This is my good coat. I even wore my Resistol." She pointed at her hat. "Mind you, that ain't a casual occurrence."

He was too slow coming up with a response. Cass brushed past him into the dining area. He followed her, calling for her to stop. She ignored him.

The dining area was large and busy. The wait staff moved with determination, making rounds with drinks and trays of good-smelling food, while managing to avoid collisions or even cause the slightest moment of disruption. They were also attired in dark tones that matched the general theme of the entire place, allowing them to blend into the dark décor and slip even more gracefully in and around the room. There were drapes, expensive paintings, crystal light fixtures, and a lot of people wearing suits or fancy dresses.

Overall, though a public locale, the restaurant did its dangdest to give an illusion of privacy. Cass finally spotted the man she was looking for, watching her from a shrouded booth in the back corner of the room. She turned to the upset maitre'de and pointed at the man. "I'm with him."

A change came over the maitre'de when he saw who she was pointing at. "Of course, why didn't you tell me in the first place? Go on in."

Alrighty then, add a little mystery to the heap. She sat down across from the red-haired man and waited for him to speak. He maintained the silence. Cass kept one eye on him and the other on the room. He'd have to say something sooner or later.

The waiter came. "What can I get for you to drink tonight?"

He looked at Cass. The man already had a drink, something the color of iced tea, whiskey of some sort probably. Cass's experience with alcohol identification was limited. Beer was pretty good, the labels were a dead giveaway. Liquor was either good or it was that stupid sweet stuff. Cocktails were something that fancy people knew the names of--except for margaritas. Cass could appreciate a good, sour, salt-rimmed margarita.

But not tonight. This was not a vacation. This was business.

"Iced tea, unsweet, with lemon."

Silence broken, the mind game moved to another stage.

The man spoke. "Miss Elkins, I hope the man at the door didn't give you any trouble. I wanted to see how you handled him. Your rather blunt approach seems to have worked."

"Well, mister, I figured it would be just as easy to ignore that fella as it would be to talk to him."

"I can see that we're going to have to work on that."

Cass laughed. "My people skills? Just 'cause I don't use 'em, don't mean I ain't got 'em." Cass's demeanor became more serious and her accent less pronounced and she said, "When the need arises, I am capable of conversing quite articulately, even politely if I must. But in my experience, more people understand the message I'm attempting to convey if I refrain from using the full extent of my vocabulary. I dislike having to repeat myself in simpler terms and explain my meaning."

The man didn't seem surprised. "I see. I must say that your appearance does not suggest such ability. Between your Stetson and your boots, you very much personify the country..."

"Hick? Bumkin? Don't hold back, Mister. I ain't offended. Takes a heck of a lot more than words to rile me up."

Cass resumed her relaxed position and less formal prose. "Where I come from, I'm considered to be rather well-dressed. This here hat is a Resistol. I only wear it on special occasions." Cass removed her hat and gently placed it in the seat beside her. "My Stetson is home with my other work clothes. 'Course, I can't judge ya too hard. I probably couldn't tell a Brooks Brothers from a JC Penney."

Before any more could be said, the waiter came back with Cass's iced tea and asked for their entrée order.

Cass had been so busy being nonchalant, the menu had escaped her attention.

Not a problem.

She glanced up at the waiter. "Steak."

"How would you like that prepared?"

Good question. Nice place, surely they had good meat. All steak was good medium. Good steak should be at least medium rare.

The man smiled. "It's good here."

Cass had already made up her mind anyway. Odds were good enough. "Medium rare, thank you."

"Cut?"

Before Cass could answer, the red-haired man chose for her. "The large filet. And same for me, as usual."

The waiter nodded. "Of course. Sides?"

The man cocked an eyebrow at Cass. "A baked potato, loaded, of course." he looked back at the waiter. "That's what I'd like."

The waiter nodded and looked at Cass. "And you as well?"

Cass shook her head once. "In fact, I'd rather have some sautéed mushrooms, so long as ya'll do 'em in white wine and butter. And some horseradish for the steak."

"Creamy or straight?"

"Straight."

"Of course." He nodded again. "Anything else?"

There wasn't.

The waiter left and the game advanced.

This time Cass spoke first. "So, mister, what exactly do I have to do to get on this show so I can win my half of a million dollars?"

"To the point. Good. You are here because you seem to possess many traits that we are looking for in a contestant. If you are as capable as our data indicates, you will be an excellent addition to our production. This meeting tonight is for me to assess you in person. I would like to begin by asking you some questions about your supposed skills. The reports we have had access to go only so far. Shall we begin?"

"Let's."

"Good." He pulled a thick file out of an attaché case that had been stashed under the table. It had Cass's name on it. "Let's start with a summary, and some of the high points. Your name is Cassidy Leroy Elkins. You grew up on your family's farm. You never attended public school. You started paying taxes when you were six years old. Hold on. That last statement must be a typo."

"No, you've got it right. I started earning a little money feeding orphaned calves on a bottle. I got audited when I was six. They decided that I had to start paying self-employment tax." She shrugged.

"Enterprising, that's good." He smiled. "Let's skip ahead to college. You passed your college entrance exams with flying colors. You also took the GED and passed with distinction. You attended the local university until you graduated near the top of your class. You received various job offers upon graduation, but instead you have spent the subsequent time living alone on the ranch you inherited from your grandfather, running an unsuccessful cattle operation. Care to add anything?"

"Who said my cattle business was unsuccessful? Was it that idiot Hearst?"

"Your tax returns show a significant loss since you took control of the ranch. No annual profit certainly implies a less than successful business. Does it not?"

"Just means that the one thing that darn accountant knows how to do right is taxes. I'll admit I've got financial problems, but it ain't 'cause of nothin' I've done. I inherited the ranch, much to the surprise of my whole family, mind you. My Grandpa was old-fashioned. Thought girls should be cookin' supper and raisin' babies. By the time I realized the difference between boys and girls, I was too far gone to come back. All the girls thought I was nuts and the boys were scared of me. Papa finally figured out that I was more cowboy that any of my cousins and he wanted the ranch to live on, not get sold or leased out of the family. I was thrilled, but the ranch came with its own pile of debt and a stupid accountant that I'm stuck with until the money is all paid back."

"So you went back to the ranch after school?"

"You bet I did. I was tired of town; tired of being around people all day long. Needed to get away. Too much civilization just don't agree with me. I like it better out in the middle of nowhere with my dogs." Cass paused a moment to let it sink in. "That answer your question, mister?"

"Yes, it does, Miss Elkins. Thank you."

Before he could finish, the food arrived, precluding any further discussion. Cass ate her tender, juicy, red slab of beef and enjoyed it. Not as good as one she'd fattened up herself, too lean, but it was one of the better commercial steaks she'd had the pleasure of eating.

The plates were cleared away and Cass started on her third glass of tea.

"What I'm most interested in is your unofficial skills. You are supposedly skilled in a variety of weapons and quite capable in hand-to-hand combat. Before anything can happen, we need to assess those skills to determine your proficiency."

"Hold on a second here." Cass sat her glass down. "I reckon ya'll know a fair bit about me, but like I told you, I ain't gonna go much further until you tell me more about yourselves and what you want from me."

"Miss Elkins, I can assure you that all will be revealed in due time. Details of the show cannot be released early. The entire premise would be compromised. If you will consent to a few tests of your abilities, and they confirm our data, you will be presented with more information should you assent to being a contestant."

"I'll do it, but answer me one question."

"Of course."

"Do you want me on the show?"

He almost smiled. "Yes. I do."

15

Washington D.C.

WALLACE DROVE Cass back to the hotel with a promise to pick her up early the next morning and take her to the main production site somewhere in Virginia. Cass decided to get some rest. There was no telling what they had in mind for tomorrow and worrying about it would do no good.

She woke up to the theme song from one of her favorite old western TV shows emanating from her cell phone as scheduled. She turned off the music and got ready. They had told her to pack. She would be staying on site for the next few days. Rather than wearing her dress duds from last night again, she dressed in her usual, more practical, attire. She put on a pair of loose fitting, dark denim carpenter pants and a black, short-sleeved t-shirt emblazoned with a picture of a fine motorcycle on a background of flames. She put on her well-worn, but still completely functional, work boots and fastened a simple leather belt around her waist. She pulled her shoulder length, dark brown hair into a ponytail and put on a camouflage ball cap.

She packed up the rest of her clothes. Everything except her black hat fit into the small suitcase. The special case for her Resistol was set on top. She did a once over of the room and headed downstairs.

Wallace was waiting in the lobby, holding a bag of breakfast food and a large Styrofoam cup. When he saw Cass, he handed them to her. "Have some breakfast, Miss Elkins. We should get moving. You can eat on the go this morning."

"Fine with me." She took the food and the coffee and followed Wallace outside to the car.

"The coffee's black. I hope you don't mind."

Cass responded by taking a long slug of the java. "Is there any other way?"

The next couple of hours went by quickly enough. Cass finished her breakfast and sat back to watch the country go by.

Possibilities and probabilities ran through her head. She didn't know much about the situation that she was putting herself into. She was doing it, but that didn't mean she knew enough. The trick to any game was knowing the players well enough to predict them and knowing the moves good enough to break them. All she knew so far was that this was a game--and she had to be the winner.

She reviewed the facts as she knew them so far. She had encountered three people that were involved. Dobbs, then Wallace, and finally the red-haired man.

Dobbs. Dobbs the geeky gopher, or at least he had appeared to her to be one. Who knew? Dobbs had approached her at home, made her a proposition spiced with enough cash for Cass to follow.

Next came Wallace. Wallace who picked her up at the airport, seemingly unprepared for her. He didn't seem all that interesting, but the way he watched her, observed her behavior.

He found it strange, but he seemed more interested than bothered. There was more to Wallace than he was letting on. Another quandary. He acted like he was used to being taken seriously. He carried a gun and other than the fact that he seemed to underestimate her, he could probably handle himself relatively well. Why was a guy like that doing nothing but driving her around? Was he there to protect her too? Or maybe it was the other way around; maybe he was supposed to keep an eye on her. That might explain why he was so reluctant to allow her to wander around by herself.

Finally, the mysterious red-haired man. The man who stands in the shadows watching. Who talks almost like a yankee, but walks like something else entirely. So far, he was the most interesting enigma. He might dress and speak like a city boy, but he hadn't always been. She was sure he was in charge.

What else? Everything. Everything so far had really been nothing more than talk. There wasn't a glaring reason to distrust these people, but that was no excuse. Distrust didn't require a reason.

Wallace finally pulled the car into the driveway of a big Virginia estate. There were multiple buildings. The main house, good-sized and well-kept, yet nondescript at the same time. Cass saw several outbuildings of varying sizes, including a relatively large barn. Beyond the structures, the trees brooded despite the sun. The bright, well-maintained clearing transitioned into shady forest. The whole place seemed to have an air of seclusion about it. Cass knew that it was difficult to find much privacy this far east. It was too populated and had been civilized for hundreds of years. There was something about this place that she liked and something that bothered her.

Wallace stopped the car. "Here we are Miss Elkins. Go in the front door. You're expected. Your luggage will be taken care of. I'll see you in a few days--one way or the other." He had a blank expression on his face and a far off look in his eyes, as if remembering something. He regained his focus and gestured to the door. "Goodbye, Miss Elkins and good luck."

"Thanks, Wallace. I'll be seeing ya." Cass got out and walked towards the house.

The front door. It appeared to be a good one, solid wood that would withstand a fair bit. There was a button beside it, presumably to activate a door bell. The door was unlocked. Cass turned the knob and went in.

As soon as she stepped over the threshold, something hit her hard from behind.

16

Virginia

CASS REACTED ON INSTINCT.

She continued her forward momentum and rolled away from the blow, mitigating a portion of its kinetic energy. But not nearly all of it. It still hurt, but it wasn't anywhere close to incapacitating. Behind her came a resounding thunk as the front door slammed shut. She came out of her roll facing the direction the attack had come from. One knee on the ground and both her hands up in a defensive formation. Ready to counter. She stood up and faced the closed door. She was alone.

She glanced around the room. The walls were uniformly white, what had appeared from the outside to be a large, shuttered window, was nothing but another blank wall. The door she had come in was steel with no visible means of opening from the inside. The outline of what appeared to be other doors were visible on two of the other walls, but again, she could see no obvious method of opening either of them. There was no furniture. Nothing. A trap.

She'd see about that.

She slapped a wall and listened to the ring. Soft steel, maybe three-eighths thick. Nothing special. It might as well have been a foot.

She went ahead and checked every surface, banging and listening for any variation.

Only the paint changed.

The white finish covered every surface, but it was not one smooth coat. There were grooves and scratches in several places. They had been painted over, but not smoothed.

They weren't tool marks. Too irregular and shallow. They looked a lot like fingernail tracks. She placed her hand on the wall. Bigger hand, but that wasn't saying much. Hers were small stubby digits. She pulled her hand back and focused on her fingertips and the flush fingernails. Only her thumbs had any nail beyond the minimum and all but one of the nails was flattened. She was a little proud of the one finger that she'd managed not to smash, yet.

So, somebody with at least a little fingernail had decided to scratch the walls. Hmm.

Didn't help though.

She moved on to the doors.

The front door was solid and well-fitted. There wasn't enough room to get a knife in the crack and a solid side-kick confirmed that it was firmly bolted as well. She hit it again along the inner-edge. Nothing. The hinges were good too.

The other two doors weren't quite so tight. It was immediately clear that they were more standard. Still metal, but there was slack. Not much, but enough to think about.

She settled in to wait it out. Something was bound to happen soon enough. They wouldn't just trap her here for no reason. She could be patient. They had to show some cards eventually.

She sat down cross-legged on the floor in the most defensible position she could find. Not much terrain to be considered in an empty room, but she did what she could. From her corner she could see all the doors and her back was to the outside wall.

She sat there for several hours, only standing up occasionally to avoid undue stiffness in her muscles. She played games in her mind, she reviewed what little she knew of her situation, and otherwise avoided boredom through mental activity. She had learned long ago how to be patient. It wasn't easy for her, she was prone to activity, but she had learned well. She'd spent many a long day in the field doing monotonous work of one sort or another since she was a child. One learned quickly how to pass the time. She'd honed that patience. She had learned to wait and wait and still be ready. She knew she could out-wait whoever was behind this.

The first few hours passed before she allowed herself to drift off. She didn't allow herself to fall completely asleep. She was still aware enough of her surroundings that she could revive if anything changed, but she knew that she needed the rest in order to stay ready. Her ears and other senses on guard, she closed her eyes and took a deep, measured breath, calling up a darkness and willing her mind to fill it.

Images played across her eyes, waking dreams conjured to fill the void. At first, almost consciously directed. She allowed her mind to replay the events of the past couple of days. She reviewed and critiqued her encounters. She replayed the silly engagement she'd had with Wallace at the hotel. She tried to fix into her mind the route they had taken here from D.C. She went over her memory of events as best she could, looking for something, anything, of consequence that she might have overlooked. She found nothing coherent, only vague impressions that there was more to the whole situation than she could see.

After a time, she unwittingly drifted farther into the darkness, beyond the will of her conscious self, until her subconscious filled the void. Scattered images. Impressions. Fighting, struggling, challenges, the usual. Her dreams were almost always like something out of an action flick. She liked her dreams. She always won.

17

O-Bar-Z Ranch

ROBERT DANSON WAS THE FOREMAN for the O-Bar-Z ranch. Had been for over twenty years. He'd lost track of the many owners that had come and gone. But no matter the money behind it, he had stayed with the operation. Taking care of the basic ranch work on a place where such things were of minimal concern to the owners--yet always important in order to keep up appearances--earned him a decent salary. He might have left if not for the other salary which had nothing to do with work and everything to do with keeping his mouth firmly closed.

To an outsider, the O-Bar-Z was nothing more than a historic ranch in the southern part of New Mexico. Bordering Old Mexico to the south, it reached up over fifty miles across the plains. It was the perfect set-up for smuggling goods over the river and into the United States.

All sorts of contraband, drugs, weapons, and people, had been smuggled in overland and dropped off at the ranch headquarters. The illegal goods were then loaded aboard planes and flown to distribution points all across the country; eventually ending up in the hands of dealers and then consumers.

Danson spent most of the day checking stock, mending fence, and doing many of the other small jobs that kept a ranch running. Just before lunch he delivered three head of the neighbors' cattle to their rightful owner and afterwards decided to make the twenty mile drive into Ebbson to eat lunch and load the trailer with feed, mineral and other much needed supplies. He finished running his errands just before dark. He stopped at the package store for a six-pack to go, then headed back out of town. In a little less than thirty minutes, he finally stopped in front of the elaborate front gate of the O-Bar-Z. The wrought-iron molding and three-foot tall letters never ceased to impress. In stark contrast to the barb-wire fence that ran away from the gate in both directions across the dusty prairie, the magnificent entryway was a blatant symbol of something, but he just thought of it as home.

Danson threw an empty beer can into the bed of the Dodge pickup he was driving. It bounced off the trailer's gooseneck hitch before joining its brothers with a hollow clank. Slowing, he pressed a remote clamped to the sun-visor and the ornate gates swung open. He sped up and continued up the well-maintained private road to the ranch headquarters as the gates automatically closed behind.

There appeared to be an unusual amount of activity going on at the main compound. He worried for a moment. Then he heard the incoming plane and understood. Tonight was a transfer. That was all he wanted to know.

The Dodge rattled as it rolled over the cattle guard that separated the headquarters buildings from the cattle in the surrounding pasture. Danson parked next to his house which was situated away from the main buildings and leaned against the door as he watched the now visible plane come in for a landing. The men were gathered near the runway as usual, waiting for the plane. They were waving their arms and motioning the plane down. One man was strangely still. He seemed to have a log or something balanced on his shoulder. Danson took a step back when a projectile emerged from the tube and flew towards the incoming plane.

Danson gaped as the plane exploded in a fantastic fireball. The flash momentarily illuminated the far end of the runway, revealing a dark colored plane that he had never seen before. He realized that those men were intruders. He dashed into his house and retrieved the Pump shotgun that he kept around for snakes. Grabbing a box of 20 gauge shells, he went out the back door and quickly made his way towards the nearby bunkhouse where the majority of the men bunked. They should be up and about now, since they slept in the day and did their work at night. He opened the door and felt the bile rising in his throat as he beheld the gruesome scene before him. They were all dead. Twenty hardened men had been slaughtered in their sleep. Most had been killed with a single, well-aimed round. Two or three had apparently woken and tried to fight back. Now, they were all laid out on the floor, riddled with bullet holes. He stood there for a long moment before finding the will to step over the bodies and peer out the window that looked towards the main house.

One hundred yards away, the large hacienda with its wrap-around porch, and classic western design, remained dark and silent. Despair hit him as he realized that the men in the main house must be dead as well. Juan, the current son-of-a-bitch-in-charge, would not have given up the ranch without a fight. Since he wasn't shooting back at the strangers approaching the porch, he must be dead.

Danson was more than surprised when Juan came out onto the porch to meet the black-clad men. A smaller man separated from the group, wearing a pilot's jumpsuit. Hands in pockets, he casually walked up on the porch and addressed Juan. They talked until the conversation devolved into a heated argument which ended with Juan angrily retreating to the house.

He didn't get the door closed in time.

The other conversant stepped to the side and turned away. As soon as his back was turned, the lead man in black lifted his AK and shot Juan in the back of the head. His body fell across the threshold and the invaders stepped over it as they followed their leader into the house. The smaller man remained outside on the porch and Danson suppressed a scream as the man turned his gaze towards him.

A cold hand gripped Danson's chest and he thought his pounding heart would burst as he ducked away from the window. He slouched against the wall for several seconds before he realized that he had better move before they came back. There was only one chance.

He ran as fast he could towards the secondary storage barn. The old one. Inside, the dirt floor was littered with hay and manure. The walls were lined with tools, saddles, tack, and more. He knelt down in the back corner of the barn, behind a stack of hay bales and started digging frantically. Underneath a three-inch layer of dirt, he found the steel hatch that covered the underground bolt-hole he had dug fifteen years ago for one of the former owners of the ranch. He was the only one who knew of it nowadays and he had stored the knowledge in the back of his mind. He'd had the feeling that he would have to use it someday. He opened the hatch, and climbed down the ladder until only his head was above ground. He felt renewed fear as a hole appeared in the barn door and lead whined over his head. He grabbed the wire of the nearest hay bale and pulled as he descended and let the hatch close after him. He heard the stacked hay fall, closing him in.

He remained as he was, perfectly still in the pitch blackness of the lightless hole for at least an hour. He held his breath as he heard the shouting of orders in a strange rhythmic language and the sounds of the invaders searching the barn. At last, after what seemed like an eternity, the sounds receded and he dared to breathe once more. Reaching in his pocket for the small flashlight he carried, he surveyed his new domain. A ten by ten, cinderblock cave greeted him. A small cot, and emergency radio, a chemical toilet and six months of water and food filled the room. With an exhausted sigh, he sat down on the cot and realized that he was still clutching the old shotgun in his hand. Never letting the cold steel go, he fell back on the cot.

18

Virginia

THREE MEN SAT IN A DIM ROOM and watched a computer screen. The image showed an almost featureless room--featureless except for the dark figure sitting cross-legged in the corner directly across from the camera. One of the men sat in front of the computer while the other two looked over his shoulders.

The Cowboy looked at the image of Cass Elkins. He put his hand on the seated man's shoulder. "Alan, how's it going?"

Alan Dobbs swiveled his chair around and looked up. "I'm not sure, sir. She's been just sitting there for the last few hours. At first, she examined the room quite thoroughly, then she sat down in the corner. For the first few hours she stood up and walked around every few minutes. Then a couple of hours ago she sat down and hasn't moved since. I assume she's just asleep." He turned his attention back at the screen.

"Hmm. Usually, the isolation causes a subject to get increasingly active and agitated. Not calmer and more relaxed, as appears to be the case with Miss Elkins." He turned to the man standing beside him. "What do you think, Wallace? You're the one who likes to profile the criminal mind."

Wallace nodded thoughtfully. "I expected her to pass the time with physical activity. Push-ups, sit-ups, the usual. She didn't strike me as the passive type. She's been wound pretty tight since I met her. This doesn't seem to fit the pattern I've observed so far. But I'm not all that surprised. She's interesting."

"We can agree on that." He turned to Dobbs. "Open the first door, Alan."

On the screen, a door popped opened across the room from the seated figure. Through the door was a small room containing a sink and a toilet. The dark figure remained still. Only the slow and steady movement of her diaphragm differentiated her from a statue.

The three men stared at the screen, waiting for a reaction.

Dobbs leaned forward and turned his chair. "At this point in the test, they are usually more than happy to make use of the facilities."

"Quite right," said Wallace.

"Maybe she is really asleep and didn't notice." Dobbs shrugged with his hand.

"I doubt that," said Wallace. "That door makes a loud noise when it opens."

The Cowboy didn't reply. He merely stood there, arms crossed, with an almost imperceptible grin.

After a few minutes without a change on the screen, Dobbs looked at him again. "What should we do?"

"You might try learning some patience from Miss Elkins." The Cowboy turned and walked out of the room, speaking over his shoulder as he went. "Terminate the test. Open the door."

19

Virginia

CASS WATCHED through slitted eyes as the final door opened and the red-haired man stepped into the room. He had changed. He wasn't hiding anymore. And he was wearing boots--real cowboy boots, not big city wannabes. They suited him.

She stood up to face him and look him in the eyes. That wasn't difficult. They were practically the same height. Nobody ever called Cass short, but she wasn't exceptionally tall either. Call it five-seven or eight. She figured that many people had foolishly underestimated the man because of his height. She wouldn't make that mistake. He was not a man to be taken lightly. This was the man she had spoken to on the phone. This was the real version.

She spoke first. "Well, mister. Or should I call you Producer. I thought it was you. How's my chances looking?" She crossed her arms.

The man smiled. "You've seen through my ruse. Though let me introduce myself anyway. As you surmised, I am in charge here."

"Do you have a name?" Cass didn't smile. "Or should I make something up?"

"My name is of no consequence. Just call me the Producer for now."

"Whatever floats your boat, Mr. Producer. Since I'm just plain 'ole folks, I reckon you can call me Cass. Now what? I must admit that I found the opportunity to be by myself refreshing, but I'm getting bored." A tight smile. "And onery."

"Soon, Miss Elkins."

"I said you can call me Cass, mister."

"Yes, Miss... Err, Cass."

"That's better. You were saying?"

"Yes, I believe you have what it takes to join our production. We will begin filming immediately."

"What makes you think I still want to? Ya'll tricked me. I ain't stupid. I know that was supposed to be uncomfortable. Most folks don't take too well to being by their lonesome. I'm an exception."

"You're curious. I can see it. You pretend to be upset, but in reality, you are enjoying yourself. The threat of danger excites rather than scares you." He looked her in the eyes. "And there's the money."

"Maybe." Cass didn't look away. "How would you know what I'm thinking, mister?"

The man paced back and forth in the small room. "Because I know you, Cass. Probably better than you know yourself." He stopped. "Follow me. Let's see if you can shoot as good as they say."

The man turned towards the closed front door. He said aloud, "Open the door. We're going outside." The door sprang open and he walked outside.

Cass followed. Shooting was always good.

The Producer led her around to a barn. Inside was a small pistol range. A bench towards one end, a bullet trap at the other and a pulley system strung between the two ends to move cardboard targets back and forth. All told, the maximum distance between bench and target was about fifty feet.

The producer stopped inside the door and motioned for Cass to enter.

She stepped inside.

Alan Dobbs was waiting for them.

"Alan set up a target at three meters and start the cameras. Let's see what Miss Elkins can do. Are you ready, Cass?"

Cass looked skeptical. "I would be, 'cept I ain't got a gun to shoot."

"We can fix that." He walked to the wall beside the bench and pressed a hidden switch.

A false panel slid to the side and revealed a well-kept weapons cache. Cass didn't hide her smile. There were guns of all kinds arrayed in neat rows. There were, of course, plenty of the pistols preferred by law enforcement and the military. Nine-millimeter Berettas, Glock Nineteens and Seventeens, Sig Sauers, and even some of the Kimber 1911 forty-fives that were specially designed for the SIS unit in Los Angeles. There were also quite a few--less common guns.

The Producer pointed to the pistols. "Pick one and we'll begin."

Cass walked over to the cache and carefully scanned the guns looking for something she would like. She knew that she could shoot any of them fine, but she had preferences--and she was here to put on a show.

She found what she was looking for and pulled it out. "This'll do." She checked it over. Mag out, slide back, chamber clear. The innards looked clean, and well-maintained. She racked the slide back and forth several times, feeling for any catch. It was fine. She let if drop and pulled the gun up and sighted. Simple wedge for the front and a notch for the back, all black. Stock sights. Not great, but this close, it would be okay. Happy with the feel of everything else, she pulled the trigger, carefully feeling the entire length of the pull and noting any rough or hard spots. Again, not great, but middling for the model. At this range, it would do.

She put the gun in her back pocket and proceeded to the next step. Ammo. There were boxes stacked beside the guns. She found the forty-four caliber loads. There were Magnums and specials. She scowled at the specials. Not gonna happen, even if they would've run in the gun. She grabbed a box of hollow-point magnums and opened the box. She took one round out and examined it. Standard brass case, a little tarnished. Primer visually intact and sealed. She rubbed her finger over the bullet. It was more tapered than rounded. That could be a problem. She hoped that this Eagle was one of the hungry ones that would eat anything.

She filled the magazine with eight rounds and gestured to the bench. "Ready?"

The producer looked at the gun she had chosen. "Interesting choice. Explain it."

"Okay?" Cass pulled the gun out and did her best impression of an expert salesman. "This here is a genuine Israeli-made Desert Eagle chambered for forty-four Remington Magnum. It's not the newest model; it's only a Mark Seven. But that's alright, it still handles the same as a Mark Nineteen which is what I'm used to. It holds eight rounds in the magazine and..."

The producer interrupted her. "I see you are familiar with it. Why did you choose it?"

"Because I like it?"

"You have no other reason? No logic behind the choice?"

"I have to explain my gun choice, really?"

"The camera can't read your mind."

"That's good to know. Fine. Here goes." Cass continued to display the gun. Awkward to hold it so very wrong. "Where's the camera?"

The Producer pointed.

She looked in the indicated direction. "The Desert Eagle is powerful, accurate, and it looks mighty fine. In this case, I was looking for a weapon I was very familiar with and used to shooting. I also wanted something that lends itself to me shooting it real accurate. You know, some guns just get along with me better."

"What would you have picked had the situation been different?" The Producer put his hands on his hips.

"Different how?"

"Combat, for example?"

"How close, how many, and where?"

"It matters?"

"Quite a bit, if you want a real answer."

"Close quarters, several, soft or unknown backdrop."

Cass cocked her head to the side. "More or less than ten?"

The Producer smiled. "More."

"Glock, nine-millimeter, pref'rably mine, but even a regular one would work."

"Practical. Very different from a Desert Eagle."

Cass relaxed and turned to the bench. "Very different situation."

The Producer and Dobbs put on a set of headphones to dampen the sound. Dobbs tapped her on the shoulder. "Would you like some hearing protection?"

Cass looked at him.

Rather too loudly she said, "What's that? I can't hear you."

Dobbs repeated his offer.

"No thanks. I'm good."

He looked confused.

She pointed to her ears. "Ear plugs. I keep a pair in my pocket."

That seemed to satisfy him.

Cass might not have been a boy scout, but she had always liked their motto.

She turned back to the bench, inserted the magazine up the well, and racked the slide to chamber a round. She checked to make sure the two men were out of the way behind her. They gave her a thumbs up. Range is live.

She looked at the target they had set up and tried not to laugh. A single snort escaped before she could contain it, but with their ears on, it was unlikely that anybody heard. It was a couple of feet wide and at least three feet tall. The target area was in the shape of a man's torso and head. And to top it off, it was only ten feet away. She almost didn't know what to aim for. Almost.

She put the gun in her left hand, took the safety off and proceeded to rapidly put eight rounds through the target. After the last round ejected, the slide locked back. She was pleased. The gun ate the ammo without a hitch.

She turned to see the two men standing there much like before. But now Dobbs had a decidedly less indifferent air about him. He looked at the target and then at Cass. His face went a shade paler and he avoided Cass's gaze by glancing down. Subtle, but she noticed.

The Producer looked smug. He spoke to Dobbs. "Alan, run get that target and set up a new one. Further out this time."

Dobbs changed out the targets and handed the old one to the producer. He ran his finger around inside the ragged hole in the cardboard. "Well, a little rough around the edges, but not bad."

With the eight shots, Cass had made a silver-dollar sized hole right through the center of the target's forehead. She didn't tell him that she'd originally intended to put them in the throat. That was understandable. She'd never fired the gun before and with all the potential variations in sight pattern and sight-in, it was always a gamble the first time.

Well, the first couple shots were an accident. She'd decided to put the rest in the same hole. No reason to adjust and skew such an impressive pattern.

The Producer looked at her. His eyes went from the target, to the gun, and then back to her other hand. "Are you right or left handed?"

"Right, mostly."

"Then why are you shooting with your left?"

"It didn't seem sporting to shoot anything that close with my right. 'Specially something that big. I wouldn't use a target that size at anything less than a hundred yards on a windy day. Two hundred on a still morning."

"I'm impressed."

"So, can I shoot as good as they say?"

He laughed. "It seems possible."

20

O-Bar-Z Ranch

"SLOPPY WORK, MR. JOHN. Have your men burn them as soon as it gets dark." Maksim Derchev finished searching the body on the porch and stood. He flipped through the items in his hands. Five hundred dollars, a gold watch, a gold-plated forty-five, a smartphone, and three pieces of peppermint candy. Careful not to get any blood on it, he unwrapped a candy and popped it in his mouth. He had resisted the gluttony that infected his father, but he blamed his mother for his very American sweet-tooth. He dropped the other items in a plastic shopping bag, tied the handles together and then added it to the garbage bag sitting by the driveway.

"Are you finished?" The man he knew only as Mr. John spoke in the clipped tones of a man who had not learned English from America, but in Europe. Like Maksim's cousin, Yuri, who had always made fun of Maksim's American English. Hell with Yuri, America was so much more fun. If Maksim never set foot in Europe or the damn Motherland again it would be too soon.

He nodded. "Da. Burn them now. I doubt that Juan had many visitors, but we should be ready. Clean this up, then the bunkhouse."

Mr. John did not respond, but Maksim took it for an affirmative. The Arab did not like taking any suggestions from a foreigner and 'infidel.' But Maksim had been hired by someone higher up the Arabian food chain and from the moment Mr. John and his followers had crossed the border, they were supposed to listen to Maksim, the expert on America. It was a mystery why they had even been sent. The plan did not require idiots wearing explosives or the usual crude methods preferred by the jihadists. Maksim admired the depth and sophistication of the plot, even the parts he had not worked out himself. These idiots were going to be trouble. He could feel it.

He waited long enough to see that Mr. John passed along his instructions before leaving them to the unglamorous task.

"Where are you going?" Mr. John stopped in the doorway and glared.

"The trucks will arrive tonight. I must make preparations." Maksim kept walking. He hated to turn his back, but it was the world he lived in. He wondered if his father would avenge him if something happened. Unlikely. His employer was even less likely to care. They needed him, but that was not enough reason to stop hating him.

He had already decided that the hanger building would house the girls and the equipment. It was already wired heavy and had ample room for the operations. All that remained was to secure it.

The large, sliding doors would not be needed. He thanked the late Juan or whoever had built it, there was a chain ready and waiting to lock it down. The single remaining entrance was around the side. It was also lockable, but a guard would be best. At the very least, Mr. John and his men made any manpower issues moot. The one called Bill had struck him as level-headed and at least moderately experienced. He would do.

Inside, it was dark and quiet. After a momentary pause, his eyes adjusted and looking for where the sun slipped in through cracks or holes, he was pleased to find that the building had been well made and well-sealed--and that the Johns had not damaged it during the mad raid to take control of the ranch. He only spotted a few bullet holes in the tin, and counted himself lucky. Satisfied, he reached out and found the light switch.

A dark green Turbo 210 aircraft was parked close to the hanger doors and other than a large locker for parts and tools next to the walk-in door, the large space was empty. Perfect.

He pulled out his cell. No service in the hanger. He had to get outside in the open for the two bars necessary to make a voice call. It rang four times and then Alexei answered.

"Zdrastwicha, Alexei."

"Mr. D? You're dead."

Maksim sighed. Alexei was not the brightest bulb in the house, but he was loyal and surprisingly competent. "Duh, this is Maksim. Are you sober?"

"Yeah, you just sound like him."

"My brother is dead and I am not him. Remember that or I will find someone else."

"Yes, sir, Mr. Max."

Well, it beat being mistaken for Junior. "Send the trucks. I want those girls working right away."

"Yes, sir."

"You get the trucks here tonight. See you soon." Maksim ended the call and stared at the sky. Now, he needed to find a place to stay. One night in the same house with the Arabs was plenty. He hadn't slept a wink, knowing they were so close. The hatred they had for him was so thick it was palpable and he'd rather not give them too much opportunity to forget how necessary his services were.

He decided that the tack room in the old barn was a good bet. He would hear the old doors creak if anyone tried to sneak in and the small room inside was just big enough to make it work. Taking a few saddle blankets from the tack room in the new barn, he made a moderately comfortable sleeping pallet. He retrieved his go bag and other stuff from the big plane he had used to fly in the Arabs and hid it in the room as well. He took the gun he had stolen from the dead Juan and slipped it between two of the blankets. His father would never stand for such pitiful accommodations, but Maksim was not his father. There weren't bars on the door. It would do fine.

But it would be best if it was secret.

He went back up to the house and found a spare bedroom and took the mattress and the bedding. Quite conspicuous, he dragged it across the dry grass to the new barn and a made a show of setting up camp inside. It was only a short distance between the two barns and he could make it out of sight from the other buildings after dark. He doubted he would sleep soundly, but there would be some rest.

For now, there was little to do but wait until Alexei arrived with the trucks. Then there would be more than enough to do. He looked around and saw no one. Maybe it would be a good time to try out his hideout. There'd be no time to sleep tonight.

21

Virginia

THE MIND WAS A TERRIBLE THING to leave alone.
Cass believed that the constant harassment of one's inner
thoughts, beliefs, and principles was healthy and more than a
little entertaining. Unfortunately, she ended up doing most of
the harassing. Other than her close family, few had the inclina-
tion or the ability to test her psyche. She looked over the room
where the analyzing was about to happen and hoped the shrink
was up to the challenge. She'd always thought it might be fun
to be psychoanalyzed.

There were two cameras on one side of the room, each
pointed at one of two chairs and a little lamp table. She picked
the one that appeared to be intended for the question-asker and
sat down, watching the door. Alan Dobbs, who had followed
her in, came over and started attaching leads and sensors. It
had been explained that for dramatic effect, she would be mon-
itored with the intent of measuring the truth of her responses.
He worked silently and she let him. After he finished and left

for the control room to run the cameras and other equipment, it was no more than five minutes before her much anticipated mental nemesis entered. She was more than a little surprised to see who it was.

"Wallace?"

"Good to see you again, Miss Elkins. Are you ready to begin?" He was eyeing her chosen seat, but said nothing about it.

She gestured to the other chair. "Ready as I always am. Have a seat and let's get this show on the road."

He sat down and had to move the little table so that he could reach the notepad and pen that had been waiting for him. "Here we go Miss Elkins. We'll start with a few standardized questions to calibrate the readings. Are you ready?"

Cass nodded and slumped in the chair. "Shoot."

Dobbs pressed a few keys on the laptop and Wallace cleared his throat. "Please answer with either a yes or a no. Is your name Cassidy Leroy Elkins?"

"Yes."

"Are you twenty-three years old?"

Cass paused to think. Age had never meant much to her and she was prone to forgetting. "No, not anymore."

"Very good." Wallace glanced at Dobbs' screen and nodded. "Why are you here?"

"That's not a yes or no question."

"Please answer all questions as necessary, Miss Elkins."

"I'm here to win a million dollars, I guess."

"You guess?"

"Yeah."

"How do you feel about authority?"

"I don't."

"You have no opinion?"

"No, I don't *feel* about it. I *think* about it," Cass said. "Let's just say I don't get along with it real well."

"You have a problem with authority?"

Cass thought a moment, wanting to convey herself accurately on a subject that was far too nuanced to easily discuss. "I have no automatic or ingrained respect of any authority. I'm just not a follower. I think too much."

"Are you religious?"

"I would say no."

Okay, moving on. Have you ever broken the law?"

"That's vague, can you be more specific? You talking about God's law, Federal law, state law, or what?"

Wallace wrung his hands together and said, "Have you ever broken a federal law?"

Cass shrugged. "I think anybody that's breathing has probably done that."

Wallace tapped something on his tablet and nodded. "How about state law?"

Cass tilted her head to the side and smiled. "Maybe."

"I'll take that as a yes."

"That's your prerogative, I reckon. You got any questions that mean anything?"

Ignoring her, Wallace continued, "And God's law as you call it, have you broken that?"

"I sure try not to and I think I'm doing pretty good, considering."

"Considering what?"

"I'm human."

"You believe that excuses any wrongdoing?"

Cass shook her head. "No, you can't be excused, only forgiven. Humans just ain't perfect, and neither am I, that's all it means."

"So, by God's law, what are you referring to? You said that

you were not religious."

"The ten commandments. And I'm not. I've got faith. No need for an institution in between. Religion is not a prerequisite for faith, it's a path."

"The ten commandments tell you not to kill. Do you believe that killing is a sin?"

"Try reading the original, mister. I try not to murder, there's a difference."

"I see," Wallace mumbled, making yet another note.

Cass doubted it, but she was willing to give him the benefit of the doubt. Unlike some people she knew, she didn't automatically assume that everyone who didn't immediately and dramatically declare their faith at every opportunity didn't have any. There was nothing more annoying than constant preaching.

"So, you are a Christian, then?"

"That seems obvious."

"Do you go to church?"

"Sometimes."

"Not a true devotee, then."

"My faith is between me and Jesus. I just go to church 'cause I like the people there."

"I see. Let's move on to your more earthly actions. Have you ever hurt anyone?"

"Sure. Hard not to."

"Do you enjoy it?"

"I don't know?"

"You don't know?"

"I've never really thought about it." Cass paused, thinking. "I don't think I'm a sadist, if that's what you mean."

Wallace glanced at Dobbs, who shook his head. "You are telling the truth. Now, have you ever killed anyone?"

"Is this a trick question?"

"No, please answer."

"You already know the answer. That's the reason ya'll wanted me. That mess back in college." Cass grew a little distant, remembering, yet again, that day. "He was a bad guy."

"Did you enjoy it?"

Cass was still in the past. She replied softly, "What?"

"Killing."

She looked Wallace in the eye and shrugged. "I beat the bad guys and saved those girls. The good guys won. I won. That usually feels pretty good."

"Have you ever killed anything else?"

"You mean a person, or just anything with two eyes?"

"Anything."

"Sure."

"What, specifically?"

"Varmints, mostly. A few critters too."

"You've hunted animals."

"Yeah."

"Why do you kill animals?"

"Killin' varmints is obvious, but critters tend to taste good and it's a good exercise."

"Do you enjoy it?"

"Sure, hunting trips are usually fun."

"Do you shoot these defenseless animals?"

Cass raised her eyebrow. "Sometimes I use a gun, usually a pistol, and sometimes they ain't defenseless. Ever heard of a cougar, mister?"

"Yes, Miss Elkins."

"They ain't exactly defenseless."

"So, you enjoy hunting predators?"

"Sure."

"Why?"

"Cause it's harder."

"Than what?"

"Than hunting prey, obviously."

"Have you ever thought about hunting a human?"

"Why would I do that? Sounds too easy."

"I see. Interesting."

"If you say so." Cass had to admit that it was amusing to lead him on. Despite her love of bluntness, she considered it a challenge to be blunt while revealing as little as possible. Then, of course, there were times to let it all out 'cause no one would believe it anyway.

"Miss Elkins, do you consider yourself to be a racist?"

Cass leaned back in her chair and continued to smile. Finally, a question to roll with. "Well, sir. If by that you mean, do I judge folks based on whatever subset of the human race they appear to be, then, no, I don't. If you mean, do I ignore such things when I'm making up my mind about something, the answer is no. I'm not stupid. Or mayhap you're asking if I avoid making jokes and poking fun based on such subsets. Once again, no. I'm afraid I'm an equal opportunity insulter. My sarcasm and irreverence is applied to all, no free passes. If they cain't handle it, that's their business, not my concern." Cass eyed the man. "Does that answer your question?"

"In detail. Thank you, Miss Elkins." He made a few notes, taking several seconds to look at his notepad before raising his gaze back to Cass. "Next question. Do you consider yourself to be a patriot, Miss Elkins?"

Cass took a deep breath and paused a moment before answering. "Well, sir. That's another loaded question. It's gonna take a bit to answer. Short answer is yes. Long answer is what I figure that means."

"Feel free to explain."

"Certainly. That's it right there. You're brilliant, doc."

"Pardon?"

Cass had to savor the look of confusion on his face. "Just like you said. I'm free. That sums it up pretty succinctly."

"Are you going to elaborate?"

Cass looked thoughtful, for effect. Then just said, "No."

"I see," he said, taking more notes, and waiting even longer before asking her another question.

"Miss Elkins, how do you feel about women in the workplace?"

"What workplace?"

"Any workplace."

"That's not a question."

"Well then, let me clarify. How do you feel...?"

"Stop right there, mister. You got me wrong. I don't feel nothing about it, that ain't how I roll. However, if you can find it in yourself to ask me a real question, I might just tell you what I think, yes?"

"Can you answer the question?"

"No, but I'll give you a related opinion. I'm tired of waiting on you to ask something sensible. What do I think about women? In whatever they're doing, wherever they're doing it? I say I think they're generally gullible, they complain too much and they don't think things through near enough."

"Miss Elkins."

"Yeah, hold on. Let me finish. I want you to know that I know that ain't the sort of sentiment that I'm supposed to express. I'm quite aware of the current societal expectations and conventions. I just don't care. I'll think what seems most logical up and until I'm convinced otherwise. For now, I'm a chauvinist. Chew on that."

"Miss Elkins, calm down. There is no need to get upset."

"That's the truth, doc. I'm just tired. I'm happy to tell you what you want to know, but only if you ask me straight."

"I think we're done for now. Dobbs will remove the sensors and then you are free to go. We'll do some other tests in the morning. Make sure you get a good night's rest."

"So what's the analysis so far, doc?"

"Most interesting." He stood and headed for the door, his notebook still on the table.

Cass picked it up and waved it at him. "You forgot this."

He paused at the door and smiled. "No, I don't forget anything. Thank you, though."

22

O-Bar-Z Ranch

ALEXEI WAS DUE TO ARRIVE with the truck at any moment. Everything was more or less ready. The Johns were lined up and armed, as visually menacing as possible. That was one thing they were actually good at. Maksim preferred them that way. Not close enough to smell, but as a distant image of hairy danger.

The truck arrived on-time. High noon was sufficiently hot and hellish. Maksim wanted it that way. Holding captives was as much a psychological effort as physical. The oppressive environment, the obvious isolation from civilization, the menace of armed guards, it was all a part of the show.

He nodded to Alexei and the two girls were brought out. Gagged and tied, they were weak from the stress, but still well enough. Perfect. Maksim stood back and allowed Mr. John to greet them. As expected, and intended, he was not nice. He gave them each a full dose of menacing maniac and punctuated his speech with a disrespectful blow that knocked them both to the ground. Right on cue, he turned and stomped away in self-righteous strides across the sand.

Maksim contained his smug smile and approached the captives. He helped them up and gave a disapproving glance in the direction of Mr. John. They were on the verge of tears, stopped only by the fact that they had no more to shed. Maksim removed the gags one at a time and let each girl have a drink from the Gatorade bottle he'd brought along. They thanked him with their eyes, still scared, but he was now the closest thing they had to a friend in the world.

They were easily escorted to the hanger where they would be staying for the duration of the project. Three-fourths of the space would be occupied by the project and the rest was makeshift living arrangements. Maksim had been involved in many kidnappings, it being the family trade. Usually, there were no accommodations made. The living conditions were abhorrent. This was different. These girls were chosen for their brains. He needed them well-rested, nourished, and as comfortable as possible.

He said little or nothing of importance, continuing to imprint himself as the nice guy. He brought them food and drink and showed them the fresh clothes that were waiting. He left them alone for a time, but never strayed far. He wanted them to see him as a protector.

He gave them one week to acclimate and then they would be working.

23

Massachusetts

CAMBRIDGE, MASSACHUSETTS, home of the Massachusetts Institute of Technology. Seeing it in person made Cass happy she had turned it down. MIT sounded cool, but Massachusetts was not somewhere she'd ever aspired to be. No car, no gun, no space, too many people.

Too civilized.

The only good thing was that she didn't have a problem keeping on her toes. The city made her nerves tingle. Today, that was very good. She was supposed to be ready for some sort of situation to arise. Wallace was to drive her wherever she wanted to go, and at some point, they would cross paths with a prearranged situation where her reaction would be filmed. It would either be her first or last episode. She had to make it look good.

She intended to make it look real good.

It would be fun at the very least. It was the first real challenge. No script. A surprise encounter. She wondered what they had planned.

"Where shall we go first?" Wallace didn't take his eyes off the traffic.

"Kendall Square."

Wallace obliged and after a few more minutes of murderous city driving, Cass was thankful that she wasn't prone to motion sickness, and she was within walking distance of where she wanted to go.

The place had a name appropriate to its location near one of the premier engineering schools in the world. The title was an invented term that implied an amalgam of high-powered coffee and raw electricity. The shop served coffee and also served as a sort of art gallery for some rather mechanically inclined paintings and sculptures. Cass was there for the coffee. According to her source, it was worth the slow service and the hip clientele.

Wallace was trailing behind her, ready with a camera, and she decided not to worry about it. There was espresso to be had.

Cass went inside and ordered. Ready to wait, she picked a small table in the back that only had one chair. She didn't want Wallace to join her. He could sit somewhere else.

It took ten minutes for her coffee to be made, less than one for her to drink it, and five more before Anne Chaves walked up to her table dragging a chair and offering a dry cappuccino.

"You always were the perfect friend." Cass took the coffee and smiled as the woman sat down across from her.

Anne had been Cass's only real friend in college. They had drank gallons of coffee together and graduated first and second out of their class. Anne won the tie alphabetically and she would never let Cass forget it.

"You were right. They make a good espresso." Cass took another sip and made another pass over the cafe with her eyes. The place wasn't bustling at the moment, but business was steady.

Cass played a mental game with herself as the patrons came and went. She kept track of what kind of coffee people ordered and whether or not they wanted flavor of some sort. She found it somewhat amusing that a large percentage of the patrons ordered something that had so many flavors or sugar or chocolate, or something else in it, that it was a stretch to even call it coffee when they were through. Seemed like very few people came into the coffee shop to actually drink coffee.

Anne watched her scan the room and waited until her attention drifted back to the table. "Still the same. Anything I should know?"

Cass smiled a little. "I was simply contemplating the infinite hypocrisy of flavored coffee."

Anne laughed. "I've never seen you turn down good coffee."

"Quite right." Cass took a deep drink. "I merely imply that a certain concentration of actual coffee must be present in order for a drink to qualify as such. So, how are you doing these days?"

"Good. School keeps me busy. How about you? What brings you this far east? I know I'm good company, but you're not here just to see me."

The show was still supposed to be a secret, but Cass was good at avoiding details. She hated to lie to her friends, the least she could do was make sure they knew she was doing it. "I came out here to see a man about a job. Had some spare time. Thought I'd look up an old friend. Here I am."

"A job? Really? Cass Elkins is considering getting a job in the city?" Anne was incredulous and her face showed it. "I don't believe it."

"Well," said Cass slowly. "Let me put it this way. Some guy wanted to make me an offer and he flew me out here to meet him. I don't have any plans to work in a city, but I'm always up for a vacation that somebody else is paying for. But, enough about me. How's school? Learning anything? Doing any research?"

"I should have known better than to ask." Anne giggled and she took a sip of her latte. "School's good. Graduate work is a little tougher than the first four years, but it's good. Not nearly as bad as all our professors told us it would be, anyway. It's more fun too. I'm getting to take part in some cutting edge research in my spare time. I can't tell you much about it. We're supposed to keep it a secret for now. But I can tell you that its potential impact is enormous."

Cass nodded in response as she watched a man dressed like a university student order a plain black cup of joe. Not impossible of course. But certainly against the odds. Anyone who tries so hard to dress trendy would likely be inclined to drink trendy flavored coffee. Maybe even a Chai or something. But plain? Maybe, but not likely.

Out of curiosity, Cass kept an eye on the exception to her previously established rule. She couldn't put her finger on it, but something else about the man was bugging her.

She looked back at her friend. "Microbiology is going places, sounds like. It sounds like you did all right when you decided to do your grad work there." Cass grinned slyly and leaned across the table. "Surely you can tell me a little about this research you're so excited about. You know me, I ain't no blabbermouth. Come to think about it, I reckon you're the only person within a couple hundred miles that I'm inclined to visit with. I'll be back home in a few days and nobody will be the wiser-- 'cept maybe a cow or two."

Cass watched as Anne contemplated her answer.

"I do trust you, Cass. But, I had to sign all kinds of papers that promised I wouldn't tell anyone about the project. I'm sorry. But, you know how it is. We were both raised to keep our word and that's what I intend to do."

Cass leaned back with a satisfied smile. "That's what I wanted to hear. I wanted to see if the city had changed you too much. Glad to see you haven't."

"Why you! I oughta." Anne pretended to throw her coffee at Cass. "I can see that you haven't changed a bit either, Cassidy Leroy. You're still an ornery rascal if there ever was one."

Cass smiled and drank some cappuccino.

Anne scowled, trying not to smile, failing. "With a twisted sense of humor to boot. You're hopeless." She finished off her latte and stood. "If you'll excuse me a minute, Amiga." She headed further back, where the restrooms were located.

Cass slowly drank the last of her cappuccino and watched the crowd with amused interest. She watched as the man with the black coffee stood up and walked towards the back. By itself, nothing out of the ordinary. But, suspiciously, three other men, who had come in just after Anne, also picked that moment to apparently heed the call of the wild. There was probably nothing wrong, but all of Anne's talk about top secret research made Cass wonder.

She knew that there was nothing more than a dead end corridor with two doors. Men's and women's. She had seen no way out when she had taken a look at the layout of the place earlier.

Before she could decide whether or not to check up on Anne. Her friend returned to the table--none the worse for wear--and took a seat. Cass mentally teased herself for being so paranoid. She knew it was futile though. She was always this way when people were around. It was fascinating how they could live so close together and appear so relaxed. She took a deep breath and leaned back in the hard chair.

"So, how long are you going to be here, Cass? I've got to

get back soon. Maybe we could get together again before you leave."

"At least a couple more days I reckon." Truthfully, she didn't really know how long. But she had three days of hanging around waiting for something to happen. She hoped it would be sooner rather than later. Running around Boston for three days was not her idea of fun, even if she did have a good reason. She would do it for the money, but she would prefer to find a way to make it enjoyable. Steak would be a good start.

"Steak?"

"Of course. How about tomorrow night? We can meet at my apartment and go from there. I know just the place. Seven work for you?"

Cass nodded. "As far as I know. My plans are somewhat unpredictable. But, unless something comes up, I'll be there."

Anne checked the time on her cell phone and stood up. "I've got to scram. See you tomorrow." She waved back at Cass as she left.

Cass ordered and drank another espresso before leaving. Nothing like good coffee to calm the nerves.

24

Virginia

"HOW DID IT GO, JUSTIN?" The Cowboy sat down in his chair and lit a cigar. He put out the match with his fingers and leaned back, smiling. "Was I right?"

"She is definitely non-typical. Hard to classify." Wallace shrugged.

"No one is unreadable, Justin. What can you tell me?"

"Well, she's probably smarter than me. I had her complete several different intelligence tests and her scores were very superior in most cases. There were a few specific areas where she was only above average, but there were complementary spikes to match. Her short term memory scores were unexceptional, but I suspect that is due more to a lack of attention, than lack of faculty. Pattern recognition scores were very good. Overall, her average IQ is definitely very superior, if not quite genius level. She's about as smart as you can get while still having a reasonably solid connection with reality."

"Excellent, but unsurprising. Continue. Tell me about her

personality."

"There is far more to it than the simple character she seems to prefer. She is a very accomplished actor in her own way, picking and choosing facades as she pleases depending on how she wants to interact with others. The arrogant persona that she has largely maintained during my contact with her is but a small portion of her true self."

"A defensive mechanism."

"In part, perhaps, but that would imply fear, and submission. Neither of which is she inclined towards. She has convinced herself, to a very deep level, that she can do almost anything. In her mind, her capabilities are sufficient to any situation. Unlike most people, she does not fear the unknown. She trusts in her own capacity to overcome any obstacle or problem."

"Mmmm." The Cowboy tapped his cigar on the wooden ashtray. "Are you trying to tell me she's fearless?"

"No, but fear is a very minor factor in her decision making process. What I believe I'm saying is that once she decides to do something, regardless of fear, she does it. No more hesitation."

"She doesn't second guess herself."

"Exactly."

The Cowboy glanced at the cigar between his fingers. "A rare trait when paired with true competence."

Wallace raised his eyebrows. "It makes her very dangerous."

"Yes, of course it does." The Cowboy's smile turned wolfish.

"I'm concerned about her reaction when she finds out the truth. She has very strict ideas about honesty. Violating her trust is an easy way to turn her against you."

The Cowboy looked at Wallace. "Then we must make sure she has something more at stake. She may never forgive, but she will overlook a deception in pursuit of something more important."

"Ah, the money." Wallace nodded.

The Cowboy shook his head. "It'll take more than that. It would be much simpler if she was that greedy. What do you think, Justin?"

"I don't know. She strikes me as extremely motivated to get the money. She talks about that ranch like it was a person, a loved one, almost. She has no intention of letting the land go."

"Well, we can hope then. Perhaps that is all that will be required to guarantee her cooperation. But I suspect that the ranch has a far different significance to her than it would to most. She probably doesn't even know her own motivations in the matter."

"What would they be?"

The Cowboy smiled. Wallace knew that expression. It was satisfied and superior. The Cowboy knew something special and he was not going to share it quickly. He would try to make Wallace arrive at the same conclusion with only the minimum of guidance.

"I have to work for it?" Wallace sighed, but it was with a smile. He couldn't complain. Ever since the strange man had knocked on his door, his life had gotten far more interesting. Being the small town newspaper man with a psychology habit on the side had been interesting on the rare occasion that something more criminal than a traffic violation occurred. There had been two actual murders where the culprit wasn't obvious. The sheriff had called him in to help profile those cases and he'd started to look forward to the next one.

The Cowboy blew some smoke and said nothing. He would wait and watch Wallace search for the answer.

"I don't see anything beyond the obvious, emotional motivations or the money." Wallace spoke mostly to himself. "Without a doubt, it was far from a good business decision. Cass's intelligence makes me believe that there would have to be a significant alternative motivation to overcome the more rational part of her. Some sort of intangible emotional motivation seems likely if monetary gain is eliminated." Wallace leaned back and looked down, deep in thought. Whatever the Cowboy was implying, he was far too sure that he was in on some sort of secret, and he probably was. The Cowboy, and Cass to a degree, showed more than a few anti-social characteristics. Wallace had always found sociopaths strangely fascinating. The intelligent ones were enigmas. They played at normalcy, but underneath, their motivations were far removed from anything a normal person would have. Not for the first time, he wondered at the Cowboy's reasons. He had the brains and the ruthlessness to be a master criminal; he had no real reason to be on the side of the angels. Yet here he was, working to save people that he probably saw as weak and even useless. It was an enigma that Wallace had some theories about, but he could never prove anything. No matter how many theories and terms they came up with to describe the workings of the human mind, it was ultimately a mystery. No one could truly understand the mind of another.

But he could try.

"You're certain it's not nostalgia? An irrational desire to keep the ranch in the family?"

"The ranch has only been owned by her family for twenty years. There's not enough history there. The actual family land is still owned by her parents and is in no danger of being lost."

"I'll have to think on it," Wallace said. "I'll let you know."

The Cowboy nodded, his gaze already distant, and Wallace took it as a signal. He stood up, hesitated long enough for the Cowboy to give him an indication, but his mind was already far ahead. He ignored Wallace in his typical form of dismissal, moving only to tap the ashes off his cigar.

Tomorrow would be very telling. She would have to show her true mettle and he suspected that her heart was made of something much more useful than gold.

25

Massachusetts

CASS PAID THE TAXI DRIVER outside Anne's apartment building. As she started down the sidewalk, the driver shouted, "Be careful. It's not safe for a woman to run around alone."

She kept walking as she turned her head and shouted back with a grin, "That's what they keep tellin' me. It's kinda hard for someone to hurt me if I'm alone, ain't it? It's when I have company that I oughta be worried."

The driver just shook his head as he counted the money and drove away.

Cass walked through the darkness with a light step. Wallace had taken her on a tour that ended with a sparring match in some park. They'd hired some sort of local martial artist to stage a mugging. The second one of the day. More material for the editing booth, she supposed. The first mugger was much more convincing, his knife was very in character, but he'd come too close with it. The second one was too flashy. She doubted a real mugger would try too hard to get into a hand-to-hand fight--or a foot-to-nerve fight, as it had ended. But it would look good for the camera. Realism, after all, had little chance on reality television.

She went up the stairs, thinking about supper. Her stomach growled. Anne had not told her where they were going, but Cass knew it would be good. They had similar taste in dining, and since it was unlikely to find a good plate of green chili fajitas this far from home, wherever they were going, there would be steak. Thick, rare, well-marbled steak--or something close.

Cass pressed a button on the wall that buzzed her friend's apartment.

"Chaves residence," came a tinny voice from the small speaker.

"It's me. I'm hungry."

"You always are. Be right down."

Cass waited. Anne came down about the same time that a cab showed up and parked along the curb.

"Shall we go and satisfy our carnivorous selves?" Anne asked as she motioned to the cab.

"That's a silly question," said Cass as she slid into the seat beside her friend."

Cass raised her eyebrow. "Where are we going?"

Anne laughed. "Now who's asking silly questions? A steakhouse. Where else would I take a barbarian like you? It's not far, we should be there soon."

She spoke true.

The sign said 'wait to be seated'. A few moments after they entered, a young woman came into view carrying menus. She looked up at her customers and upon seeing Cass's black cowboy hat, said excitedly, "Well, hee yaw. Where are you from, Texas?"

Cass hid her amusement and said with a straight face and a pronounced accent, "I'm from around there, ma'am. I live on the Texas-Arizona border, to be exact."

If the waitress was aware of the geographical ambiguity of the statement, she didn't show it.

"Well, howdy partner. Please follow me to your table," said the waitress, sounding out the greeting with a strange cadence and emphasis that made it almost unintelligible.

The corner of Cass's mouth turned up slightly and she traded a glance with her friend as they followed the waitress down to the main dining area.

"Not as good as McNally's, but not too bad either." Cass wiped her face with the cloth napkin before tossing it onto the empty plate. She took a long swallow of freshly brewed unsweet tea before continuing, "I'll have to remember this place in case I'm in this part of the world again."

"You're impossible," said Anne. "I swear you're never satisfied. This is supposed to be one of the best steakhouses in the city, hence the prices and the clientele. If this McNally's is that good, how come nobody's ever heard of it? I still think you just made it up."

"Think what you will, my friend, it exists and if we're ever on the other side of the country, a little up the Kern River, south of the Sequoias, I'll prove it to you. 'Till then, I guess you'll just have to take my word for it."

"You're incorrigible," Anne said. "Speaking of geographical locations, I'm still curious about what might bring a bitter American like you this far east."

"That's a story for a more private venue and a large pot of strong coffee"

"If you're gonna be that way, let's head back to my place.

I've got a good press and I might even have enough coffee to keep you for a while. How about it, amiga?"

"Coffee and less people? You have to ask?" Cass stood. "Lead the way, amiga."

They paid the tab and went outside.

"It's less than two miles back to your place, right?" Cass put her hand in her pockets and took a deep breath of the less than fresh air. It still stunk, but the cool evening air was better than the stuffy, stinky, oxygen-like stuff inside. "Let's walk, work off some of that meal. You lead the way."

"All right. I suppose you can protect me."

Cass smiled. "Eh, I've only beaten up two muggers today, I might be a little out of practice. Still care to take the risk?"

Anne laughed. She was used to Cass's sense of humor. "Let's go."

Cass looked around. "Which way?"

Anne pointed to the right. Cass started walking. Her friend had to hurry to catch up, but in a few moments, she was keeping pace. "I forgot how fast you walked."

"Do I need to slow down?" Cass paused.

"No, it reminds me of old times. It reminds me of how we got to be friends."

Cass resumed her normal pace and thought back. "Hmm, as I recall, that was a slightly embarrassing situation."

"For me. I think you enjoyed it."

"It was amusing. Your mother, of all things, asked you to ask me to accompany you when you had to walk between buildings. She was afraid for you to walk alone."

"I decided it was cool. I was the only freshman with my own bodyguard."

"It was kinda fun. And we never yakked like any other pair of girls."

"Yeah, not like she said, he said, she said, he did with her... We were more inclined towards laughing like crazy people and sharing stories of the dumbest things that happened to us that day. I'm not sure either of us would have finished without the venting."

"We almost decided to quit every couple of months, as I recall. It's a wonder we made it through."

"No, I needed the degree to get a job and you..." She trailed off, grinning.

"Me what?"

"You were just stubborn. Still are, I'm sure."

"Can't argue with you there, my friend. You're undoubtedly correct."

They were still laughing and talking of old times when Cass heard the distinctive sound of a slide being racked. "Trouble." She went from casual observation to full on alert. The sound had come from behind and there wasn't any cover around. It was several yards to the nearest parked car and she wasn't nearly skinny enough to hide behind a light post. There was the slim chance that they were not in danger, but it seemed unlikely. Just a few steps more and she would have a decent hand to play.

But of course, no luck. "Put your hands in the air, ladies. You're coming with us. Turn around slow." Cass turned around to see the hree men from the coffee shop, each holding a Glock small-frame handgun. Nine millimeters, judging by the size of the bore. Glock Nineteens, then. Looked like stock magazines. They'd just racked the slides, so no more than fifteen rounds apiece.

Small bullets. Not that it mattered at this range.

The man in the middle gestured with his pistol and the other two approached.

Anne looked at Cass, a question in her eyes, and a hint of

fear. She raised her arms up and stared at the muzzle of the gun.

Cass raised her hands as well, but she was watching the man holding the gun, waiting for an opportunity. She rocked up so that her weight was on the balls of her feet, and bent her knees slightly, ready to move.

The men got behind them and pushed them towards a dark car parked at the curb. They were close, but there were two of them. Cass could do nothing about the one who was herding her friend around with the muzzle of a gun. She'd gotten Anne to come to her self-defense classes a few times, but Anne didn't ever make it to the serious stuff.

This was definitely the serious stuff.

She needed to act soon. The odds of escape and survival decreased drastically if she got into the car. If she could get the leader... He was only a couple steps away. The gun was in his right hand, held at waist level, not really aiming, just pointing. His attention seemed to be on Anne. Foolish.

Cass had it planned. Keep walking towards his right side, when he was in range, roll around his gun arm. Grab the top of the slide with the left hand, then control his arm with the right. Control the arm with the other hand. Continue the spin and leverage the wrist to get the gun free, hopefully breaking the trigger finger. Gun in right hand, roll around behind the man and use him for cover and shoot the other two before they realize what's happening. Can't shoot boss guy, he's unarmed. Shame.

The first man and his gun were a step away from being close enough to take when Cass felt a sharp blow from behind. She saw Anne fall, felled by a similar strike. It stunned Cass for a moment, but didn't knock her out and she was only one step away. She took the step and started to turn, her raised arm moving down to grab the gun, but the second blow was harder and

Lee Brown

she ended up on the ground.
    The third blow knocked her out.

26

Massachusetts

CASS NEVER STAYED OUT for long. Her and a few sparring buddies used to practice knocking each other out in order to familiarize themselves with the process--on both sides. Cass had always been hard to put under. It didn't take long to make sense of the voices.

"Yes sir, we got the girl like you asked. No sir, no trouble at all. Right away, sir, I'll deliver her personally," said a man's voice from the front seat.

Cass listened to the near end of a telephone conversation. It sounded like this wasn't an accidental kidnapping. Of course, the guys in the cafe... They must have been after her all along. She wondered what this was all about. Then she remembered that she was on a reality show and was supposed to be waiting for things to happen. Doh. A kidnapping would make sense, a revisit of her past. The more she thought about it, the more sense it made. The guy on the phone even had a hint of a Slavic accent. She stifled a snort. Anne was probably in on it too. She'd do that. Cass relaxed as she decided that she was right. Guess it was a good thing she hadn't gotten around to shooting these guys back there. She berated herself for being so blind. When she'd heard that gun, she'd forgot about everything but the situation and how to survive it. She'd have to be more careful in the future, she didn't want to kill any actors.

But they wouldn't use real guns. She smiled as she realized that she hadn't nearly killed a couple of innocents. Now the fun could begin. Time to put on a show.

She considered her position. She was in the back seat of a car. Her hands were tied and she was gagged. But her feet were still unencumbered.

Same mistake they'd made last time.

She was slumped across the seat next to Anne, who appeared to be unconscious. Next to Anne was one of the men. The other two were in the front seat. The apparent leader was sitting on the passenger's side, talking on a cell phone. The car was moving fast, probably on a freeway.

She wondered where they were going, not that it mattered. She knew little or nothing about the area and her normally accurate sense of direction didn't work so well in an urban setting.

She nearly giggled as she heard more of the phone conversation.

"One more thing, sir. What about the other one? What should I do with her?" A short pause ensued before he finished, "Very well, I'll have Marco do it, he enjoys that sort of thing. We'll be back soon." The man ended the call by closing the cell phone. Then he returned it to a pocket and said," Marco."

"Yea, Pete?" said the man in the back seat.

"The boss says we don't need an extra. We'll let you out up here and then you take care of it. I'll have Jimmy come back for you after he drops me off at base. Got it?

"Sure, I got it. No problem."

Cass pondered the exchange and could not come up with any reasonable interpretation other than that they wanted Anne safely out of the way--and the writer was more than a little melodramatic. The whole situation belonged in some cheap action flick. But she was no one to throw stones, she'd watch it--probably more than once.

She just relaxed, letting her head rest on the soft seat. The ride continued in silence until the driver stopped the car.

"This'll do, Marco," said the boss. "Wait until we're gone and be sure to clean up."

Cass was expecting the man called Marco to drag Anne out of the car. She was momentarily surprised when he reached for her. She continued to feign unconsciousness while the big man maneuvered her out. He unceremoniously dropped her on the ground several feet away before returning to slam the door closed.

Guess they wanted a one-on-one bit. Cass watched the car drive away down the street. She quietly rolled around and got her feet under her. She looked for an escape. The narrow, dead-end alley offered no hope. The only way out was past the man standing in the narrow mouth. That was okay, running away didn't make for good television.

An inconvenient streetlamp illuminated the opening to the extent that she would never be able to sneak past him convincingly anyway. She could run for it, but he supposedly had a gun and if he could shoot half-decent, her odds were bad. Embracing the need for a more direct approach, she stood and took a few steps back until she was cloaked in the deepest shadow the alley provided. She smiled grimly. It was only one man.

He turned towards her and looked at the spot where she had been.

He twisted his face into an ugly smile as he looked around and said, "Come here, little girly. You can't hide from me. You've got nowhere to go." He stepped farther into the alley, hands out in front of him, like he was going to catch her.

Cass stood still and watched him advance.

He was taking his time, kicking the profuse garbage that littered the alley. He stumbled a little, his eyes not adjusted to the darkness yet. Ah, the drama.

Cass had been careful to keep one eye completely closed while in the light in order to preserve her night vision. She figured that she could see several feet further than her enemy. She had an edge.

It was not that she needed one, but she was of the opinion that every edge should be taken advantage of. Nothing was too small to swing the odds just a bit more in her favor. That would make a good voice-over or interview clip... She'd have to remember that.

Back in the game, she watched as he foolishly came further into the shadowed alley, calling to her in his thick Boston accent.

"Come on, baby. Come on out."

She held her breath as he came close and then walked right past her. The way out was clear, but she turned away from the street. Her eyes were bright and a tight smile crossed her face as she silently stepped away from the grimy brick wall at her back.

Marco stopped a moment to scan the alley. "Don't be afraid, little girly, come to papa." His vision was improving. He paused again when Cass came out of the shadows.

Cass quickly hid her confidence behind a timid facade. She wasn't very good at faking submission, but it only had to work for a moment--and it was nice and dim.

"Come here," he grunted.

Cass raised her arms slowly. She stopped just shy of arm's length. He was reaching out to grab her when she raised her eyes. He hesitated for a moment when their eyes locked. A moment was all that was necessary.

Cass attacked.

She threw a ridiculously slow, but pretty kick towards his head, trying to play along with the drama level she'd observed so far. He ducked, and she followed with a double roundhouse. He dodged the first kick, but caught the second. With impressive strength, he threw her against the alley wall.

"You stupid girl. Now I'm mad. I was gonna make it quick." He shook his head and pulled out the Glock.

Cass tried to overcome the instinctive urge to try and kill the man. She kept telling herself it was not a real gun right up until the bullet tore through her left thigh. Cass looked down, shocked. It must have been a solid core 9mm, not a hollow-point, because it went right on through. It hurt like the dickens, but she could hardly feel it. She was angry and that made her more focused on causing pain than feeling it.

"Now you won't be trying any of that kung fu crap on me, babe. Let's have some fun."

He moved towards her, teeth bared, and a look in his eye that said he wasn't going to kill her right away. The moment he'd fired that gun, Cass had forgotten all about the show or anything else other than the right here and now. She was no longer playing by any rules.

She'd pulled herself up into a sitting position, her back against the grimy brick wall, her hands curled up against her left shoulder. She kept her eyes glued to her target as she waited for him to get close enough. The seconds were eternities as he walked up, then knelt down over her. He reached out with his free hand and felt of her hair. His other hand, still holding the gun, was against the ground, helping to hold him up. It was the end.

Cass's tied hands moved in unison towards their target, one just an inch behind the other. The edge of her right hand struck the man's throat. The other hand followed right behind, adding the strength of her other arm. A blow that was dangerous with one hand became deadly with two. There was a wet sound as he tried to breathe through his partially crushed trachea.

He jerked back to his feet, hands grabbing at his neck.

The gun was out of play.

Cass stood and set herself against the wall, using it to steady her injured leg long enough to kick with the other. The kick wasn't pretty, or high, or any of the other things that look good on a television screen. It was only nasty. Cass's foot hit him right above the groin. He took a step back, still searching for air, then he collapsed, no longer capable of standing.

Cass fell down, unable to maintain the balance needed to recover without both legs working. She got her good leg under her and picked up the gun, but there was no need for it. The kick, as intended, had not only knocked the wind from her enemy, but dislodged the cartilage connection of the pelvis, damaging the structural integrity of his body. He was not going anywhere.

Cass put her boot on his right arm and let her other knee fall on his chest, provoking a violent gasp. He continued to moan as she searched his coat and found an extra magazine for the Glock and a switchblade knife. She stuck the mag in her pocket and used the knife to remove the bindings from her wrists.

"Listen here, bub." Cass aimed the gun at a discolored spot of skin between his eyebrows. "Where is my friend? Where'd ya'll take her?" Her voice was a low growl, unsteady. But her hand was not. "Tell me."

"D..D..Derchev," he coughed between ragged breaths.

"Derchev? Is that a man? A place? What are you saying?" Her accent became more pronounced as her anger and her fear for her friend grew. "Tell me where those punks took her so's I can go an' get her."

"You..you..cannot..." he gurgled. "..you..just..a..a..little girl."

"I reckon I am, bub." Cass grinned, letting her eyes stray from the sights to lock gazes with her prey. "But that never stopped me before."

Before she could do or say anything else, the man died.

Cass stood up, keeping the gun ready, and listened. There was nothing extra to hear over the standard racket of a city. She started walking towards the street, staring at the darkness.

She had to find Anne. Who knows what they intended to do. Nothing good, for sure. Cass used a word she saved for special occasions and started looking for her cell phone. It was gone, of course. She started walking as fast as she could manage with the bum leg. She had to find her friend before something happened.

She would make it right either way.

BOOK 2

Strike

28

Massachusetts

"THANKS, WALLACE. I'M OBLIGED."

Cass fumbled herself into the passenger seat of the car. Her leg was beginning to hurt. The excitement was no longer keeping the pain suppressed. It still seemed to work, more or less, but she hoped that the bullet hadn't caused too much damage. She needed to be ambulatory to go get Anne when she found her.

Wallace replied evenly. "It's what I'm supposed to be doing, keeping an eye on you. Where have you been?" He noted the blood still seeping from her leg, despite the makeshift tourniquet she'd fashioned from her belt. "What happened?"

"I thought we already established that I don't need you to babysit me everywhere I go."

Wallace sighed. "I don't doubt your ability to handle trouble. But I'm starting to wonder about your ability to avoid it. I don't know what you've gotten involved in, but it isn't good for you."

Cass looked at him with a scowl, "I don't care if it's 'good for me' or not. Somebody kidnapped my friend and tried to kill me. I don't know what that means around here, but where I come from it means I got some work to do."

"I understand your feelings, Cass, but you can't just go after a criminal organization on your own. It's suicide."

"That, my friend, is your opinion." Cass looked sideways at him. "And if you're so darn worried about me going it alone, I reckon I wouldn't be opposed to the idea of you taggin' along." She raised an eyebrow. "If you ain't too scared, that is?"

Wallace looked out the window. "I have more pressing concerns. What you're proposing sounds contrary to those goals. Surely you understand?"

Cass grinned. "Oh I understand all right. But I can't say I sympathize with your feelings. I've got my vices, but obedience ain't never been one of 'em."

"Alright, Miss Elkins. Where to first?"

"I knew you had it in you, Wallace," Cass said, looking around the car for something to use as a makeshift bandage. "Let's start with Anne's apartment. I'm pretty sure that this was no random kidnapping. Them fellas had a plan and knew who they wanted. I've been trying to figure out why they were after Anne. Maybe there's something informative at her place." She looked up. "Where's the duct tape? And I assume you have some sort of good rags? Shop towels? Blue paper towels? Even just some regular paper towels, maybe?"

Wallace shook his head. Cass was struck again by the frustration of being so very far from where things made sense. What kind of rig didn't have duct tape? A sorry one.

"Where exactly is your friend's apartment?"

"About a mile from MIT, half-a mile from this little coffee shop. I can't remember the name of the street, but it was four lanes and sounded like a weed."

"Let me take a look at the map." He reached down beside his seat. But what he retrieved was a small unmarked aerosol container.

Cass was opening her mouth to ask him about it when he discharged some of the contents in her face. She coughed a few times before her eyelids got heavy and she found herself unable to move. She tried to speak, but little more than a moan escaped her lips. Deprived of a vocal outlet for her thoughts, she did her best to stare daggers straight through Wallace's big yankee brain as he put the car in gear and drove off.

"Sorry about that, but as I said, you left me little choice. I'm sorry about your friend. I'll inform the proper authorities." He paused and looked at his watch. "I'll wake you when we get there."

Cass had no intention of sleeping but the drug was making it very hard. Within a minute she drifted into unconsciousness.

She woke to see the same white room where she'd ended up the first time Wallace tricked her. As the tranquilizer wore off she began to regain control of her muscles. She was lying on her back on a simple cot in her favorite corner. She slowly sat up and gripped the edge tightly as a wave of lightheadedness nearly overcame her. She recovered after a few seconds and the events preceding her slumber rushed into her mind.

"Anne," she mumbled to herself softly. Then with a violent clenching of her jaw, she growled, "Wallace."

The pain was getting more annoying as time wore on and when she sat up, she found that her injury had been treated and bandaged. Her pants leg was gone. She pondered it a minute before reaching for the knife she'd taken off the dead man. It was gone too. She growled again and tried to stand. It took a couple of attempts, but she made it happen. She stood and stretched thoroughly before making use of the facilities. At least they had left that door open for her.

She had to get out of here. She'd been right. Things were not as they seemed. More important, Anne was in trouble. Cass took a deep breath and squashed the maddening panic that threatened to rise up every time she thought of her friend. It was no good in here. She was no good in here. She was no good to anyone until she got out, away from these people and whatever they were really up to.

This wasn't real, so neither was the money. Not that it mattered either way. Friends were more important than money.

But there was still an act to put on. Had to play along to get out of the trap. That was the only option she could see. If her stupid leg wasn't shot, maybe the interior door would fall to a good side kick, but Cass wasn't about to produce a good one. No, it was down to a mind game.

A game that she had to win.

After splashing some cold water on her face, she sat back down on the cot and looked up at where she decided a camera ought to be. "Morning, big brother. Where's breakfast? Where's coffee?"

29

Virginia

PATIENCE WAS A VIRTUE. Cass kept repeating it to make it more true. After hours of sitting and waiting, a second door opened and added something interesting to the featureless white room.

The producer walked in, followed by a man that she had never seen before. A little older than herself, she guessed, he was wearing a white polo shirt, some sort of tac-pant, and his shoes were clean and probably expensive. She noted that the pockets were flat except for what looked to be a small clip knife on his left side. His face was unmarred and a little pale under the stylishly-tangled brown hair. An indoorsman, more prepared than the usual, but not overly; clean, the white shirt was spotless and...well, he was wearing a white shirt. More than a little vanity. His look was calculated. He didn't just throw on whatever was on top of the pile.

But she had to admit that under the swagger, he had a decent stride. He wasn't helpless, just soft. He stopped beside the

Producer and waited with his arms crossed.

"Congratulations, Miss Elkins. Welcome to the final part of the show," said the Producer, pointing to the man. "Let me introduce you to the only other remaining contestant, Robert Bartleby."

Cass nodded and reached out to shake Bartleby's hand. "Pleasure. I'm Cass. Cass Elkins." She smiled as she spoke, but it didn't reach her eyes. She had nothing against him, but he was the competition. At the moment, friend wasn't an option.

He took her hand and smiled back with a more earnest expression. "My name's Bobby. Known to most as Bobby Blade. Robert Bartleby is my father's name, an old name, I never have liked it. I need a name that fits the new age."

His handshake was firm, but a little too quick. He wasn't all that interested in meeting Cass, something else was on his mind. But he seemed alright, if a little pale and his Yankee accent was offset by the precision with which he pronounced his words. Not too annoying for someone from back east. "That's fine, Bobby. You can call me Cass. Never been much for conventions either."

"I like you," he said, pointing his finger at her and grinning. He looked at the Producer. "What does she do?"

Cass resisted the urge to remind him that she was standing right there. She decided that he was making up for the lack of an annoying accent in other areas. Like being an idiot.

The Producer just turned and left the room, leaving her alone with Bartleby. There was no chance she was going to call him "Bobby Blade."

He scratched his hairless chin and spoke at her. "Oh, the silent type. Very mysterious and frightening. Guess I had better watch my back in case you pull out the ninja voodoo." He waved his hands through the air pointlessly to emphasize the end of the sentence.

Cass was more than happy to let him think whatever he wanted.

She walked past him on her way out and without looking back, she said, "Don't worry. I'm not from Louisiana."

"No voodoo, then. Good to know," he called after her.

She continued walking, but she had heard. Good to know. Bobby Blade was sharper than he looked.

She waited until the man she wanted to talk to came out. The Producer. He swaggered by and she fell into step beside him.

"What is it?" he said.

"I didn't say nothing in there because that boy might not be in on the trick yet, but it's time for you to spill the beans, mister. I ain't playing anymore."

"As expected. Follow me and we'll have a sit down and a cigar. I'll explain."

30

Virginia

THE PRODUCER LED Cass through the house into a more comfortable room, one that was free of gadgets and monitors, one that did not seem so out of place in rural Virginia. The room was furnished in oiled wood and leather and smelled of cigar smoke and secrets. The Producer sat down in the chair with the best view and Cass took the next best one. It was comfortable and smelled good, but she was too preoccupied to relax and enjoy it. She leaned forward and glared at the man across the room. "Spit it out."

The Producer smiled. "Much of what I'm about to tell you is highly sensitive information that cannot leave this room." He handed her a non-disclosure contract and a pen. "Before we can continue, I need you to sign this."

Cass took the paper and read it all the way through before signing it and handing it back in silence. She could be quiet; it was one of her favorite pastimes.

"Thank you. Now onto business. It's quite simple. I have

brought you here to offer you a job."

"That don't require near as much hoopla as this."

He nodded. "I had to make sure that my information about you was correct."

"I hate tests." She popped one of her knuckles absently. "Even when I can ace 'em."

Only his eyes moved, but she got the impression he was enjoying the confrontational atmosphere that had filled the air between them. "You have a decision to make."

"Hold on a second," Cass paused her knuckle popping. "Answer me one question before I answer you. Why should I? You've done nothing so far but deceive me. What in the world makes you think I'd want to work for you now?"

He didn't hide the small grin. "Cass, I've spent the last thirty years in this business. I've seen people of every kind. Most people are sheep, they are victims; they don't understand that there are predators out there. Most predators prey on the sheep, but a rare few don't settle for weakened prey. You and I are the same, we are not sheep. That's why you isolate yourself. Because you're afraid of what you might do. You're afraid of yourself. What I'm offering you is the chance to become a protector. You have the skills that I need. You can make a difference and probably enjoy yourself at the same time."

Cass considered this. She still doubted the legitimacy of this entire setup. It was not right. A lot of things were off, but she was worried about the most obvious.

What if they had something to do with the kidnapping? It seemed a little crazy, but so did everything else that was happening. She couldn't forget that they had lied--a lot.

She looked at the Producer and said, "You're telling me that you work for the CIA? Excuse me for my ignorance, but this thing doesn't smell like a big government agency operation.

There's not enough paperwork and too few people. You're still not telling me something and to be honest with you, I've just about had it with this cloak and dagger misdirection. If you really want me to work for you, tell me what's really going on or put me on a plane. Your choice. Lay it out or let me leave."

The Producer sighed. "Has anyone ever told you that you are too smart for your own good, Miss Elkins?"

Cass leaned back and crossed her arms. "Nope. Might have been a few people thought it, but nobody ever told it to my face."

"Well, I guess I would have been disappointed if you didn't live up to your reputation as a stubborn and annoyingly discerning young woman. You are correct in your deduction that I don't work for the Company. This is a small operation that the CIA doesn't even know about. Myself, Dobbs, Wallace, Bobby, our benefactor who will remain unnamed, and now you, are the only people who are aware of its existence."

Cass nodded. "I see. Now that I know what I'm really here for, we can do business. What would you have me do if I say yes?"

If this was the master plan, it would do to see how far it went. She needed to know exactly what the man calling himself the Producer, wanted from her.

A look of satisfaction crossed the Producer's face. "I'm sure you're aware of the many threats facing this country; enemies from abroad and from here at home. The major government intelligence agencies and the military can take care of most situations. However, the bureaucratic nonsense that they must go through, aided by the policies of the new administration, severely limits their ability to act in certain situations. They can handle the big stuff, but there are times when a single, unhampered individual is needed. The government, by nature, is virtually incapable of doing anything that small." He paused for a moment.

Cass cocked her head to the side. He was making sense, but he was still a liar. "You're just preaching to the choir so far, mister."

"So it seems. You'd be surprised how rare it is to find people who understand the reality of the world rather than believing the lies that are told to comfort and mislead the weak. But I digress. Back to your question. If you say yes, quite simply, due to the range of your skills and the variety of situations that might arise, there is a multitude of possible answers. In a nutshell, your job will be to solve problems that arise with a minimum of fuss and minimal assistance. At times you may be called upon to use your mental skills to gain information. Other times, you may be asked to use your martial skills. Let me put it this way, the reason we exist is to handle problems that require immediate action and adaptability. I chose you for a very simple reason. You are self-sufficient and competent in a broad range of areas. You should be able to handle virtually any situation that comes along. You can adapt."

"I'm flattered," Cass said with an edge of sarcasm. "One more question. What do I do when there's no heads to smash? I hope you don't expect me to stay around here. If I had to take up residence this far east, I'd likely become a threat myself."

The Producer chuckled. "When you're not activated, you can do whatever you want. As far as I'm concerned, you can live just as you are now. As long as we have a means of contacting you. Stay on your ranch and write a book or whatever it is you do out there."

Cass realized that he was winning her over. What he was saying made sense in a weird sort of way.

If he was telling the truth--this time--then maybe he could

help. Maybe this was just what she needed to find Anne. It wasn't likely to be easy. Cass was stubborn enough that she had a chance alone, but if she had a better chance with these people, she had to take it. She had to do everything possible to find her friend.

Right now, the producer looked like a manipulative, possibly nefarious, lying jackass. But he was the best thing she had going.

Cass made up her mind. "Alright, here's the deal, mister."

31

Virginia

"I'LL DO IT--on one condition." She had thought it over and she'd made up her mind. She would join them, for now, but not as a lowly employee. She didn't do things like that.

"What condition might that be?"

"The condition that you accept all my conditions... I have a few." Cass took the lack of response as an invitation to explain. "Here's the deal. First, I want ya'll to help me find Anne. I reckon you have access to a fair bit of information. I want you to find out about this 'Derchev', and anything else that'll help me find the people who took her."

"And how would that benefit us?"

Cass smiled. "Simple, I'm goin' after them whether you help me or not. So if I'm valuable to you, it would seem that your best interests lie with me gettin' this over with. The more info and support I've got the better off we'll all be. That make sense?"

"I see your point. Very well, I accept you terms. Give me a

moment." He sent a text message of some sort and then looked back up at her. "Alan is on it. He'll let me know the instant he has a lead. You can settle down. We'll find your friend. I guarantee it."

"That's a big promise. I'll hold you to it." Cass took a breath. It wasn't much, but maybe it was all that could be done at the moment. It wasn't like she had a clue where to start. She turned her attention back to the Producer. Sometimes, slow was the best you could do. But she wasn't finished. "I ain't done yet, mister. I need something to shoot. I don't like running around without a decent aresenal. 'Specially with a limp." She pointed to her leg. "That doable?"

"I think I can arrange something." The Producer crossed his arms. "What else?"

"Just one more thing. If you want me to do something, you tell me all about it. And I don't mean that 'need to know' junk either. You lay it out plain as day--or clear as mud, whatever the case may be--but you tell me everything. I've never been inclined to do anything half-cocked and I ain't about to start now. If you want me in this little organization of yours, you bring me in all the way or not at all. Savvy, mister?"

"It's not that simple. We can't just..."

Cass cut him off. "No, that's not what I said. This is the million dollar question. Yes or no? I'm either in or out, but I won't settle for in-betweens. Make up your mind."

He shook his head and smiled. "Welcome aboard, Miss Elkins."

"I reckon so." She looked at the man called the Producer. "Now, first things first, seeing as how we're now in business together, I reckon first names will do. You call me Cass and I'll call you..."

He hesitated and started to argue but Cass preempted

him.

"Now, don't start that. We agreed. I'm in on it all. Now, what can I call you other than 'The Producer'?" A mischievous look crossed her face. "You better come up with something or else I'm gonna make something up and it might not be to your likin'. Your choice."

"Cowboy," said the man. "They call me the Cowboy."

"That's still not a name. You can make something up for all I care, but it better be a name."

The Cowboy sighed. "Fine, if you insist, you can call me Carlos."

"Well howdy then, Carlos." Cass stuck out her hand. "Pleasure doing business with ya."

They were shaking hands, when one of the dark wood panels that lined the walls swung inward like a door. An older, but decent-looking man in a grey suit stepped into the room and the secret panel closed behind him with a soft whoosh. Cass heard the noise behind her and turned to look as the Cowboy spoke, "Dirk, meet our newest recruit, Cass Elkins. Cass this is..."

She interrupted the introduction. "It's an honor, Mr. Vice President." It had taken a moment for her to recognize the man out of context, but upon realizing his identity, she stood and tipped her hat to the man.

He seemed almost embarrassed by her reaction. "Please, let us forgo such formalities. I'm no longer in office and to be honest I'd prefer it if you just treat me like the regular person that I am." He noticed Cass's rather stiff pose. "Relax, Miss Elkins. No need to stand at attention." He proffered his right hand.

Having realized that she was standing stiffly, she smiled, somewhat embarrassed. "Sorry, sir. It's not every day that a girl gets to meet someone she admires." She shook his hand. "Still an honor to meet you, sir. Cass Elkins at your service. But, I'd appreciate it if you'd just call me Cass. I'm not much for formality either."

"Glad you're of a like mind, Cass. Call me Dirk."

He took a seat in one of the nice leather chairs and reached for the small humidor sitting on the mantel of the large fireplace. "Mind if I smoke a cigar? The Cowboy always has such a fine selection."

"Not at all. 'Specially if I can have one too."

"You smoke?"

"Not really. But occasionally I've been known to enjoy a good stogie. That a problem?"

"No." He passed the humidor to her. "Here."

She got herself one of the proffered cigars and put the box back on the mantel. She rolled it between her fingers and looked at it thoughtfully. "They say these'll kill ya."

The Cowboy finished lighting his own cigar. "They might be right."

"Yeah. I reckon they might at that." She lit hers. "But it don't really matter."

The Cowboy savored a mouthful of smoke, blew it out, and then looked at her. "Why not?"

She smiled and leaned back in her chair. "Cause I know something else that will kill ya fer sure and it ain't an occasional smoke. Cracks me up how people go on about how this might kill or that'll kill ya. Well, they can spend their whole life with their panties in a wad, worryin' about it, but I ain't gonna waste my time. I don't worry s'much because I know somethin' they all seem to forget. Fact is, life'll kill ya no matter what ya do. Might as well enjoy yourself a little 'fore it does."

The Cowboy laughed. "Indeed, Cass. You're right. But

tell me. How did such a young person come to such a cynical conclusion?"

"Experience. When you live a lifestyle where danger is an everyday occurrence, you realize that there ain't no guarantees."

"The Cowboy told me you were new to all this," Dirk said.

"Sure, I'm new to this, but I grew up doing two of the most deadly jobs around." Cass grinned, pausing for effect as they pondered the answer. After a few moments, she explained. "Farmin' and Ranchin'."

"I'm still not quite sure what you mean."

Cass sighed, but she wasn't surprised. It was hard for out-siders to understand what that kind of life is like. "Let me give you an example. On a typical day, you might have to pen an angry two-thousand pound bull and if you're lucky, he's poled."

"Poled?" Chandler said.

"Means no horns. But as I was sayin'. If you don't have to do that, you might need to crawl under a huge plow that could kill you right quick if one of the hydraulic hoses blew and it came down on top of you. You might have to load a huge spiked piece of said plow in your pickup with nothing but grit and your little brother. But if you slip, a few hundred pounds of spiky steel falls on you. I could give you examples like that all day. But here's the kicker. Every now and then, something crazy happens and you have one of those days when everything seems to go wrong and worse."

"Worse?"

"You know, a bad day."

"Right." Chandler nodded a little too vehemently. Cass maintained her 'duh' face, but it was difficult not to laugh. It was always fun to mess with people like that. She blew a little smoke and kept on rather nonchalant, enjoying the reactions as she went. "Like one time when we had a couple of near record hot days in a row. A hundred and ten at least. Murphy and his Law decided to stop by, of course, and so on the two hottest days of the year, the water tank runs dry. The cattle ain't got nothing to drink. To make it worse, 'stead of gettin' out and breaking down the fence to get to the neighbor's water, they have a bizarre attack of restraint and decided to stay in and be thirsty. When we realize what's going on, they been dry for a couple of scorchers. So, guess what. They're too far from their regular water-tank, which we fixed, so the only way to get'em healthy enough to herd is to haul water."

Cass paused for a moment, catching her breath. "Don't sound too bad right? Well it wouldn't be 'cept for the fact that water-starved bovines ain't rational by a far piece. They get dehydrated and most of 'em just get stupid. They wander around kinda confused and weak. The problem is that way too many don't get dumb, they go nuts. The kinda nuts where when they spot you across an open field and you haven't even bothered 'em yet, they decide to kill you for no apparent reason. I remember one time, I had to personally fight off three homicidal cows in one day."

"What do you mean fight off?" the Cowboy asked.

"Exactly what it sounds like," Cass said, pleased to have his attention. "The first one was early in the day. Me, my brother, and my sister had taken our motorcycles down to see what we could do about pushing the cows back to water. We didn't realize yet how dehydrated they were. We expected them to respond well to the cycles 'cause we had 'em trained to herd with 'em. Normally, 'bout the time they heard us on our bikes comin', they'd start headin' back where they belonged. Not this time. After a few minutes of failed attempts to get them cows to move, my brother and I approached another bunch that we hadn't messed with yet. Now keep in mind that cows can get mean, but they're predictable, even rational about their behavior. But this time, we found out the hard way, was different. We stopped a hundred yards from them cows, just surveying the situation. Then from the far side of the herd, this black cow came a runnin' at us. She had them crazy eyes and I could tell she intended to run one of us over. My brother popped the clutch and got out of there, but I wasn't so lucky. That cow was too close by that time, so I just planted my foot and got as stable as I could. Luckily, instead of hittin' my cycle head-on, at the last instant she ducked around the side and tried to take out the back end of my cycle, flank me, per se. Well, I had my right leg up and when she got close enough, I let'er have a nice shin kick to her ugly nose. I musta hit 'er hard, 'cause she backed off long enough for me to get myself and my cycle outta there."

"You kicked the cow?"

"Yep, and that was just killer cow number one that day. Number two was a few minutes later. We'd come to the conclusion that movin' the cattle to water in their current state was not gonna work. We were waitin' on our folks to arrive with some more substantial vehicles and come up with a new plan. To pass the time, I was talkin' with a couple of the neighbors over the barb-wire fence. The nearest cows were a ways off and we weren't botherin' 'em. I'd gotten off my ride and had been pokin' at the dumb cows with a big tree limb I'd picked up. I was standin' there leanin' on the stick, talkin' to the neighbors over the fence when my brother hollered for me to watch out. I looked and another dadgummed cow was runnin' at me. Now, normally the thing to do in such a situation--which ain't terribly uncommon--is run and climb on or get in something where she can't get ya. Well you can't take cover in or on a motorcycle, you can't climb a barb-wire fence, and I can outrun a cow for a ways, but not for half a mile which is how far it was to the nearest good cover. So again, I stood my ground. That cow squared off with me and charged. Not havin' a better option, I hit'er in the nose with my stick. I's lucky again that I had the stick. Every time she came at me, I'd hit her again. I bet she charged me fifteen times--and I never missed. After a while, she wore herself out and backed off. I still look back on that, wonderin' what in the world I was thinkin' but also wonderin' what else was there to do? Anyway, at that point it was 2-0 in my favor."

Cass paused again. She cleared her throat and finished her story. "Cow number three was the unlucky one. She caught me without a stick and more unawares. I was near the back of the trailer we'd been using to haul water to them cows all day. Most of the cows had had some water and were closer to their normal selves. Quite a few were gathered around close, havin' figured out that the trailer meant water. Again, from out of the back of the herd, another crazy cow came runnin'. This time, my brother's warnin' was a bit too late. That dang cow put her head down an' hit me, well, like a fifteen-hun'erd pound cow that's out of her mind. Wouldn't of been too bad, but she hit me so that she rammed me into the side of the trailer too. End result was that I got hit hard on both sides. The only good thing was that she hit me on the leg. Any higher and I'd of likely had broken ribs or worse. So as you can see, it ain't no walk in the park." Cass grinned and added, "S'more like a runnin' fer your life in the pasture sorta thing."

Chandler took a puff on the rapidly shortening cigar and regarded Cass with a mix of wonder tinged with skepticism. "Your story seems a bit fantastic to me. Are you sure you're not exaggerating it a little?"

Cass thought for a moment before replying. "Maybe the cow only weighed fourteen-fifty, I can't say for sure. Never weighed her, she killed herself later that day by goin' crazy and flipping over. Broke her own back." Cass shook her head. "Crazy." She looked up and eyed Chandler. "My numbers are rounded, but the story is about as true as they come. I've been guilty in my life of exaggeration, but this story don't need it. It's crazy enough as it is, I reckon."

"You are certainly an interesting individual," the Cowboy commented, more to himself than anyone else.

Wallace knocked on the door. He came in. "Miss Elkins, there is a room upstairs for you. No need to go back to the city. I also had your things brought from the hotel."

Cass, not particularly happy that her stuff had been messed with, was nonetheless grateful. She was shot, and feeling it. There was work to be done tomorrow. She needed rest. "Thanks. That bed sure sounds good." She turned to the other two men. "Mind if I call it a night, guys?"

"That's fine," the Cowboy said. "We'll talk more tomorrow."

"Dang right we will. We've got work to do finding Anne," she said. "Alright then, see ya'll in the mornin'." She yawned and gestured for Wallace to lead the way. "Disfidonia de man-llana," she mumbled as she went through the door, not really caring as the various languages she knew ran together.

It'd been a long day.

32

Virginia

THE DOOR CLOSED and Cass Elkins was gone.

After a few moments of silence, the Cowboy addressed the other man. "So, what do you think of my choice, Dirk? You've read her file, seen my report, and now you've met her. Impressed?"

"I can see why you like the woman. She's certainly interesting. I've never met anyone quite like her. I'm worried though. I don't see her blending in very well."

"Trust me, she'll do fine. She may like to play the part of a hick, but whether she knows it or not, it's merely how she chooses to behave. I've gotten a glimpse of her true intelligence and capabilities."

"I'll believe it when I see it."

The Cowboy grinned. "You just did. She had you hooked. Wove quite a story."

Chandler scowled. "She was lying?"

"No way to tell. Not that it matters. It's likely that at least part of it was true. We'll never know."

"Well, if she can fool you, I'll say that I am impressed. What do you have in mind for her first? I assume you want her in the field as soon as possible."

"Indeed. Even if I thought she needed it, there's no time to waste with training. I've got to get her doing something quick or I'll lose her. She'll be operational immediately. I give her a week before she forgets about that leg."

"Very well, good luck. I've got to get back to D.C." The former VP put his hand on the door knob. He turned it and took one step out the door before pausing. He turned back to where the Cowboy was still sitting, "How'd you know? She could've said no."

"Because this is my job. I know."

33

Virginia

Cass woke before daylight, and found herself in an unfamiliar room. It was a few moments before she remembered where. She lay there, eyes closed, thinking. She was still unsure about the wisdom of her decision to join these strange people in doing whatever it was they were doing. But she knew that they were her best chance of saving Anne. She'd made up her mind for now. They might not be completely straight up, but they knew more about what was going on than they had told her. She had a feeling that this Derchev character was known to them and she intended to find out everything she could about him. Then go find him.

She had been reassured by the presence of the former Vice-President. She believed him to be an honest, if devious, man. She respected him and that was a rare thing for her when it came to anyone involved in the government.

She got up, decided that the loose pajama bottoms were

fine until the dressing on her leg lost a little bulk. She'd rather not cut up any more good britches. She dressed otherwise, putting on her boots and shirt that said, "Bullets make me happy." She tried the door and was happy to find it unlocked this time. With a slow and awkward gait, she went downstairs, trying to avoid putting more weight on her injury than was absolutely necessary. She realized why single story houses were better. No stupid stairs. It was a revelation she'd already had, but this nailed the coffin shut. She's always thought two-stories were neat. Having grown up where there was plenty of room to build out instead of up, it had been a fascinating novelty. College had stairs. Yet another reason to hate 'em--and another reason to hate college back.

She fumbled for balance as the bad leg tried to give out. She sat down on the steps for a minute and then finished the ordeal. As she limped down off the last step she had another thought. Why'd they make her sleep upstairs? No tellin'.

She started down the hall with her stomach urging her on. There was no one else around that she saw, so she decided to go ahead and find something for breakfast. Food made her mind work better. Even though it was early, she knew she wouldn't get anymore sleep. Too many things were rambling around in her head.

She quickly found the kitchen. She was making an omelet when she sensed someone enter the room. Whoever it was, they were quiet. But not quiet enough.

"Morning," she said without turning. Standing still was good. Moving hurt more. She flipped the omelet over in the air. "Hope you don't mind. I was mighty hungry."

"I won't mind if you share," the Cowboy said. "I smelled that and it woke me right up."

"Can't blame, ya. It does smell tasty. If you'll get a coupl'a plates from wherever they're at and tell me that Dobbs found a lead, I'll split it with ya. I always fix too much anyway."

"Sounds like a good deal to me," he said and retrieved plates and forks. "Alan hasn't slept all night. Eat your breakfast and we'll go talk to him. It won't do you any good on an empty stomach."

It was hard to argue with logic. Cass shoved the food relatively evenly onto the two plates and the Cowboy sat them on the table.

"Hope you like strong coffee." She finished off the cup she had been drinking before refilling it with thick black liquid. She then got another mug and filled it. She sat both down on the table and took a seat across from the man called the Cowboy. Again they ate in silence, each studying the other.

Cass noted the way he held his fork, the way he didn't balk at the thick coffee, how much pepper he put on his eggs and many other small details. By the time the food had disappeared she was all but sure that he was not from around here. "You want s'more coffee?"

He did, so she refilled both their cups. She stared at him. "So where in Texas are you from?"

He deftly hid his surprise, but she noted the reaction.

"What makes you think I'm from Texas?"

"Lots of things. You're not the same as these Yankees. You do a good job of pullin' the wool over their eyes, but I learned how to spot a Texan a long time ago. In fact, I'd wager a guess that you're from somewhere 'round Dallas. Not from the city, but some small town in that part of the state. Leastways, you're accent makes me think so."

"You are full of talent, Cass. But then, I wouldn't have recruited you otherwise. You are fairly accurate in your deductions. I haven't been home in so long; I'm surprised you can tell.

What gave it away?"

She contemplated his question. There were many things... It was difficult to explain. The combinations and intangibles were more telling than quantifiable attributes. But there were a few big ones. "The way you walk," she answered at last. "You walk like you mean to cover some country, but you ain't in a hurry. And there's just enough of what these Yankees call a swagger. They don't understand that it's just normal back home."

Shortly, Wallace came in. He looked like he hadn't gotten enough sleep. "Sir, I need to talk to you. There's been a development."

"What is it?"

Wallace hesitated, looking at Cass. "Are you sure you don't want to... um... come into the command room?"

Obviously picking up on what Wallace was worried about, he nodded to Cass. "This is her operation. She needs to be briefed. Go ahead."

"Yes, sir. I've isolated two other kidnappings similar to the Chaves case. I think I've found a pattern."

"Curious," the Cowboy said, standing up and finishing off his coffee. "Maybe not random then. Let's see what you've got."

Cass got up, and after refilling her coffee mug, followed the two men down a hall and then down two flights of stairs. 'Ow' and more 'ow.' She didn't ask for help and they went on without her. A few minutes later, she made it down to the lower level. Undoubtedly underground now, the walls were plain concrete and the doors were heavy steel. The last door on the left was open. Limping in, she found herself in a high-tech hub. Hardware and more hardware. Her brother would go nuts. The walls were covered in large flat screens and the notable lack of a computer or server made her surmise that the processing machinery was big and powerful enough to be housed elsewhere. Yeah, he'd lose his mind in about two seconds.

The Cowboy went up behind the man who was sitting in front of a smaller screen and a couple of keyboards. "Alan, fill us in."

Dobbs, who was dressed in shorts and a T-Shirt that said "Mind the Crap," removed the headphones from his ears and turned in his seat. Dobbs looked more comfortable now than anywhere else Cass had seen him.

The Cowboy motioned to Cass. "She's in charge."

"Sure," said Alan Dobbs, looking sideways at Cass. "Welcome, welcome. Since we're on the same side now, I hope you still don't want to shoot me?"

Cass smiled. "Not today. But for your own sake, call before you come visit next time." She found something to lean against and looked at the data scrolling across the big screen above Dobbs. "Alright, let's get on with this. What can you tell me?"

Dobbs began typing. An image of a man came up on the screen. He had several crude tattoos showing beneath his sleeves, a shaved head, and enough visible scars to indicate a hard life of some kind. But he wasn't musclebound or huge. Not tall, not wide, just taut. Mean."

"Maksim Petrovich Derchev, youngest child of Pyotr Derchev, one of the biggest names in the Russian mafia for the last twenty years. Twenty-seven years old, he's been locked up for almost half that time. After his most recent exit from prison, he fled Russia and has been making the international crime scene for the last few years. Lately, he's been hanging out with some radical groups in the Middle East. Working as a middle-man, setting up deals, running guns, he does the stuff that his Islamic friends can't or won't do." Dobbs pointed at the screen. "He may not look like much, but he's killed and schemed and worse."

He produced a grainy image of two men. "This is a photo taken last month in Mexico. The one on the right is Derchev and the other is a known terrorist. We don't know what the meeting was about. But it can't be good."

"What are you getting at?" asked Cass.

"Right, we're not sure what their nefarious plan is, but I think they've been kidnapping college students. Your friend made three, enough to isolate a decent pattern. I've spent the night backtracking from there to find the motive and means behind the snatches. The name really sped things up. I checked it first and hit pay dirt by cross-referencing their traceable activities with the kidnapping pattern. It's well-removed, but eventually, everything leads back to the boss." He grinned over his shoulder. "Or, if you have me, 'eventually' is 'extremely soon.'" He paused and hit a few keys before turning his chair around and facing Cass. "Over the last year, the Derchev organization has taken more girls than I want to count, but they stick to a standard, low-risk profile that keeps them from making the news too often. Pretty girls who won't be missed right away and in non-repeating quantities, locations, and timetables. Very effective, very hard to catch. But these three girls. They appear to have been taken during one of the Derchev runs. They snatch a few in sequence, having already set them up, and then disappear before it gets too hot. The timing, the methods, it all screams Derchev slavers, but the girls are all wrong. These three, one in California, one in Indiana, and now Cambridge, they are too noticeable, too important."

"So where's Anne?" Cass was feeling tired. Stupid leg.

"At first, it appeared that it was just what it appeared to be, an expansion of their operations or an error in judgment. However, there's something else at work here. There has to be."

Three girls' faces and files popped up on the screen. Anne's was one of them.

"That's Anne."

"Yes, Anne Chaves, your friend, is just one of the latest in a line of promising young women to be snatched. All these ladies were doing graduate work in Biology, Genetics, or Agricultural Science. They were all involved in research and were expected to become leaders in their fields after graduation. Over the last few months, they have all disappeared. Evidence leads us to believe that the Derchevs were involved in all cases. These girls are being grabbed for a reason. What we need to do is find out what that purpose is. Because of the terrorist involvement in this, we need to find and stop whatever they are planning because it's not going to be good for this country."

"How bad?"

"It has to be expertise that they're after. These girls are smart and deep into some serious science. So it could be, like, biological WMD bad." He leaned back and smiled. "It's a great plan. Who's going to figure that these girls were snatched for their brains?"

"What else?" the Cowboy asked.

He paused a moment and entered more commands into the console. "That's where I'm at. I'm running all the data to see if I can find any specific correspondences. The Derchev organization is not small. Until I can isolate something smaller, there's not much to go on. But Maksim is smart--and ambitious. If I'm right and he's the player, it's going to get interesting."

Cass stopped staring at the picture of Anne and turned to the Cowboy. "What can I do?"

34

O-Bar-Z Ranch

THE WOMAN WAS DEAD. There was no question. The Arabs were gathered around the body, faces impassive. He looked carefully at each one, searching for a twitch, a sign that would betray the culprit. All too many of them were failing to hide the contempt they felt and even amusement.

Maksim had been roused from his daytime nap by the screaming. Five hours a day, that was all he asked. Five hours without anyone being stupid. It was obviously too much to expect of these idiots. He wished Alexei was back. At least he knew how far to trust the familiar dimwit. It didn't matter now. The deed was done and now there was a problem that needed handled. A diplomatic approach might keep things in order or maybe Maksim could just take a leaf out of his father's well-used book of persuasion.

"What in the hell happened here?" Maksim stared at Mr. John. No matter the actual culprit, he was to blame.

"Nothing of importance," John said. "She was trying to escape."

Maksim looked down at the body. There had been quite a struggle. The sparse covering of dry grass that normally held the ground down was gone. The body lay near the edge of a ten-foot area that was now nothing but deeply scarred and mildly stained sand. There had been a drawn out battle here, uncharacteristic of a simple apprehension. "Why didn't you just bring her back? We still needed her expertise."

John huffed. "It was best to teach a lesson. Now, there will be no more attempts to escape, I think."

Turning away from the body, Maksim locked eyes with John. "Exactly."

John was clearly offended, but he shrugged it off and nodded.

"Now get your men to dig a hole somewhere. We need to get rid of her." He picked a spot of bare ground and pointed. "There. Pack it down and level it. The wind will hide it before we're gone."

He waited until they returned with shovels and made sure they knew to dig it deep enough. He exaggerated the depth a little, just in case they decided to get lazy. He wanted to make sure the body would be well hidden.

Maksim didn't want to wait around to watch the men dig in the dry dirt. The baked ground was hard and it would take some time and effort to dig a usable hole. It had to be done well or not at all. When they left, there could be no evidence that indicated anything more than a simple case of drug-related violence had transpired. The locals would not question it and neither would the authorities. It would be just as they had expected. The best sort of lie, so close to the truth that no one would see it.

Maksim turned away and headed towards the runway, too

angry to be afraid of the men behind him and just angry enough to wish one of them would try something.

He walked as slowly as he could manage and only relaxed a little when he could no longer hear the sound of dry scraping that the shovels made. It was irritating, reminding him of fingernails against the hardened walls of prison. He pushed the past away as he always did and pulled out his cell phone. He needed another girl to finish the project. The dead one had been critical. A replacement had to be found--fast. The goal was in sight and the time was getting short. There was a well-defined window of opportunity for everything to work and for Maksim to get his money and his skin clear of the entire thing.

As much as he hated it, there was only one man who could arrange the grab fast enough to satisfy. Maksim set his jaw. He dialed a number from memory and put the phone to his ear, almost dreading the answer on the other end.

"How did you get this number?" Pyotr Derchev answered.

"It's me."

"It's who? I don't know who the fuck this is."

"Maksim." He felt history bubbling to the surface and tried to keep his voice level. He hadn't talked to his father since he got out except for a brief Christmas message once a year. A message that did not require more than a few seconds.

"What are you doing? Where have you been? Your brother is dead and I still haven't seen you."

Maksim cut off the rant he knew would continue. "Not now, father. I called to talk business. That's all I have time for right now."

"What sort of business?" Pyotr still sounded upset, but he was above all else, a businessman.

"I need a girl."

Pyotr laughed. Maksim could practically hear his face purpling, the sound was still familiar. "I can do that. What sort of girl? I just got a new shipment gathered. Many choices. Young and pretty."

"I doubt it. I need something special. I want a graduate student that specializes in genetically-engineered crops. Nothing else will do. And I need it yesterday. Money is no object. Can you make it happen?"

"Boy, what do you take me for?"

"Can you make it happen?" Maksim said again, slower.

"You are a very lucky boy today. I will call you soon with a price and transfer arrangements. *Da*?"

"Good enough." Maksim ended the call without another word and approached his plane. He started his checklist and tried to keep his mind busy. He had to keep his focus. There was too much to lose. He was in a dangerous position. It was possible that not everyone involved would prefer him dead, but no one was in any way invested in his survival. He didn't want to die and he planned on making sure that didn't happen.

He sat in the plane for a while, stashing the anger down deep where it wouldn't get in the way. It took a lot of work. Speaking to his father never left him in a good mood. He considered what he had to do. If his father could get a replacement half as fast as the old man implied, he could make this work. He could make the other one work for a few days, but not without diminishing her ability. She would have to be made to work without much sleep. Maksim realized that he still had a problem. He could afford no mistakes at this stage. The Project was over halfway complete and it could not be interrupted. It had to be smooth and continuous.

Two girls had seemed like the best plan at the beginning. Low profile, no pattern. But now, he could take a little more risk. Had to take the risk. The operation needed to finish. Success was his best way out.

He had already scouted an alternate, just in case, but the perfect time for her snatch wasn't until the end of the month. If his father had a girl now, he could grab the other one then.

Three would prevent anything like today's problem from happening again. Losing one wouldn't jeopardize the operation. More manpower and a failsafe, he decided. The professor would get the coded email by morning, authorizing the initial payment to proceed with the setup.

One more girl and no more chances.

35

Virginia

THE COWBOY'S MANSION didn't appear to be such on the outside and that was exactly as planned. The true interior was much more interesting.

Everybody had one room in the underground level for whatever they needed to store. Dobbs' was full of computers, so much so that he got two rooms. Bobby had only had time to get a chair, a TV, and a couple of car posters. Wallace had filled his with a desk and lots of books.

Above, the two-story house was not small, but it was not conspicuous for the area. High to middling in apparent value, it was nice enough that it was generally avoided, but not monstrous, not an attraction, nothing special to see.

Except for the white room, the ground floor contained all the basic, traditional elements of a home including the kitchen and the Cowboy's living quarters. He was the only one who slept on the ground floor. The rest of the team got the upstairs. There were four bedrooms on the second floor, all occupied now that Elkins had joined up. During an operation all the members stayed close. He had little choice. Much like her, home was far away. Dobbs clearly had a lair within a day's drive because he did disappear sometimes, not spending the night, and Wallace was certain he wasn't out cavorting. Bobby was less tethered. He had a place too, undoubtedly, but he didn't have a home in the truest sense. He was the modern drifter, traveling the country with nothing but his fancy car, no destination, no hurry, nothing.

A strange group, not a healthy mind among them, but an amazing set of skills between them. Wallace hoped that the Cowboy knew what he was doing.

A knocking sound broke his reverie. He looked up to find Cass leaning against one side of the door frame and rapping on the other with a lazy back hand. She smiled, but he could see the weariness in her body. The injury would slow her down for a time. He looked at her eyes, and was struck by the awareness. Her mind was working hard, fast. Despite her body's weakness, she still had a clear sense of purpose. No apparent dejection. That was good. Athletes, soldiers, and such physical types were prone to respond unhealthily to serious injury. When they couldn't perform, they sank into depression.

"They won't let me do nothing 'til I talked to you."

He cleared the books off of the extra chair and she took the invitation to sit. She didn't try to hide the relief of getting off her feet. "Do you want to talk to me?"

"I don't mind." She grinned, eyes twinkling more than was comfortable. "Just keep your hands where I can see 'em."

Wallace leaned back and put his hands in his lap. "I'm sorry about that. You left me no choice."

"Eh, it's done. Just don't expect me to thank you for it--or forget it."

"How's the leg."

"It has a hole in it. Not as bad as it could have been, but it still ain't particularly good right now."

Wallace nodded. "I hope you feel better soon."

"When my leg works right, I'll be good."

"I see. So how are you feeling right now?"

"Uh, tired, and things hurt."

Wallace, not surprised by her avoidance of anything past the physical, was ready to be patient. "How do you feel emotionally?"

Her answer took a couple of seconds, but not too long. "Hmm, irritated." Wallace could almost see her take a step back, but not in fear, just consideration. She seemed much the same as during their last interview, when she'd thought it was all a game, before her friend had been kidnapped in front of her, before she'd killed a man. Maybe a little less jovial, but not disturbed, not even worried. Interesting.

"That's all?"

"I don't know. I mean, I'm really irritated, not just the normal kind."

"Maybe you're angry." Wallace ventured. "Surely you're angry at someone for what happened to you friend?"

She seemed to consider the idea seriously. "Probably, but blame don't accomplish much."

"Someone is responsible."

"Exactly. Responsible. That's it right there. Somebody is responsible."

"This, responsible party, what do you feel towards him or her? Anger? Fear? Hatred? Something else?"

She shrugged. "Hadn't really thought about it."

"How about what happened to your friend? How does that make you feel?"

"Not good."

"Can you be more specific?"

"I don't know, maybe angry?"

"When you think about the other night, what comes to mind?"

"That Anne is kidnapped and I need to find her."

"Let's be more specific. What do you remember thinking about when the kidnapping took place?"

She thought for a few moments. The longest pause yet. Wallace hoped that meant she was actually thinking back to that moment and not just looking to come up with a good answer.

"I was figuring out how to, eh...*disarm*...the dumbasses."

"That was your first thought?"

"Pretty much, far as I can remember."

"You don't remember being scared, surprised that you were attacked?"

"Well, I guess I was surprised. That's pretty obvious and I guess it was scary. I don't know. That stuff wasn't important."

"But you did feel something?"

"Look, you want the truth? I'll tell you how it works and you can tell me that I'm a little crazy. I don't mind."

"Please go on."

"It happened so fast that there was nothing to do but figure it out. That make sense?"

Wallace could swear that she grinned a little at his confusion. "Not really."

"Yeah, that's about how it is unless it's happening. When something like that happens, it's the clearest my mind ever gets. Everything slows down, a whole bunch of possible solutions run through my mind all at the same time and then I do the best thing. I do what needs done. It's simple, but it's how it is."

"A well-trained reaction to danger. Impressive."

"I don't know about the trained part. It doesn't get that way in practice and that's how it works for as long as I can remember. Nobody told me how to do it and to be honest, I thought that's how it always worked. My family all does it about the same as far as I can tell."

"You've never panicked?"

"I guess not."

"So you *think* in the face of danger?"

She nodded, as if relieved that he finally understood. "Yep."

"Of course."

"Are we done now?"

"No. I want to talk to you about the other incident."

"The guy."

"Yes. You killed a man. That needs to be discussed."

"Okay. That's probably a good idea."

"Good. Tell me about it."

"Well, you heard the first part. They knocked me out and put me and Anne in a car. I woke up and next thing I know, they throw me out with this guy and drive off. We're in this dark alley, of course, and the guy comes after me."

Wallace interrupted. "You didn't try to escape at that point."

Cass shook her head. "It wasn't a good idea."

"How did you know?"

"I already told you."

"And you're never wrong?"

A shrug. "Never have been."

Wallace nodded. "Continue the story."

"Sure." Her eyes unfocused. "The guy was there, I let him get close and then the fight started." She frowned and tensed. "Oh, wait, yeah. I remembered about the show and realized that it was all fake. That it wasn't real." She blew air out her nose and looked at Wallace, eyebrows raised. "That's when he shot me."

"So then you knew it wasn't an act."

"Yes. That was when I got mean."

"You decided to kill him?"

"No. I decided to win."

"Is there a difference?"

"I don't know. Could be."

"I see. Go on. What did you do?"

"I hit him in the throat."

"So you wanted to kill him?"

"It was the best idea. The opening was there and there was no reason to go for anything less. I saw the chance. I used it."

"You intended to crush his trachea."

She looked up, thinking. "Yep. That's how it's supposed to work. Guess I did it right." She looked back at Wallace, her confidence suddenly increased. "I definitely meant to dislodge his pelvic cartilage connection with that side kick. That worked out right too."

"So, the first blow killed him?"

"I'd say so, yeah. The punch to the throat was very effective."

"It sounds like very straight up self-defense."

A strange look fell on her face. "Guess so."

"I have one last question. You killed the man. That's no small thing. What was your first thought after he died?"

"That he didn't say much."

"And later?"

"I was trying to figure out where to start looking for Anne."

Wallace finally let a sigh out. "And now, what do you take away from it?"

She stood up and walked to the door. She turned back, one hand on the door frame. "That's a really long last question."

"I promise it is. One last answer and you can go."

She smiled. "I'm glad I got him--and now I know that those techniques work like they're supposed to. I always wondered." She turned to go. "Later, doc."

36

Virginia

"ARE YOU READY?"

Cass kept her cool at the Cowboy's question. "Course I am."

"How's the leg?" He pointed.

"Better."

"Enough?"

"Good enough for what you got me doing."

The Cowboy nodded. "Be ready in an hour. We have to move fast before they move her."

"Okay," Cass said and went downstairs.

There was a lead, a location. Some sort of Derchev stash house. Anne was supposed to be there. Cass would do what it took. Her leg would just hurt and that was something that could be overcome.

The Cowboy had a plan and it sounded like it should work. Her job was to be the gun in the rear, watching the big picture and making sure no bad guys got the drop on the guys in front. It might be because she had a bum leg at the moment, or it might be because she was the man for the job. She didn't really care. It was a job she could do and it needed done.

Cass opened the door to her 'gear room.' She'd been more than a little happy to get it--and the gear to go with it. The Cowboy had let her go shopping. Four guns to start with. That's what he'd said. She hadn't even tried to hide her excitement. The only thing better than guns you already have, are guns you don't.

She'd thought about it for a couple of days, narrowing down a list, trying to come up with a set that would cover all the bases, all the options. She needed a sidearm, a long range rifle, a close-range rifle. That would be a good core. Number four was harder to pick. Something extra. Maybe a shotgun? A lot of protection close-in, but not much else. Nothing extra that the first three wouldn't already do better. There was no point in another rifle. Two was a lot. Yet another reason against the shotgun. Three long guns were more than it was handy to carry. Two was already a mess.

She decided that she wanted to be able to carry all her guns with her, usefully. That narrowed it right down to another side-arm, another handgun. A logical decision and one that made her smile.

Her new room was now tastefully outfitted with a recliner, a desk, and a peg-board wall to display her guns. Since the room was hidden in a secret bunker, she figured it would've been re-dundant to put them in a gun safe. It was silly, to display them, but she'd always wanted to. It certainly looked cool, all of them hung there on the wall.

She was wearing dark grey cargo pants and a matching com-pression shirt. Both allowed plenty of movement and the tight shirt wouldn't get in the way of anything. She put on a gun belt. Black webbing with a stiffener to better hold up and distribute the weight. She put the holster on the right and extra mag pouches along the left, careful to follow the marks she'd made days before. She wanted everything exactly in the right place. Exactly where she'd practiced drawing and reloading from. All set, she took the Glock 34 from its place on the wall. It was a loose-fitting, black plastic, ugly chunk of a gun, but it would work when hell froze over and then some. Lots of bullets, completely reliable, and accurate. All its shortcomings were minuscule in comparison.

She checked the chamber, ran the slide a few times, making sure everything felt right, and did the same with the trigger and the reset. She smiled as she dry-fired. It was sweet. It was not stock. The first thing she'd done with the gun was modify it. Stock Glocks were good, but she'd had plenty of time to make it better. A fully-adjustable fulcrum trigger had replaced the pitiful bit of hard squishiness that it had come with, a full-length tungsten guide-rod replaced the plastic one, a few springs, a race connector inside, some purposeful polishing, and she'd finished with a weighted, beveled mag-well.

It wasn't to any police or military spec. It was better. It was up to competition level.

Satisfied that is was perfectly operational, she pressed a loaded magazine up the well and racked one into the chamber. She then released the magazine, sat the gun down, and put one more bullet in the magazine before putting it back in the gun. Fully loaded with 23 rounds of nine-millimeter, sub-sonic hollow-points, she finally holstered the gun on her hip.

She took three more magazines, all extended beyond stock to hold twenty-three instead of the standard seventeen. Hers were loaded to twenty-two for maximum reliability and ease of reloading. Each fit tightly into a vertical mag pouch on her left side.

Last, she stuck a very high-end suppressor in her pocket. That was something new. She didn't know much about it, but the workmanship was good and it really did the job. Eventually, she planned on making a modified holster that would fit the 34 suppressed and still draw fast and easy. She'd make do for the moment.

Next, she took down the long-range gun. Made by FNH, the SCAR17 was a highly engineered, well-made, reliable, battle rifle. It came almost perfect. The only thing she'd changed was the stock trigger, replacing it with a two-pound single-stage.

It was only a .308, but in this part of the world, that was serious long-range power. Too many trees. Too many people. It was not likely to be needed. She shouldered the gun and looked through the long-range scope she'd added. Everything was clear. She ran the bolt once, dry-fired the trigger, and then put the rifle in a short, black case. With the fully-folding stock, the SCAR made a surprisingly small package. Four 20-round magazines and she zipped up the case.

There was no good reason not to take it along.

The AR-15 she'd picked for a close-in rifle was anything but stock. It was almost an exact duplicate of her brother's 3-gun rifle, custom-made by a little manufacturer in a small town in New Mexico. It was setup with a full-length, spiral-cut, anod-ized, free-floating hand guard. It had a two-pound, double-stage trigger, and all the little bells and whistles, including her favor-ite kind of holographic sight. With that in mind, it also had a set of flip-up iron sights. Just in case.

She checked it out and put it in another case along with a handful of 30-round magazines and one 60-round Surefire mag full of subsonics. If it took more than that, noise was gonna be the least of her problems. She zipped it up, glad that her favorite little gun maker had been able to fill the Cowboy's order.

Last but not least, she strapped a nice, leather, double-band-ed thigh holster onto her left leg, backwards. Stupid gunshot. To fill it, she took the last gun off the wall. Number four. Mr. Redundancy. A Mark VII Desert Eagle, Forty-Four Magnum. Bought used, she'd replaced the recoil springs and the gas cylinder after checking all the other parts too. Then, she'd fired ten boxes of varied ammo through it to make sure that it was going to eat anything she fed it. As much as she loved the guns, they were sometimes cranky. She had to be sure this was a keeper. It was.

She went through her drill. After everything checked out, she put one in the chamber, topped off the magazine, put the safety on and secured it in the holster. She laughed at herself. Only nine rounds, and the very opposite of silent, it was a little nuts, but who wouldn't want nine rounds of magnum force as backup?

She grabbed the two bags, a pair of clear shooting glasses, and the handy-dandy electronic, auto-adjusting, Bluetooth-ca-pable earplugs that Dobbs had given her. She couldn't help but look forward to what was coming next.

37

Virginia

CASS DIDN'T KNOW what to call what was about to happen. A raid? An attack? There was lots of jargon. She figured it was a rescue. That was the point, after all.

The house was just that, a house. It looked like a hundred other doublewides Cass had seen before. Pale, earthy siding, cheap trim, and it still had the mobile steps that it came with. She guessed it to be at least ten years old, but no more than twenty. Very inconspicuous.

She was honestly relieved that it was a familiar design. After seeing all the weird sorts of houses that Yankees liked to build, she'd been a little worried before the briefing. If it'd been one of those silly stuck-together jobs that were so popular, it would have been a lot more work.

As it was, the only thing that really differentiated it from the same sort of house at home was the trees. There wouldn't have been trees at home--or at least none worth noticing. These trees were big and old.

Five people, every member of the team, were sitting in a mid-nineties pickup. Dobbs was driving, the Cowboy had shotgun and she was sandwiched between Bobby and Wallace in the back seat. She was ready to get out.

They were parked about a hundred yards from the house, dawn was approaching. There was no visible activity. All they knew was mostly nothing. Anne was supposed to be there. The bad guys were bad and there was no reason not to shoot them. As for actual targets, she was certain there were no more armed bad guys than could be fit inside the house--and she doubted it would be full.

"Are we about ready?" she asked, glancing left and right at her surroundings. "I'm ready."

The Cowboy laughed once. "Just a few more minutes."

"Okay."

He turned and addressed the back seat. "Everyone know what to do?"

Cass nodded, Bobby grinned, and Wallace said, "Yes."

He looked back at the house, and nodded to Dobbs, then turned back again and said, "Okay then, let's go."

Wallace got out and waited on Cass. She was to go first and set herself behind a tree with a good line of sight around the house. She should have ridden on the outside. Next time.

Wallace got back in and closed the door. Cass headed straight for the nearest tree.

It was barely light enough to see as she moved from cover to cover towards the house. She got within an easy twenty-five yards of the house and growled a signal to the other guys. "Set. Both doors."

As she'd hoped, the house had a front door and a side door. She could see both. She had three guns. After she'd learned of the actual layout, there was absolutely no reason to bring anything for long range. Even the AR was overkill, but it was usable and for what she was supposed to be doing, it was very well suited. She could easily make good shots with the Glock at this range, but the rifle would be just a little easier, a little faster.

But there were guns that could have been better. The AR was really too much gun for this area. A carbine in nine millimeter, maybe. That would have been perfect, easy to make quiet and more than enough gun at these ranges.

As it was, the AR was suppressed and she'd loaded the sixty rounder with subsonic. It wouldn't pack a huge punch, but all she was shooting at was people. She knew it was a strange idea, but to her, people were easy targets. Slow-moving and thin-skinned, they were small game. It didn't take much bullet.

She leaned against the tree, both eyes open, the bright red reticle of the holographic sight clear.

Bobby and Wallace went in the front door slowly, hoping not to wake any sleeping bozos. They would clear the house from their entry point. She would watch for anybody to come out the side-door.

She kept her eyes moving, scanning for movement, anything out of sync. She also started looking for safe points to shoot, checking the background. The best spots were in front of trees or with the house behind the target. With that in mind, she tried to decide which way people were likely to run depending on which door they came out. With that, she made three separate sequences of shoot points, predicated on the targets initial direction. The first was at the front door. Anything that got beyond that point, she'd take at the trees.

Knowing that the odds of her routes being exactly right were slim, she had a plan to make slight adjustments to the target's run if needed. The ground was always a safe target and a well-placed shot would probably steer the runner in another direction. Like herding cattle, only less dusty.

She was figuring the best angle for such shots, depending on the runner's route and the distance from her position. She was laying out imaginary yardage lines every ten yards or so and finding associated landmarks. That way, if she needed to fire into the ground, she already had a basic target instead of just guessing.

It was all data. When something actually happened, it had to already be in her mind, because there would be only deciding at that point. But the more data to base those decisions on, the better.

And there was no more time. Shots, loud ones. The side door was opening. Time slowed down and Cass moved the red dot to the door.

38

Massachusetts

BOBBY HAD ALWAYS LIKED GUNS, even before he'd finally learned to shoot. His father had been a suit with no time or interest in that sort of thing and his mother was the standard representative of the "Guns spontaneously kill people" mentality.

He put his silenced SigSauer in his pocket when he reached the front door, wishing he had his revolver, but the need for silence was more important tonight.

Wallace stood to the side, his gun at low ready, while Bobby opened the door.

Bobby had a new set of titanium picks and he stuck them into the keyhole. A few moments of feeling around and he knew that he could get it. It wasn't anything special, just a lock like was on so many other front doors in so many other places. Very familiar. Very easy.

Bobby felt the rake engage the last tumbler and he used the torque bar to carefully turn the lock. He hit ninety degrees and felt the mechanism do its thing. He removed his tools and put them away. Turning to Wallace, he grinned and said, *"Allon-ze."* Then he pulled his Sig back out and turned the door knob. It didn't want to move. He knew it was unlocked. There was no doubt in his mind, but the stupid thing didn't want to turn. He put his strength into it and pulled back against the doorframe. Reluctantly, it released. But there was a little sound. The latch was old, cheap, and desperately needed lubrication. The hinges were much the same.

Hating the sound as he did it, Bobby slowly pushed the door in.

When there was enough gap, he quietly moved in. Then he swept his eyes and the gun along the left side of the room as he came through the door. A step behind him, Wallace would be doing something similar along the other side. As Bobby's pan approached the center of the room, he heard the muffled sound of Wallace's gun, and then again. Wallace must have shot something. He resisted the urge to take a look and completed his cycle of the room.

Done, he turned and saw the two holes in the back of a couch and two matching feet beyond.

There were two exits from the room, an open hallway to the right and a closed door to the left. Wallace indicated the right. Bobby agreed. They followed the same routine, clearing the kitchen and dining area next. There was no one, just two stacks of canned chili. One stack of full cans and the other of empties.

There was again a choice. Two hallways. One left, one right. Bobby thought a second. The side door was to the left.

Before he could make a decision, Wallace nodded to the right.

There was a bathroom, clear. Then two adjacent doors, both open. Wallace took the one on the right and Bobby the other. It was a bedroom, but there were no beds or people, just a bunch of stuff. Bobby checked everything that could be hiding a man before going back to the door. He didn't see anything in the hall, so he emerged and moved across to Wallace's room. There was a set of bunks and he could see the feet of the two occupants. Wallace was midway up the ladder, his gun in one hand. As Bobby watched, the slide cycled.

He nodded an acknowledgement to Bobby and then crossed the room and they met back in the hall.

The end of the hall was taken up by a closed door. Bobby was the designated door-opener. There was nowhere good to be. The only thing he could manage was to crouch down as he turned the knob and Wallace flattened himself along the wall.

It might have helped with bullets.

The door opened and a large man in nothing but boxers stumbled over Bobby and tackled Wallace to the ground. Bobby found his feet and cleared the room. It was empty. He ran to help Wallace.

The mostly naked man was lying on his face in the middle of the hallway, the maroon carpet darkening beneath him.

Wallace got up, but slow. There was no blood, but he was hurting from something. Bobby moved past him, moving fast now, very aware that the underdressed attacker had not been silent.

He ran back to the main room and made for the closed door. Wallace took the hall.

Bobby ducked to the side, turned the knob, and bullets hit the door as soon as it moved. He stuck his foot across and kicked it open. Too hard. The door returned and slammed shut. Damn it. Bobby reached for the knob again and more bullets came through. Now along the wall, above his head. He had to move. The walls were worthless. He kept low and ran back around into the kitchen. The dividing wall was covered in a floor-to-ceiling cabinet and a refrigerator. He had some cover. He thought about throwing a few shots back, but if he had to guess, that was the last room and it probably opened into the hall that Wallace had taken. Wallace might be coming into that room at any time. Bobby opened the nearest cabinet and found a large pan with a handle. He threw it around the wall towards the defended room. It hit the wall and the gunfire intensified. He waited a few seconds, threw another pot, and then headed across the kitchen towards the hall that led to the side door.

He suddenly remembered that he had a comm device in his ear. Duh.

He wouldn't have felt so stupid if he'd figured it out before Wallace's voice said, "Get out the side. We're done."

Bobby did what the man said. He even remembered to tell Cass not to shoot him.

"Bobby coming out..." He twisted the door knob. "...now."

Cass didn't shoot him.

Wallace was already in the trees and Bobby followed. "There's somebody in there with a lot of bullets," Bobby said, not bothering to whisper.

He heard Cass say, "Okay."

There was a pause. Cass again. "Anne?"

Wallace replied. "No."

"You sure?"

"Unless she was in the last room with the gunman. We couldn't get in there. I had a quick look, but I didn't see her. "

"So, no."

39

Massachusetts

"WALLACE. COMING OUT THE SIDE."

Cass didn't change the planned movement of the dot. She followed the figure until she was sure it was Wallace. It was. He came out alone, not fast, hurt, but not too bad. She heard him tell Bobby to get out and she repeated the process. Following the figure out the door again, she verified and returned to the door.

She spoke to them. Saying what needed to be said. Then she remembered.

"Anne?"

Wallace answered, but she didn't like it.

Anne might still be in there.

Cass considered her options. Going back inside was stupid. But there were lots of windows.

"Where's the last room?" she queried.

"Whatever it is..."

She cut them off, not even noticing who it was. "No. Tell

me now."

"See the side door?" Bobby.

"Yes." Impatient.

"To the right. All the way to the back wall."

Cass didn't respond. There were two windows that should work. She decided on the back wall. Nothing had happened in that direction. No reason to look that way.

She slung the rifle behind her back, drew the Glock and twisted on the silencer. Needed to make that holster.

She didn't run straight towards the house, but made a wide arc, keeping her distance until she was on the back side. She used what cover there was, but the last ten yards were clear. It wasn't safe. It wasn't even all that smart. Was there an alternative? No.

Cass needed to know if Anne was in there.

It took an eternity to cross the space, but very little time in the real world. She reached the window. It was almost too high up. She'd seen a loose cinderblock. It made the difference. She stepped up and looked in.

A man with a gun, his side to her, not looking. Clothes. Trash. Chairs. She looked hard. She looked for blind spots. There was nothing. She could even see in the closet and the bathroom.

The man's gaze drifted her way.

She looked again. Nothing.

The man looked again.

Cass was on the ground.

Anne was gone.

Cass picked herself up. Stupid leg had decided to get squirrelly at a bad time. It was cramping in all sorts of unhelpful ways and her toes were numb. She slapped some sense into it, but it was still unreliable. She was afraid that it would give again before she made it across to better cover.

"Somebody keep an eye on the side door, I'm coming around against the wall."

Careful to stay below the windows, she stumbled around the corner and down the wall towards the door. When she got there, she'd have to make it on her own, but it was more of a straight shot than her original, circuitous route.

She grabbed the thin metal railing of the mobile steps with her left hand and picked a path.

Her senses were on high-alert and she thought she heard something inside the door. It might be nothing, but she saw a good hedge. They should have put in a better porch. She easily pushed the steps over, leaving nothing but three feet of air for anybody coming out the door.

She started moving. Ten steps and her leg did it again. She gasped at the sudden spike of pain and started to get up. Someone grabbed her arm and pulled her to her feet. She pulled her gun in tight to her body and looked. It was Bobby. He gave her a silent smile.

She quit pointing the gun at him and they headed for the pickup.

He didn't have to support her much, but having help allowed her to move fast, not worrying about the leg. They made it in good time. Wallace had the door open and Bobby helped her up and in before following.

The middle seat again. She thought about swearing.

Bobby closed the door and they left.

"You okay?" Bobby asked.

"Guess not," Cass scowled at her leg, as if it was its fault. "Thanks."

"No problem at all." Bobby was annoyingly happy.

Cass was imagining somebody falling out the side door

thanks to her. It made her smile.

Wallace noticed. "What're you smiling about?"

She told him. Turned out, they thought it was pretty funny too. The back seat occupants made with the laughter and shared varied images of the potential results of her sabotage. Any worry or seriousness evaporated and for the first time since that morning Dobbs had knocked on her door, Cass relaxed.

40

Virginia

THE UPSTAIRS was more than Cass wanted to tackle. The downstairs wasn't much better. Her leg was still rebelling and had started to cool down and add stiffness to the list. Bobby and Wallace helped her inside while Dobbs volunteered to raid his migraine stash for something to dull the pain. The Cowboy followed them inside and directed them towards the den. Cass fell into the first chair and let out a breath she hadn't even realized she'd been holding.

"Heh, that was fun." Her smile was betrayed by a grimace of pain.

Wallace disappeared and Bobby stood around like he didn't know what to do. Before the silence went on too long, Dobbs came up with an unmarked medicine bottle.

"Take a couple of these," he said, proffering two good-size cylindrical pills. "Nothing crazy in it, but it does the trick."

Cass didn't like taking medicine, but there was a time. "Thanks." She took the pills and realized what was missing.

"How 'bout something to wash 'em down."

"Sure." Dobbs disappeared into the kitchen for a few moments before returning with a glass of water. Cass took a sip and put one of the pills in her mouth. She followed it with water and managed to choke it down. It was one of the things she'd never gotten used to or good at. Swallowing pills was not part of her repertoire. It took three tries with the water to get the second one down and it was not nearly fast enough. The pill had a bitter, chalky taste that had time to get a good hold in her mouth. She drank the rest of the glass, but couldn't quite get rid of the taste.

"I'd drink some more," she said, her face anything but relaxed. "Hope them pills work better than they taste."

Dobbs laughed and took the glass. "Be right back."

Wallace showed up before he did, carrying the blue duffel that served as his medical kit.

The Cowboy was right behind him. He pointed down the hall. "Bobby, Justin, let's put her on a bed."

First floor, that meant the white room. Cass really didn't want to go there at the moment. It was not an easy place to sleep. "I bet I can make the stairs. It's hard to sleep with all that white."

The Cowboy shook his head. "My room."

By the time she got situated on the Cowboy's bed, the painkiller had started its work. The sharper pains were spiking a little lower and her head was running a little off. She looked over the room while Wallace did his doctor routine. She pulled the Desert Eagle out of the holster and laid it beside her before letting Wallace take the thigh holster off. When it was gone, she could relax her legs more naturally and Wallace had room to work. He took scissors to the outside of her right britches leg. She wanted to complain, but decided to let it go. These weren't her favorite.

The room wasn't great big, but it wasn't small either. It had a bed, a big boring dresser, a desk, and a very nice, very wide TV. All the furniture was heavy, industrial, and black. The walls were paneled in a dark, well-figured wood, and anything else that might be called part of the decor was reddish-orange. But what really stood out was everything else. Other than the basics, there wasn't an order or a theme. The desk was home to papers, gun parts, and both loaded ammo and some empty shells. She guessed the dresser was where he unloaded his pockets. There were coins, shell casings, unreadable wads of paper, and a few green bills.

There were a few garments on the other end of the dresser and she picked out at least two pistols in the pile. The pattern, or lack thereof, repeated with minimal variation throughout the entire room. Piles of clothes, papers, ammo boxes, DVDs, and books, all interspersed with magazines and weapons.

The only unique items she saw were the three framed movie posters on the wall and the white Resistol that was hung on the corner of the half-open closet door. She nodded to the posters. "Good movies. Some of my favorites."

Wallace finished the new bandage and looked up at her. "You tore your stitches and didn't do yourself any favors. Stay off of it for a few days." He gave her a stern look. "I mean it. If you want to get better, you've got to give it time to heal." He packed up his bag and stood. "I'll check it again in the morning, the Cowboy is letting you sleep here so you can avoid the stairs."

Wallace left Cass alone with her gun. She put her hand on it and fell asleep.

41

Massachusetts

TWO BULL-FACED MEN flanked the door of Pyotr's private office in the back of the restaurant. The Cowboy wanted to go through them, but he'd learned to practice better sense. Brute force was not always the best answer in the grey world which he had chosen to rule. Enemies could be most useful so long as they were not too aware of their status as such. Everyone could be used, and people who would talk to him were the easiest to manipulate.

He maintained a light persona, his face carefully plastered with something more jovial than a scowl and less challenging than a real smile. The men were not easily put off guard and he did not expect them to be, but small details were what stopped them from seeing him as an immediately actionable threat, or worse, ignoring him completely.

It was a fine line, such critical acting, but the Cowboy did it with the ease and authority of far too much practice.

He approached slowly and kept his hands in the open. He'd

chosen a tight fitting shirt and well-cut blue jeans. The attire straddled the line between casual and sharp. He hid nothing but scars.

"I need to see Pyotr," the Cowboy said, addressing the one on the left. That one seemed just a little more relaxed, more professional.

"Do you have an appointment?" the left one said in perfect English. His voice lighter than his powerful form would suggest. A pleasant voice for an unpleasant man.

"Yes," the Cowboy lied. He raised his hands and indicated that they should search him.

They found nothing because there was nothing. He did not rush them, but took it with the casual acceptance of one who knows the drill. They finished and he nodded towards the door. "Thank you."

Left one opened the door and the Cowboy walked through and heard it close softly behind him.

Pyotr's fattened form was turned to the side, focused on an open cabinet that dominated the right side of the room. The doors blocked the Cowboy's view of the contents, but the moaning sounds were more than enough.

"Mind turning that off, Pyotr? It's difficult to have a conversation with all that excitement."

Pyotr Derchev glanced at his guest, turned back to the video, then looked at the Cowboy again. His head bobbed, disturbing the layered jowls of sweaty skin. "You!"

"Uh huh. Last time I checked."

"Get out."

"Uh uh. Need to talk to you."

Pyotr's right hand clenched in midair and he turned the chair to face the Cowboy. He scowled and glanced at the door. "Them?"

"Fine. Thorough. But not very good secretaries. Not their fault. But damn lucky."

Pyotr made a low noise in his throat and leaned forward, placing his restless hands on the big wooden desk. "What do you want?"

The cowboy stored away the smile of victory before it reached his lips. He'd won, but this was not the time to gloat. With a seriousness that Pyotr would enjoy, he said, "To find someone."

Pyotr gained confidence and poise as his mind turned to business. His business. The one thing he was surprisingly good at, despite his obvious shortcomings and his misguided sense of the dramatic. He was sometimes amusing and that was something the Cowboy appreciated.

"Who can I find?" Pyotr said.

The Cowboy smiled. "Who do you think?"

It took a moment for the reply.

"She escaped."

Pyotr was lying.

"That's not an option." He stepped up to the desk and leaned close to Pyotr's sweaty purple face. Not fast, not hard, not loud. "Bring her here now and I'll be going."

"I do not have the girl anymore."

"Yes you do. I know you do. You have to have her. I'm here for the girl. Get her." The Cowboy finally smiled. "You want me to leave."

"Yes. Now."

The fat man did a good job of not cowing, but he knew the Cowboy.

The Cowboy knew too much. "Get the girl here."

Pyotr's hand moved sideways, too smooth. The Cowboy slapped his hand down in its path. "Nuh uh, Petey." He lifted his right hand in front of Pyotr's eyes and wiggled his fingers slowly. "You be good."

"You are not good."

"That's the reason. Get the girl."

"I don't have her."

The Cowboy rolled his eyes. "Petey boy. No. No. No. You can't be this stupid. I'm gonna ask one more time nice."

Pyotr decided to laugh at his own forgetfulness. "You are old, alone, and unarmed. I don't have this girl."

"Fine. Be that way. I guess you're getting forgetful in your old age or maybe they just get lost in all that flab." The Cowboy's eyes stopped the constant movement that was their usual state. He pinned them on Pyotr. "I've always wanted to grab hold of them jowls and twist, but you stink. I've got one better."

Pyotr flicked his eyes down and then stared back. Defiant. Dumb. "You have nothing. Leave."

The Cowboy played a Jack. "I know who shot Junior."

The criminal executive flinched and his face grew sullen, the permanently drooped face drooping impossibly lower. The nerve had been struck. Pyotr's weakness had always been his sons.

"Tell me."

"No. Get the girl. Then..." He let his voice trail off, promising.

Pyotr shrugged. It was a bulky, dramatic gesture. "She is, not close by. I'm sorry."

"You failed." The Cowboy stood up, let his gaze wonder around the room for a few moments, then let out a breath and settled his attention back on Pyotr. "I thought we had an understanding."

"We do." Pyotr started backtracking. "Let me make a few calls. I can get her back. It was just a temporary arrangement."

He smiled. "An opportunity for profit. Do not worry. She's being well treated. If I'd known you wanted her back so soon..." He shrugged.

"If you know where she is. Tell me."

"On the way to an airport in South Carolina. She's being taken to meet the plane."

"What time is the rendezvous?"

"Noon, tomorrow."

"I see." He turned to leave. "Goodbye."

"Are we good?" Pyotr said.

"Nope." The Cowboy closed the door gently as he left.

42

O-Bar-Z Ranch

THERE ARE TWO DIFFERENT WAYS to fly a plane. The smart way is safe, easy, and if maintained, makes air travel a very reliable way to get around. The other way is reserved for any sort of idiot dumb enough not to care about his or her life. Maksim liked to think he was smart. He had never aspired to be daring. He'd rather be the one who lived.

He'd gotten up before daylight and ran all his preflight checks twice. He checked the fuel and made a reasonable flight plan. When he took off at dawn, he had no intention of being anything but smart.

He made the mistake of not turning his cell phone off. Technically, it was frowned upon, but he was alone on a private aircraft. Nobody was gonna care and nobody was gonna know unless the cell phone carrier tattled--and they never did. They liked their customers more than they liked the government. The only problem with a cell phone in-flight was the coverage. Cell antennas were optimized for horizontal transmission and reception. They were never meant to cover the air. The result was a lot of dropped calls and a lot of towers fighting over the same signal. Basically, it worked, it just didn't work well.

It didn't even work well at making planes crash like everyone believed. A little interference, sure, but all that it amounted to was maybe a buzz in the headset. Not a big deal.

It was much handier to leave on. Most people couldn't even use a real radio. In the modern world, a man without a cell phone was a man disconnected, cut off from the world, just like in prison. Maksim didn't like that feeling. He kept his cell phone on, all the time, even when it was annoying--or worse.

He was still climbing when he got his father's text.

He reached cruising altitude and set the power on a conservative fifty-five percent. At that rate, he'd make the rendezvous in less than ten hours. Less, if the weather and the currents were in his favor. When he was sure that everything was going as it should, he looked at his phone. The message wasn't good.

Pyotr had screwed up. Someone wanted her back and knew both the when and the where of the transfer. It didn't take much to figure out who must have spilled the information. Maksim didn't need any more reasons to be angry at his father, but for all his failings, Pyotr Derchev was not a cowardly man. It would have been no small thing to get information out of him. Whoever Maksim was now racing against was not to be underestimated.

Maksim put the phone away and swore. That's exactly what it was now, a race. Success would rely on how fast he could get to the little airport outside of Greenville. A leisurely, reliable flight was no longer an option.

The plane would go faster. Pushed hard, he could cruise better than two-hundred knots, but it was never that simple. He mentally calculated how much fuel he thought he had.

When he'd taken off, the main tanks were almost full. He'd topped them off at the nearest airport after his last run, so he had most of ninety gallons there. The crew had done a good job, not chickening out when the level got close to the top of the wing. To get ninety gallons, the tanks had to be completely full, not an inch from the top full. Taking into consideration the wingspan of the tanks, an inch was a lot of fuel. But he'd gotten the ninety, he'd made sure of it. That was enough to make it, maybe, but only if he kept his speed reduced to minimize fuel consumption.

Normally, there was nothing to be done. But, luckily, the green 210 was not quite stock. Its last owners hadn't kept it around to fly the family back and forth on vacation. It was a runner. Its purpose was all business, not pleasure. It was either for smuggling or for escaping. Distance was a weapon and it had to be armed. There was an auxiliary tank in the baggage area.

Maksim had checked the level, and it was full, but there was no way of knowing the exact capacity. His best guess was somewhere between twenty and forty gallons. There was no standard. Aftermarket tanks varied widely. He added the extra fuel to his calculations, and he wasn't too happy with the result.

It was possible, but it wasn't smart. If he pushed the plane, he could probably make a good one-ninety to two-hundred knots. He checked the total distance on the flight plan he'd printed out. It was so close, he had to be exact. At that speed, he could make it in seven hours, give or take. If Pyotr's men left when they were supposed to, that would have him arrive a little before them. He could be refueled and ready to leave when the girl showed up. No down time. That was what needed to happen.

At that power, he'd be lucky if he got twelve gallons to the hour, then for seven hours. He hated math. The numbers added up, but only just. If...IF... there was at least thirty gallons in the extra tank and everything went perfectly, it could be done. But there would be nothing left. No forty-five minute reserve. It was all or nothing and all he had to risk was himself.

But he'd made it this far, running slow, that would be worth a gallon or two. It was insane. He decided to do it and he didn't really know why. There was the project, dire, but not completely. There was always another project, more money out there to be found and taken. It was his father's mistake, not Maksim's. It wasn't his fault. It was Pyotr. But if he could fix Pyotr's screw-up, he'd be holding the cards. Pyotr would have to accept that his least favorite son had done better than he could, had solved the problem that Pyotr could not.

He put his hand on the throttle and eased it forward. He checked the airspeed monitor and smiled. Maybe hell was waiting.

Been there, done that. Still here.

43

Virginia

THE COWBOY DECIDED to send Bobby and Wallace. They were healthy, competent, and most of all, there were only two seats in the Lamborghini. He'd called as soon as he left Pyotr and explained the new situation. Wallace and Bobby were on the road in less than twenty minutes.

"Having fun yet?" Bobby was grinning like a madman in the driver's seat while Wallace maintained a white-knuckle grip on whatever he could find to hang on to.

Wallace glanced at the gauge cluster. "I know that we are in a hurry, but do you realize how fast you're going?"

Bobby glanced down and his grin widened. "I always know. That's part of the fun."

Wallace shook his head and mumbled something about some sort of disorder.

Bobby laughed. "Guess you're a different kind of driver."

He'd seen Wallace work in the city. The man was good in traffic, and that was an impressive skill. It took a certain flavor of madness to do well. But it was always interesting how one sort of crazy didn't always translate. Bobby hated traffic, but he loved to go fast. It wasn't stressful, it wasn't really scary, it was just great. An amazing sensation, and it just got better the faster they went. He wondered what sort of driver Cass was?

She'd been more than a little upset to be left behind. She'd said that she understood, but it didn't really change her mind. She wanted to go, even if it was a bad idea.

Bobby needed both hands at speed, so he usually couldn't change any settings while he was driving. Then he'd met Dobbs. He touched a sensor on the wheel and said, "Play driving music."

Voice-activated. Hell yes. The first song up was an old rock song about trains. It was fast and it was moving. Bobby's head made small bobbing motions in time with the beat and he watched the needle climb. It was a seven hour drive to Greenville. He figured to do it in five, maybe less. But definitely five.

BOBBY DIDN'T KNOW that a black face could turn so white. Wallace had his hands clenched and was doing a very good job of keeping his expression neutral. But his face, if not his expression, showed just what he thought of Bobby's driving.

Bobby slid the car to a stop at the edge of the airstrip. "We're here."

Wallace nodded, but his eyes conveyed their thanks to the sky.

They'd reached 200 mph, three times, but Bobby wasn't ready to stop the rush. It was just time to change the instrument. He let the door swing up and got out with his hand on the revolver in his jacket pocket.

The airport was dead. Nothing going on anywhere. He looked up and around, but there was nothing to see.

"I'm going to check the office. Right back." He didn't wait for the reply.

The office was a small tin building that had seen better days. The edges of the roof and the metal near the ground was severely rusted and gave the structure a gaping ring of mysterious black space all the way around the bottom. A white vinyl sign with foot-tall black letters indicated the building's purpose, and fluttered in the breeze as the wind pulled it against the cord tying it in place.

The screen door was more or less secured by a piece of moldy rope. Bobby went inside and didn't have to look far to find the lone attendant.

The body was beside the only desk, shot at least twice. There was too much blood soaked into the off-white shirt to really tell, but at least one in the chest, and one very messy hole through the man's cheek and the back of his skull. Bobby ran outside and leaned over. He didn't puke, but he felt like he should have.

Wallace got out of the car, still pale, and walked over.

"What happened?"

Bobby realized that he was done and straightened. "Dead guy in there." He glanced towards the office. "Bad."

Wallace nodded, but he seemed more interested in Bobby than the problem. Freaking shrink.

Bobby didn't want to see the body again, but he didn't see another option. He followed Wallace inside. Everything was just the same.

Wallace paused for a moment at the sight, but only for a moment. He stepped around the blood and examined papers on the desk.

"They didn't take the flight log." He tossed a sheet of paper down. "Either he was dead before the plane came in or it never did."

"Either way, looks like we're screwed." Bobby stuck his hands in his pockets and tried to look anywhere but at the dead man.

"Possibly, but although I did not enjoy our drive, we did make good time." He dipped a pencil in the pooled blood and held it up, watching it drip. "It's very fresh."

"Great." Bobby's voice was a little too high-pitched. "We still missed 'em."

"Maybe..." Wallace's voice trailed off. He was carefully poking around in the dead man's pockets. After a moment, he stood with a satisfied expression on his face and a walkie talkie in his hand. "...not."

"Yeah." Bobby perked up. Wallace was right. "That's one of those cheap, short range radios." He smiled at Wallace over the body. "There might be somebody else working here."

Wallace brought the radio to his lips and pressed the talk button. "Hello. Come in?"

There was only a click of static, but that was enough.

They found the other guy near the fuel tanks. The other guy turned out to be a young woman with a hole through her shoulder. Shot, not dead, but still very messy. Bobby was happy to let Wallace be the one to talk to her.

"Call an ambulance." Wallace pointed a focused finger at Bobby just long enough to get the message across before turning back to the injured woman. "We're here to help." Wallace did something with the wound and the woman winced out loud. Bobby cringed and turned away, concentrating on the phone ringing.

"What happened, exactly?" Wallace took the woman's face in his hand.

"Three men. Shot me." She started weeping.

"They were here to meet a plane. Did they? It is critical that you tell me."

"No." The woman looked down and continued making sobbing noises.

Wallace looked up at Bobby with a conflicted expression. "The ambulance, is it coming?"

"Yeah." Bobby slapped his pants pocket where his phone belonged. "Be here in a couple of minutes." He shot a worried look at the woman. "Is she...gonna be good?"

Wallace stood and glanced down at her. "I've done what I can. Let's go."

"We can't just leave her..." Bobby shrugged and looked sideways at the woman.

Wallace had no time for it. "It's out of my hands. The plane must have landed somewhere else and we need to find out where before another life is lost." He pointed uncomfortably at the Lambo parked on the tarmac. "Drive."

South Carolina

MAKSIM WAS FAMILIAR with many variations of trouble. Prison had been a concentrated example of the simplest forms. Surviving his fellow man had taken everything he had and more. In there, instinct was the key. It didn't matter how a man fought, if he called it an art or a style or just throwing punches. The how was second to the experience. Every fight a man lived through was an opportunity to learn. Each time, a few more things became obvious, some were discovered, and more importantly, some became instinct. If a man survived long enough, learned enough, absorbed enough, he became a master of whatever he practiced. That moment was indescribable and undefinable, but it happened. Everything became a little clearer. Instinct became indistinguishable from thought. Reaction adapted as if conscious. Instinct became so adept as to be creative.

Instinct had saved Maksim many times. It was great for the simplest and most common sorts of trouble.

Maksim forced himself to keep steady as the alarms began to blare. This wasn't that sort of trouble.

His instincts couldn't fly a plane, but they could sure as hell crash one.

He'd known the alarms might be coming, but he was unprepared for the barrage of sound and light that indicated engine failure. Without thinking, he pulled back on the yoke. It was a quick mistake, and a bad one.

With no power, the only thing left was airspeed, the faster, the better. That instant of reaction had done the opposite. It had slowed him down.

Back in charge, he pointed the nose down and tried to get back some speed. The plane stabilized into a controllable glide and he spared some attention for the nav system. He saw the screen and cursed himself. He'd known he was close, and hoped he was close enough, but that moment of panic had cost too much. There was no way he was going to make the intended rendezvous.

He had to find another, closer place to land. On his own, unfamiliar with the area and in such a rush he didn't do any contingency research, he was screwed. He made a slight adjustment and smiled. The nav system was very modern. It was constantly keeping track of nearby airstrips, doing the job that the pilot should--preparing to land at any moment. It was more prepared for an emergency than he was and quickly gave him a new destination. A private airstrip, just within his accidentally reduced glide range, and on a heading that wouldn't require much correction. As long as he didn't do anything else stupid and needlessly lose more airspeed, he could make it work. A small change of plans. Everything would be fine. All he had to do was survive the landing.

He kept the plane in a smooth glide for as long as possible, nothing to it. All too soon, the easy part was over. Landing was always the most dangerous part of any flight, and with no power, he only had one shot at it. No second chances.

He tweaked the heading so that he was properly lined up on the runway. He was going to make it. Gear down. Deep breath. He got one last good look at the runway and then he flared. He pulled the controls back and the nose came up. The airspeed needle took a dive and in a few moments, the stall speed indicator started blaring. This was it. He hoped he was still on the runway and close to the ground.

Stall. No more lift. No more magic flying. Just two-tons of machine, falling to the ground.

An eternal moment of nothing, then the landing gear hit the surface of the runway--and--that was it. No ballooning, no crashing, just a good landing.

Maksim let out a breath he'd been holding and smiled. Damn near perfect.

There was nothing quite like survival. The thrill of beating the odds; making it through a gauntlet of probable disaster. He was alive. He tried not so seek out these moments of danger that made the heart race and the mind quicken, and he knew why. It was addictive. For a little while, the world was a wonderful place. No worries, no weakness, just the glow of ultimate victory.

Then there was the let-down.

Maksim leaned back in his seat and popped a peppermint candy into his mouth, breathing deep as the hardened sugar melted in time with his nerves. After a few moments, he crunched the candy into small bits with his teeth and disembarked the aircraft. Back to the real world.

He climbed down and examined his surroundings. There was the runway and a small shed that must serve as the office, and most important, fuel pumps.

A simple setup at the edge of the tarmac, but it was a long way to move a dead airplane. Maksim alone couldn't push the plane to the pump and a quick examination revealed the impossibility of stringing hose back to the plane.

He would just have to wait until Pyotr's men arrived. They would be able to help him roll the plane nearer the pump. It would delay his departure, but the plan had already gone far afield and there was no other option. He started checking the plane for any damage. At least he would be done with his checklist. That was something he could do while he was waiting.

He was examining a small dimple on the left wing and thanking Cessna for the spring-steel landing struts, even though he made a relatively soft landing, he was always amazed at how durable the landing gear had to be. Even a nice landing put a lot of force on the gear. Or maybe he just liked to say spring-steel. Either way, he always remembered that feature of a 210.

"Can I help you?" The voice came as a surprise and Maksim turned quickly to face the unknown speaker. A man, forties, but well-built and well-kept. He wore no uniform, just the standard blue jeans and t-shirt that were so common. There was nothing special to the eye, but there was more to the man. Maksim detected a wariness and a confidence that suggested more than the usual amount of danger.

The man's arms hung at his sides, loose and ready. "This is a private runway. I don't know you."

"It was an emergency. I ran out of fuel and had to glide in. This was the best option. Sorry. Soon as I can, I'll be on my way."

"I've been here all day with the radio on. Didn't hear your distress report."

"Comms were on the fritz." Maksim lied quickly. "Planned

to get that fixed. Didn't realize how bad it was. Thought it was just a short in the mic, but looks like it's worse. Just one thing on top of another, you know?"

The man smiled slightly, but remained on guard. "I see. Well, there's a guy I know that's good with radios. I'll get him on the phone. Meanwhile..." He gestured towards the small building. "Let's get that plane over to the pumps. I'll go get my truck and a tow strap. Be right back."

45

South Carolina

"HOW THE HELL are we gonna find 'em now?" Bobby put his hand on the door, but he didn't pop the hatch. He was staring over the low-slung car at Wallace. "There's no way to know where they went from here." He slapped the roof of the car and sighed. "Or even if any of this is legit?"

"You doubt the Cowboy's intelligence?" Wallace was stone-faced, more unreadable than usual.

No, but I don't trust him. Bobby didn't have time for that discussion, so he kept it to himself.

"Let's go back to the office. I have an idea," Wallace said.

Bobby popped the hatch. "More than I got." He started the car and the purr didn't make him feel any better. "Away we go."

A very short drive later, they were back at the rusted building. Bobby followed Wallace to the door, but refused to go inside.

"You drove here awful fast to stay outside." Wallace didn't

appreciate the ride, again.

"An empty runway." Bobby leaned against the doorframe and looked back at his car. "The destination?...not the point." Without turning, he yelled to Wallace inside. "What are you looking for?"

There was no answer. Bobby looked in and immediately regretted it. Ugh. But Wallace was fine, just on the phone. The sight made the smell suddenly worse and Bobby closed the door and went back to lean against the car and wait on Wallace to pull something out of a hat. He wasn't optimistic.

Apparently, neither was Wallace, but that didn't stop him from trying. The sleuth came out after a couple of minutes with an uncharacteristic glint of something in his face. It might be in his eyes too, but they were hidden from view by the round little shades he sometimes wore.

"Solve the case, Sherlock?"

Wallace gave a rare smile and pointed his finger up in the universal light bulb position. "It's slimmer than slim, but I have one lead." He handed a note across. "Take us to this place. It's all we've got."

Bobby looked at the unreadable note and started the engine. "You shoulda been a doctor." He handed the scrap of paper back. "You read it. I'll drive."

It was a good idea, because it was the only idea.

"I checked the potential alternative landing locations in the immediate region. " Wallace seemed a little proud of himself. "And determined the most likely."

"How's that?" Bobby kept his eyes on the road, but he wasn't past a hundred, easy driving. "You flip a coin?"

Wallace dramatically huffed. "I called them."

"And what? Asked for the criminal? They put you on hold?" Bobby raised a finger off the wheel as a shrug.

"One of them didn't answer. A small strip at a private, residential complex that caters to those families who own small aircraft."

"Small, private, maybe they just weren't there. Not like there has to be someone to answer the phone."

Wallace returned to his impassive routine, the brief interlude of levity complete. "There is nothing else I can think of."

Bobby nodded. "And we're out of time." He accelerated. "Good as anything. Hold on."

46

South Carolina

THE GATE WAS LOCKED and Bobby was not going to ram it with his car. Wallace seemed disappointed. Bobby gave him a glare and spun the Lambo to a stop.

They climbed over and made their way down between the rows of homes that made up the community.

"The strip is just past the last houses." Wallace was a little out of breath, but so was Bobby. Excitement did that.

They paused before moving out into the open area between the houses and the airstrip.

"Hell if you weren't right." Bobby leaned against the dull brown siding of the last house and surveyed the situation.

A green plane, four guys, and one Anne Chaves right in the middle of it. It was about a hundred yards to the strip and just a little further to the crowd of bad guys. Way too far to take a shot with a pistol and there was no time to go back to the car for the AR. Just as well, it was still a long shot.

Bobby rolled back around to face Wallace, out of sight of the enemy. "Any ideas?"

"Sadly, no." Wallace looked at the ground. "Nothing good, anyhow. There's no cover, we would be outnumbered, and there is the girl to worry about in a firefight--assuming we have a chance at all."

"Well, shit." Bobby was up for stupid, but not suicide, and that was all he could see.

He looked back towards the strip and watched with a growing sense of dread as the plane started moving. There were only three men visible on the tarmac. So one in the plane with the girl. As he continued to watch, helpless, the plane took off and the three men got into a Dodge Magnum and started to drive towards the houses; towards Bobby and Wallace.

"Be ready. There's only three. I'll get the rear tire, you get the front." Bobby checked that he had a good two-handed grip on the pistol and waited.

The car was moving slow for a Magnum and it gave Bobby the several shots he needed.

Minus two tires got the attention of the three men. They didn't have to stop, but they did. Bobby kept his gun pointed right between the collarbone of the passenger and Wallace was pointing his gun too, hopefully at a different guy. The window rolled down and a gun came up. Wallace fired and the passenger died. Bobby moved to the figure in the back seat and hoped that this time Wallace took the other guy. But, he didn't leave it to fate this time. "I got the guy in the back."

"Exit the vehicle with your hands in the air immediately." Wallace chuckled. "Or die."

"Okay, do not shoot." The driver had a thick accent, but the Boston was way worse than the Slavic. Once the two men were no longer a threat, Bobby called the Cowboy.

"Good news?" Bobby could hear the Cowboy's apprehension. That made for two.

Bobby shrugged out loud. "Meh...and not so good."

47

Virginia

"I COULD HAVE MADE THE SHOT." Cass didn't have eyes for anybody in the room. She was staring off into space as Bobby and Wallace recounted their failure to rescue Anne.

"There was no way to know." Bobby's eyes pleaded. "Besides you were injured. You couldn't come."

"There was not a thing you could have done." Wallace looked a little distracted when he decided to chime in.

Cass continued to glare into space. "I should have been there."

The Cowboy leaned forward, his elbows on the table, his palms up. "We have more than before. We will find her."

Cass nodded. "We better."

"We will." The Cowboy steepled his fingers and smiled tightly. "I may already have something. When ya'll called, I did some talking--persuasive talking. Based on what I've learned and can guess, I intend to have your next move right away." He looked at Cass. "You, I want ready to leave by morning." He turned his attention to Wallace. "And you."

"Where are we going?" Cass didn't really care as long as it was somewhere useful.

"I'll let you know. I need to narrow it down more." He stood. "But, pack for academia."

PART 3

Set

49

Colorado

JESSICA BRIGHTON was a certifiable genius in Genetic Engineering. Her specialty was the new and exciting field of pharmacrops. Using genetically modified strains of wheat, corn, and other common grains to produce specific proteins to be used in medicine and other biological applications. The potential for cheap production of rare custom proteins was remarkable and could revolutionize modern medicine and the production of vaccines and treatments. All in all, the twenty-five year old student was doing what every Oprah watching American dreamed of. She was making the world a more civilized and controlled place.

She was also an idiot.

Cass had e-mailed Brighton about the roommate situation expecting to arrange an in-person interview and then convince the graduate student that Cass would be a good choice for a roommate. Unbelievably, the girl had accepted Cass without so much as a single inquiry or hesitation.

"I am so happy to have a new roommate! You can move in immediately. Can't wait to meet you. Sincerely, Jessica Brighton."

Cass scowled at the message on her phone one more time, and knocked on the plain white door of APT 4B. Confirming Cass's first impression, Jessica Brighton opened the door without asking who was there or any other such reasonable precaution. At least she'd be watching the right target, because Brighton was the easiest kidnapping victim that Cass could imagine.

Having replaced her natural scowl with a less scary smile, Cass greeted the woman. "Anne Chavez, at your service. You must be Jessica."

"Yes, that's me! Come on in. This is going to be so much fun. I've always wanted an apartment and a roommate. Can I help you with your stuff?"

Cass didn't take her hand off the simple rolling suitcase that she had brought. "No thanks. I got it just fine."

As she entered the room, she took its measure. Clean, but not new, the walls were papered with dull floral designs that turned Cass's stomach--figuratively, anyway--and the floors were off-white carpet. There was enough usable furniture in pastel plaid to satisfy a complement of half a dozen guests in front of a modern, but small, flat screen television. Most notably, to someone of Cass's mindset, the couch and both chairs were all facing the TV and away from the door.

After the door was closed, Brighton offered to pour up some coffee. She went into the small kitchen and Cass took the opportunity to check the other rooms. There was indeed a small kitchen with one door and a window with a view of the alley, two stories down. Two bedrooms and a full bath between them. It was a corner apartment, so one of the bedrooms adjoined the hall and the other had two outside walls. Cass's choice would be the inside room with the outside walls. Accordingly, and unsurprisingly, that very room was empty and waiting for Brighton's new roommate.

Cass adjusted one of the pink stuffed chairs so that it afforded an acceptable view of the door. She was sitting there, contemplating the complete lack of security, and the painful color scheme, when the coffee came in.

Accepting the proffered mug (decorated with flowers, of course) from Brighton, Cass sipped the flavored water. It was a testament of her self-control that she didn't let the distaste show. If proper coffee could float a horseshoe, then this brew wouldn't float a scrap of paper.

Brighton took a seat and began chatting. She explained to Cass exactly how old she was, where she'd lived, been born, what kind of car she had, how her last boyfriend had departed, and continued to essentially bore Cass immensely while simultaneously revealing enough information about herself that, if Cass had been a bit more unscrupulous, she could have had a nice, new stolen identity.

The rather one-sided chat continued for almost an hour, with Cass inserting neutral monosyllabic guttural responses at appropriate intervals. At the end of that time, Cass knew far more than she wanted to about the girl, and had told Brighton nothing. It was better to allow the girl to fit Cass into whatever profile suited her. Cass suspected that Brighton would not understand or approve of the truth--not even counting the new bit about being a secret agent and such.

"Pardon me, Jessica, but I think I'd better unpack and get settled, if that's alright?"

"Oh, of course! Is there anything I can do to help?"

Cass informed Brighton of her self-sufficiency and desire to take a siesta because of the fatigue of the trip. Satisfied, Brighton allowed Cass to retire to the empty bedroom.

The door was closed and the suitcase was opened, revealing a couple of T-shirts and a pair of jeans. Cass sat the clothes on the bed and extracted the rest of the contents.

There was ammo for her new Glock, a second secure mobile phone, a four-inch knife with a razor edge, and three extra mags for the pistol. She had everything she'd asked for. Time to get to it.

Cass put the stuff away, and then waited half an hour to make the nap story mesh. With the gun concealed under a loose shirt and the extra mags and the knife stowed on her person, she reemerged into the main part of the apartment. Brighton was watching some sort of shopping program on the TV and talking on the phone.

"I'm starved," Cass said. "Where can you get a good steak around here?"

50

Colorado

CASS REMEMBERED exactly why she had decided not to continue her college education. Just two days of hanging around campus and she was already fit to be tied. The fact that she didn't slap half the students she encountered was either a miracle or a fine testament to her self-control.

Brighton, the genetics guru, was obviously familiar with every beer-serving restaurant in town--and with the Coors factory just up the hill, there were plenty--except for the one that must serve a decent slab of beef. Unwilling to let Brighton out of her sight for more than a few seconds, Cass was doing her best to be the girl's friend, and when she didn't get invited, she still followed, just less conspicuously.

In all honesty, stalking the girl was easier than having to interact with her friends. They didn't have much in common to talk about, and at times, were downright annoying. But that was easily put away because of her purpose. She was concerned with finding Anne--and her captors. Not slapping a few wannabe hippies was a small price to pay.

The afternoon lecture by Dr. Archodore was proving to be less than satisfying. Rather than talk about medieval literature, as one would expect, he did more preaching and rambling about his personal opinions and life stories. Cass found him shallow and dull, and thought he was a sorry excuse for a professor. Nonetheless, he was apparently enthralling most of the audience.

She kept scanning the auditorium and finding no one else looking away from the stage. Having decided that Cass was not enough fun, Brighton was sitting in the second row with some of her more chatty friends. Cass was in the back row of the lower tier, close to an exit and with a good view of her task.

Halfway through the two-hour indoctrination, a ten minute break was called. Cass carefully tailed Brighton through the suddenly thronging crowd of sheep all the way down the corridor to the restroom. Five minutes later, without anything amiss other than the unfortunately overheard conversations in the women's bathroom, Brighton returned to her seat and waited for the rest of the speech.

Cass watched as the auditorium filled back up. At the ten minute mark, the buzz of chatter died down a little as Archodore returned to the mic.

In the middle of his latest childhood anecdote, her phone buzzed. It was The Cowboy. Brighton was still in her seat so Cass slipped out into the hall and put the phone to her ear.

"Yeah," she answered.

We've got a problem. The target has changed. It's not Brighton.

"Huh, who is?"

All we know is that it's one of the other women in her department. Probably a classmate. I'll send you a list. Try to keep an eye on as many as you can. I'm sending Wallace and Bobby in. Looks like we're gonna need more eyes.

"Alright, I'll do what I can. Later."

She hung up the phone and returned to her seat. Within a minute, a list of names appeared on her screen and she went through them. It was a short list, only three names, but it was going to be a chore trying to keep tabs on them by herself. At least after the lecture. For the moment, all but one were sitting in the second row, near Brighton. Cass looked up to confirm and realized that she was wrong. One of the girls had not returned to her seat after the intermission.

It could be nothing, but it wasn't worth assuming. Cass got up and went to the second row. Sitting down in the missing girl's seat, she leaned over and whispered to Brighton.

"That girl, Gilbert was her last name, where'd she go at the break? She was with you, right?"

Oblivious to anything amiss, Brighton answered absentmindedly, "I don't know. She said she was gonna go ask Archodore a question. I think she wanted his autograph. She said she actually read one of his books and liked it."

"Thanks," said Cass briskly. She went out the side door by the stage, not even bothering to be subtle anymore. She was in too much of a hurry to be sneaky. She checked the halls, both public and not, the restrooms and everywhere else she could find. She was making a round outside the building when she found the purse. She only found it because she saw a flash out of the corner of her eye that turned out to be the sun reflecting off the rhinestones that covered the small bag.

It was shoved up behind the trash can by the least-used, back door of the building. Cass opened it up and found exactly what she was afraid of--it belonged to the student named Gilbert. Money, cards, driver's license, nothing of value was missing. Cass dialed her phone.

"Carlos. The one named Gilbert. She's gone."

"How do you know?

"She never came back after the intermission. Brighton said she was going to get Archodore's autograph and I found her purse outside."

"That's all circumstantial. You can't be sure."

"You've been in the city too long. I just know it, alright. Call it instinct. They've got her."

Ok, we'll see if we can trace something. Keep up your surveillance till the end of the week, just in case. I'll get back to you.

"Right." She stabbed the button to end the call with a calloused finger.

She was waiting at the same door thirty minutes later when Archodore emerged. A trail of adoring students followed him and she slipped into the crowd and used them for cover. He stopped at the honorary office assigned to him for the duration of his stay and proceeded to sign autographs and bask in adulation for the next hour. Cass kept rolling to the back of the line, staying close, but never actually entering the office. There was only one door, she'd know when he left. She wasn't going to hurry this, she knew better. She'd already picked her spot, she just had to wait for him there. As the sky darkened outside, the line disappeared and she slipped away to wait and watch in the dark.

In addition to keeping tabs on Brighton, she had been tracking the good professor too. He was a creature of habit and vanity. She knew that he would eventually grow tired of this and head back to his room. The on-campus apartment was just three buildings over from the office. He took the same route every night, and ate his evening meal by himself in the same place. He was a strict vegan apparently and only ate food that he bought and prepared himself. He also believed in global warming and the evils of internal combustion. So he deigned to walk rather than drive around. It would be easy enough.

She waited silently behind a sculpted bush, just off the sidewalk. An hour later, Archodore came into view. He was walking along slowly, the ups and downs of the mountain campus taking their toll on his rather large and out-of-shape body. She heard him breathing before he came around the corner into view.

He passed by and she followed him, keeping in time with his pace and avoiding any angles of light that would cast her shadow where he might see it. She took long steps and gained on him quickly. She got within a step and took a deep breath, running the plan over in her head one more time. She'd never actually tried it before, but that didn't matter.

She closed the distance and reached her right arm around and clamped her hand over his mouth. He froze for moment, his mind and body not knowing how to react. In that instant of indetermination, she delivered a precise strike to the side of his neck. She grinned as he went limp. It worked. Neat.

He was heavy, but she was stout and had parked her cover-appropriate car in the nearby lot, just yards from where she had dropped him. Which was the main reason she had picked the spot. No use trying to carry his weight any farther. Grabbing an arm, she got him over her shoulder and off the ground. Just like a feed sack, only bigger--and smellier. A short time later, he was in the trunk.

She drove out of town and pulled off onto a side road. Armed with duct-tape and nice-sized tree limb that she picked up in the barditch, she opened the trunk. He was awake and started moaning and yelling and talking. Cass ignored him just like she would an ornery calf that wouldn't quit bawling. She taped his hands and mouth and then directed him to get out of the trunk. She kept hold of one of his thumbs and twisted it enough to show him that she was in control.

"Ye're too dang slow to get away, even if I let you. Do what I say and we'll all be good. Got it?"

He nodded, his eyes showing a combination of fear and confusion.

"Good." She led him around and opened the passenger door. "Get in."

He complied and after he was sitting, she taped his ankles together too. Throwing the branch in the back seat, she got in and turned back onto the interstate.

After a few minutes she ripped the tape off his face.

"Don't want nobody to be suspicious, now, do we," she said. He started to speak and she cut him off. "No. You shut up for a minute. I know you been helping some bad guys kidnap some stupid girls. So there ain't no good reason for me to be any kind of nice to you. But if you tell me what I want to know and don't get on my nerves, I'll be nicer." She held the gaze for several long moments before turning back to the road.

"You're crazy!" said the professor at last. "I don't know what you're talking about. You kidnapped me! I'm gonna have you imprisoned!" He continued to ramble on for several minutes.

Finally, Cass spoke again. She was getting tired of his ranting. He must not have understood her to be telling the truth. "Shush, mister," she said slowly, eyeing him again.

He shrunk back in the seat. Better. Maybe he was getting the message.

"I don't think you understand how serious I am." She pointed a finger at him. "You're the bad guy here. I want to know about the Russians and anyone else they're working with. I'm gonna find out where they're taking those girls and then they are gonna regret the day I found out about all this." She paused, letting her words sink in and keeping her attention on the road as she passed a truck. "You got anything to tell me?"

He shook his head and turned his eyes away. "I know nothing."

She shrugged. "Suit yourself, fella. You got a few hundred miles to change your mind. Then I might get mean. Don't say I didn't warn ya." She turned the radio on to classic country and started singing.

51

New Mexico

THE RANCH that Cass had inherited from her grandfather was mostly up on top of a large mesa. It was as flat as it was dry, the short grass shaded only by cactus and the occasional juniper tree. Hard land, but workable if not stocked too heavily--and so long as it caught a decent rain on occasion.

Cass parked the car under a shed that was half-full of large hay bales. The low-riding vehicle had barely made it up the deeply rutted road and she was glad to get out of the cramped space.

Without removing the rag she had used to blindfold the professor with, she helped him out of the car and led him to the other vehicle parked under the shed. It was an older pickup with peeling white paint and less than nothing in the way of amenities. It was barebones except for the four-wheel drive system and the big block engine. It had a flatbed with a feeder mounted on it for delivering cake to the cattle. It would go anywhere it was needed and a few places it shouldn't. It was the perfect example of what locals called a cowboy rig. All business and absolutely nothing fancy.

Cass put the professor in the passenger seat, took the key out of the ignition, and closed the doors. She threw the branch on the back.

"Stay put. Don't bother trying to get out, the inside door handles haven't worked in years. I'll be back before you get too hot."

Even in the shade, the temperature was over a hundred degrees and she knew from experience that it would be like a dry sauna inside the closed cab. He could sweat while she got what she needed from the barn.

The barn was old, built out of wood and tin; it looked like it could collapse at any minute. But Cass had shored it up inside. It wasn't gonna fall until a tornado hit it or somebody drove through it with a tractor. It was full of parts, feed, and horse tack. Cass went all the way to the back, stepped behind a rack of saddles, and knelt down on the dusty concrete floor. She shoved the nearest rack aside to reveal a hole. She dropped down into the darkness.

With a confident aim, she reached out with her left hand and flipped a switch. A couple of bare light bulbs came on and shed their dim light on the underground space. It was a small room, with dirt floors and walls, maybe ten-foot square. The walls were supported by crude wooden shelves that held boxes of ammunition, gun cases, knives, a few boxes of canned food, and a collection of holsters. At the far end was a large gun safe with a combination lock. Cass spun the lock and opened the safe, smiling at the contents. Her prized possessions were organized neatly, in contrast to the general disorder of the rest of her stuff. She chose a 5-inch Smith and Wesson forty-four magnum revolver and a Remington semi-auto carbine in 30-06. She closed the safe and locked it.

Turning her attention to the shelves, she selected a good, quick holster for the revolver and attached a sling to the rifle. She got an extra box of ammo for each of the guns--they were already loaded, of course. She also grabbed a camouflage bag with something already in it. Almost as an afterthought, she grabbed a large bowie knife and its sheath. She turned off the lights, and returned the way she had come, concealing the entrance to her stash again.

When she got back got into the driver's seat of the cowboy rig, she was armed and ready for bear. Or in this case, cougar.

"I'm going to die of heat stroke!" the professor moaned. "Turn the A/C on."

"Shut ye're trap. You ain't that bad yet. You've only been in here for a few minutes." She rolled her window down and started driving. "I'll roll yours down too. The breeze will cool things down a bit. I'm afraid that's all the air-con this rig's got. Welcome to the desert."

He did as she suggested and sat silently for the rest of the ride--much to her delight. His whiney voice was getting on her nerves.

After half an hour of driving, she killed the engine and got out. She slung the rifle across her back, grabbed the camo bag and the tree branch, before letting the professor out and removing his blindfold.

He stopped and looked around. A worried look came onto his face as he realized just how far he was from civilization. "Where are we?"

"Nowhere. Nothing but us and a few critters for too many miles to worry about." Cass grinned. "That bother you?"

She had figured that it would. Very few folks appreciated freedom. Most were scared of it. The professor didn't disappoint.

"There's no one else out here? Just us?"

The fear in his voice was tangible. Cass was pleased. She didn't want this to get ugly. Maybe fear would be enough. "Yeah, just us--and the cougars." She let the words hang in the air.

She made him walk in front of her as they left the rig behind and approached the edge of the mesa. The land dropped off steep and sudden along most of the edge and the juniper trees became very thick. There was the occasional ravine that cut into the cliff which provided a path down that was not too steep to walk. They went down one of these gaps and emerged onto a large shelf of land part way down the side. There was nothing but cliff below and above. The only way out was the way they came in.

The shelf was about a hundred yards across and almost as wide. Cass opened the bag and took out what looked like a camouflage flashlight and a remote. It was actually an electronic game call. She placed the larger piece under a tree near the edge and put the remote in her pocket.

"What are you doing?" Archodore asked as she programmed the call. "What is that?"

She finished and turned the call on. It started emitting a strange, high-pitched screaming sound. "That's a call, mister. Right now, I've got it set to sound like a deer in distress." She looked him in the eyes. "And last time I checked, that was the favored meal of every mountain lion I ever met. You getting the idea?"

He looked at her and then at the call. A look of horror came over his face. "No! I'm defenseless."

She smiled. He shivered and sweated and babbled. She grabbed his face. "Get a hold of yourself. I warned you, mister. This is me gettin' mean. Here's the situation. You tell me what I want to know. I mean spill every bean in the pot...or you can stay here and have it out with the next hungry cat that comes within earshot."

She handed him the branch. "Here you go. I heard you were one of them greenies, against guns and pickups and such. I knew one once, he told me that I didn't need my pistol to fight a cougar. He said I just needed a beat stick. I reckon you'd agree with him on most issues, and I don't want to make you a hypocrite, so you can prove him right."

She backed away, close enough to talk, but in the open and with a good view all around. It wouldn't do to be blindsided. She said nothing for a few minutes, giving the man a chance to assess his situation.

"Well?" she said after a while, projecting her voice over the noise of the call.

He looked around, frightened, but still not convinced. "You are crazy. No one would bring down one of nature's great predators on themselves. You are bluffing." Having convinced himself, he calmed down and let the stick hang at his side. He glared his challenge at Cass.

She just grinned. Staring right back at the foolish man. She had never been afraid of a challenge. In fact, some might say that she had a weakness. She could never resist the chance to beat a trial--or call a bluff.

"Why are you laughing? I see nothing funny at all here."

She stopped, but the reckless grin remained. "You're amusing me. Cougars are tough cats, no doubt about it. But God didn't put no cats at the top of the food chain. That spot's reserved for the two-legged breed." She shifted the rifle a little to be more accessible. "My Daddy didn't raise me to be scared of no cat, mister. Are you?" She raised an eyebrow.

Before he could reply, she pretended that she heard something. "Hear that? Sounds like you're running out of time."

"I can't tell you anything. You don't understand. They will kill me!" He clutched the branch uselessly.

Cass glanced towards the ravine they had come down. She didn't really expect a mountain lion to show up. They were notoriously hard to call. She'd seen a few and gone on a hunt with hounds on a neighbor's place. She figured some coyotes might show up, maybe a bobcat if she was lucky, but nothing was also a distinct possibility. The point was to scare the fellow, and by the looks of him, it was working.

She kept her eyes roving, looking for movement. Even if she was just putting on a show, she couldn't let her guard down. She was telling the truth about one thing, cougars were pretty scary.

Again, she pretended to see something and jumped a little, a quick move of fake apprehension. She looked at the professor. "As we've established, I'm curious to know who it is you're afraid of, mister. What I think you ought to do is tell me so that you live long enough to find out if they really are as scary as you claim. I ain't got nowhere else to be and if you don't talk, I ain't got no use for you."

Before he had a chance to reply, there was movement, real this time and she turned her attention towards the spot along the trees. It was a coyote, a big one, walking along. She flipped the gun around on the sling, took the safety off as she aimed, and fired. The coyote fell.

She grinned at the professor and returned the rifle to its previous position on her back. If he said anything, she couldn't make it out, her ears were still ringing. There'd been enough adrenaline to help block the noise, but even excitement can't overcome the sound of a big rifle with a short barrel, and in all the planning and just plain oddness of the situation, she'd forgotten to put anything in her ears.

Looking at the dead coyote, she came up with an idea. She

went after the carcass.

She'd hit a little higher than necessary, but still in the vital area. It was good and dead. It was in good shape too, not all mangy and ragged like they were sometimes. She put it on her shoulder. Even the biggest coyote weighed less than a sack of feed.

Walking back to the professor, she threw the carcass on the ground in front of him and started the process of skinning it out. It was a nice hide. She could give it to her sister to tan and make something out of it. She gagged the man, no point in letting him talk when she couldn't hear.

Using her bowie knife--which wasn't really the best tool for the job, but she figured would look the part better--she started cutting up the belly. When she had it slit open, she picked it up, drained the blood, and pulled out the guts so that they splashed mostly on the ground at the professor's feet. He didn't seem too happy about the bits that landed on him and his fancy shoes.

It smelled bad and it took a while, but she eventually got the hide off and in mostly one piece. She stood up, a bloody knife in one hand, bloody coyote skin in the other and looked down at the professor. Her ears were more or less back to normal and she hoped he was ready to talk. She was getting thirsty. She wanted to get back, get some iced tea, and get on the road towards finding Anne.

He looked like he was ready to talk. "What? I'm almost done. Then we'll get back to you."

She glanced around and didn't see anything to worry about, so she turned the majority of her attention to her captive. "Okay, I'm about tired of this, so you can talk, or I can go back home." She shrugged. "Without you."

She took the gag off and crouched down, putting the smelly hide over her shoulder to give herself a free hand. He wasn't saying anything. In fact, he was almost smiling.

"What is it? You think I'm joking around here?" She realized that she was joking less and less. She only planned to scare him, but if it meant finding Anne, she wasn't sure how far she wouldn't go--and she found that, for the moment, she didn't have a problem with that.

"I don't think either of us is going to go home," he said.

He hit her in the leg with the stick and she glared at him. It stung. She took the stick away and tossed it over her shoulder. "You're supposed to be smart. That wasn't very."

He pointed behind her. "We're all dead."

She felt a weight on her lower back and pain on her sides. It took a moment to comprehend what was happening, but she was already moving. It was a mountain lion. She kicked behind, and reached down to where the claws were digging into her sides. It was trying to knock her down and climb to find her neck. She fought it, but wrestling something that was on your back was hard and shooting it was out of the question. It didn't look like much as the cat's claws dug into her and then retracted for another swipe, but it felt like something. Lines of blood appeared on her arms as she fought to keep its mouth off of her and deflect the paws. She dropped the knife and after a few moment of wrestling, the cat was more on her side and she could try and restrain it. She managed to hold both front legs off long enough to kick it in the chest and knock it back. It landed on its feet--of course--a few feet away, and she drew the revolver as it launched itself towards her. Her hand was slick with blood and it ached from the cuts the cougar had inflicted, but she didn't notice either as she pulled the gun like she had practiced so many times, and all that was in her mind was that the cougar was her target. She fired once and the cougar's left shoulder exploded. She took a step back as it landed disturbingly gracefully for a three-pawed cat, and she was aware for the first time of it growling as it bared its teeth in pain. She now had both hands on the gun and before it had a chance to do anything else, she fired again and the back of its skull sprayed out and it collapsed.

It was hard to tell how long it was before she did anything else. She'd zoned out, time slow, brain fast, world very small. The wider world came back slowly, she unnecessarily toed the dead cougar with her boot, gun still aimed and she still ready to fire. Then the realization of what had actually happened presented itself in her mind and she felt the rush of fear and the thrill of survival in a sensation that made her stomach queasy and her neck shiver. She was breathing hard and she focused on that as she remembered the professor. He was trying to creep up to the rifle that had somehow ended up on the ground a few feet away.

She fired a shot into the ground between him and the gun.

He jumped back and looked at her oddly, different than before. "Stay back. You are crazy. I knew it!"

Cass just stood there, staring at him. She was thinking simply. She was tired, in pain, angry, scared, excited…and she was all out of patience. "It's time you talk."

He just nodded.

52

New Mexico

ARCHODORE HAD BEEN READY to tell the woman everything. But she'd gagged and blindfolded him again and she'd remained silent as she gathered her things and then herded him to the pickup truck. She drove in silence.

She'd tied his feet and hands and left him in the spartan front room of an old ranch house. Two worn leather couches and a rustic coffee table were the only furniture. The cold sandstone floor was uneven and the native stone fireplace was the only source of heat or light.

He sat on one of the couches. He was cold, frightened, and still wearing the same, bloody, stinking clothes. He avoided thinking about all the blood and grime that he was covered in. How had it all gone so wrong? The money he had been paid for setting up the kidnapping victims seemed so far away now.

He watched warily she filled the two mugs and sat down across from him, propping her feet up on the table. She had been gone a while, and had not changed clothes either, but seemed

233

completely unconscious of the fact. She took a long swig of the thick, black liquid and finally spoke. "So, get to talkin'."

"What do you want to know?"

"Where are they? Where are the girls?" She spoke softly, between sips of the vile liquid that she called coffee. There was an undertone in her voice that she tried to hide, but emphasis was hard to miss. Archodore knew that she was dangerously serious. He could not escape the image of her, covered in cougar blood, laughing. In recent months he had become all too familiar with the sensation of being in the presence of madness.

He took a deep breath to keep his voice steady and started to tell his story.

She cut him off quickly. "No, no. I don't want to hear that. Your life story ain't what I'm interested in. I don't care why or how you got involved. All that matters to me is that you know something that can help me find those girls. Now." She poured herself another cup and spoke slowly. "Tell me about the location. Anything you know about the location. Got it?"

He almost declared his resentment, but thought better of it. He nodded and tried again. "I think it's a ranch. I don't know where exactly. They only took me there once and I was blindfolded and it was dark. I don't think I can help you." He shrugged helplessly. "I really don't know much."

She scowled and he flinched. But after a few moments she seemed to calm back down. "I reckon I knew it wouldn't be that easy. We'll just do it the hard way then. Tell me about the place. The grass, the dirt, the smell, anything about it you can remember."

Archodore thought hard. He hadn't really been paying that much attention. He'd been scared. "It was dark when they let me off the plane. I don't even remember if I saw any grass. Just the runway and dirt as they took me up to the house. I do remember the smell. I was...it smelled just as bad as it does here."

She frowned again. "A runway? You're sure it was a runway, not just a road?"

"It was lighted."

"Right. A ranch with a lighted runway. That narrows it down quite a bit." She looked at him again. "What else do you remember? Any mention of a name? Either a person or a place?"

"In the house, the Russian who approached me in the first place, greeted me and waved the guards off. If I recall correctly, he told them to go let off some steam in town. That they would fly me back out in the morning. I think the name of the town was Edison or something like that. It was strange."

"Ebbson?" she asked. "Was it Ebbson?"

"Yes, I think that was it. You know it?"

She grinned. "Yeah, I reckon so. And I think I know what ranch they're using too."

"What happens to me?" asked Archodore, worried.

She shrugged.

53

New Mexico

CASS GOT HER ANSWERS. The professor didn't know enough, but now she knew more. She put him in an old hog-trap under the shed, beneath a tarp. Tied, blind, and muzzled. She needed him out of the way.

Despite the fact that she figured her family was more than capable of handling the truth, that had not been the agreement with the Cowboy. She intended to keep her word--shy of any reasonable alternative, anyway.

The wounds were bleeding and they hurt. Nothing seemed too deep, but it needed some attention, nonetheless.

She thought about getting her sister's help. Glenn had the skills and the stomach to fix up her back, and a few cougar scratches were in no way outside the possibilities of her day-to-day operation. But there would be concern. Cass would have to sneak out, and they would wonder. She didn't have the time. She had to find Anne. She had a direction and she intended to pursue it now, not later.

First thing first, some medicine and a phone call. The pain was beginning to get more than distracting. She made a pot of thick coffee and poured some vodka into an empty mug.

Then, Cass dialed the Cowboy.

He answered, not sounding pleased.

"What's happening?"

"I found them. That's what's going on."

"What?"

"Archodore. He told me. I know where the girls are. I'm going after Anne. Can you have someone pick up the professor? I'll leave him in the hog trap under the shed."

"I'll take care of it. You were supposed to wait for backup."

"Hey, what was it you said about initiative? Don't tell me you really expected me to follow orders?"

"What's done is done. Tell me where and I'll send the boys. You'll need them."

"Fine. They can meet me in Ebbson, New Mexico. I'm heading out in a few minutes. Later."

She hung up and poured coffee into her mug. She drank it, felt a little better, and started to see about her cuts.

She had gauze and a gallon of disinfectant around for injured cattle. She figured it was going to take more than band-aids. A shower washed the worst of it off and started some of the deeper scratches to bleeding again.

Cass gritted her teeth as she poured and pushed disinfectant into all the wounds and then she started the process of closing the ones she could. The smaller ones, she pinched closed and covered in super glue. They needed stitches, but even if she'd had time, some were out of reach for that, but with a long swab and some glue, she got them more or less taken care of. The bigger ones really did need more, but she did them the same, but more carefully, and finished by wrapping clean gauze around her ribs and on the worst places on her arms.

It wasn't a final solution, but she could still move, and she was too close to stop now. Some of the things the professor has said made her worry that time was getting short and reinforced her conviction that Anne was in real danger.

She filled a thermos with fortified-coffee, put on a clean set of clothes, and headed outside.

Cass loaded up some weapons and other handy supplies and started the car to let the A/C cool it down while she checked on the professor.

He was just where she had left him, hobbled and locked in the live trap under the shed. She stared at him for a few moments, trying to think of any more questions to ask him, and after coming up with none, she headed out.

54

New Mexico

THE DRIVE TO EBBSON was shorter than the drive down from Colorado and she made it in less than four hours.

By the time she rolled over the rough pavement that served as a state highway and a main street, she had enough of a plan that she quit thinking about it too hard. It was nearly dinner time and the noon crowd would hit the little café called Jo's soon. With that in mind, she pulled up and went inside the little diner.

It was a simple place. Mismatched chairs and well-worn tables made up the décor along with a couple of retro tin signs and a trophy rodeo saddle in the corner. The name on the saddle was Jordan so Cass figured it belonged to the owner. She nodded in appreciation as the waitress walked by. "All around cowgirl. Impressive."

The waitress heard and laughed. "That was a long time ago. I was pretty good and I liked it, but you know how it is, you've got to be the best if you want to make enough to keep at it. I just wasn't quite good enough."

Cass smiled and nodded. "Yep. I know exactly how it is. I used to be a pretty good heeler, but never the best. 'Sides there ain't never been any glamour in heelin', the headers get all the money. When my good horse died, I quit the rodeoin' and counted myself ahead. Nice place you got here."

"Thanks. It ain't much, but it suits me. Can I get you something to eat?"

"You bet. I'm starved. What's the house recommend?" Cass headed for a seat at the nearest table.

The waitress quickly cleaned the table, deftly picking up the salt, pepper, and hot sauce. "The green-chili cheeseburger is my favorite, but it's pretty hot. The plain burger might be the best choice."

"The day I don't love a good, spicy, green-chili cheeseburger is the day ya'll might as well shoot me and be done with it."

"Didn't mean to offend, I can never tell with strangers. Iced tea to drink?"

"Yep," Cass said. "No offense taken. I reckon I'd think the same thing. I may not be from here, but you can bet I'm from close enough." Cass held out her hand. "Cass Elkins, from over on the east side, pleased to meet you."

"Call me Jo," said the waitress, shaking the hand firmly. "I'll have that burger out right away."

"Thanks."

Fifteen minutes later, Cass was staring at an empty plate and working on her third glass of iced tea. The noon rush was well under way and a likely suspect had just sat down at a nearby table.

The man was probably in his fifties, eating the house special, wearing dusty work clothes, and packing what looked like a Ruger Vaquero on his left side. His only companion was the sweat-stained hat he took off and sat on the opposite side of his table.

Cass smiled to herself. It was just like home. Knowing that he would be happy to have the conversation while he was waiting for his food, Cass turned her chair towards his table, leaned back comfortably, and spoke. "Ya'll had any rain around here this year?"

The man answered automatically, rain being the favored topic of all ranchers and farmers of the desert state. "Not enough. We got a couple of inches so far, but it dries up as soon as it hits the ground." He paused, turning to look at Cass for the first time. Realizing she wasn't a local, he asked, a note of suspicion in his voice, "Where you from?"

Cass smiled and answered calmly, "Over on the east side. Guess we're at least a little better off than ya'll. I think we've had three whole inches this summer."

He nodded, smiling now. He was relaxing more. "Good for you. Send some this way next time, huh?"

"I'll do what I can, but you know how it is."

He nodded. "Yeah." He took a long swallow of his drink and turned back to Cass, sticking out his hand. "Andy Jimenez. I've got a place out south of town. Nice to meet you."

"You too. The name's Cass. Cass Elkins." She returned his shake, not too hard, but good and firm. She approved and it looked like he did too.

"So, Ebbson seems like a nice place. Never been here before, but Jo's green-chili burger makes me want to come back."

He nodded, fully at ease now and ready to visit. "Yep, she makes a good one. Can't believe how grown up she is. I remember when she used to come out and help me gather cattle on the ranch. She wasn't more'n six years old, but she made a good hand."

Cass just smiled. She'd been there. Age was no reason not to work when you grew up on a ranch. "Say, you wouldn't know anybody has a good cow-horse for sale? My best one got tangled up in a fence last year and I still ain't found a replacement."

He thought for a few moments before replying. "I can't think of anybody. My neighbors always have a bunch of good stock, but I ain't never seen 'em sell any. They're a strange bunch. I just leave 'em alone as much as I can. 'Cept when the cows get out. But I try to keep the fence in good shape." As Cass watched he got more animated and more than a little angry. But not at her.

He glared at his boots. "Most of the trouble is the human kind. Ya'll get that down your way?"

"Yep. Dang poachers, and lately even a few rustlers. I haven't been lucky enough to catch any of the latter. But I've got a good rope behind the seat, just in case."

Jimenez grinned at that. "Yeah, I wish that was all we had around here. But as far south as we are, we get the cartels in here too. I swear, they ain't got no respect for fences. Just a couple of weeks ago, I found where somebody cut my fence and drove through. I lucked out and only a couple of cows got loose. Damn neighbors with the airplanes and the exposions are getting to be a real pain in the ass. I can't do nothing about it, but not everybody around here makes their money on cows. The O-Bar-Z ain't paying for those fancy gates with honest money."

He was getting pretty wound up and realized it. He drank some more tea and about that time his food arrived.

Cass finished off her drink and nodded to him as she stood up. "Nice talkin' to ya. Hope you catch your troublesome critters. Adios."

"Thanks," he said, already starting on his hamburger.

Cass left a twenty on the table and left.

55

New Mexico

WALLACE ARRIVED just in time for supper and she was happy to treat him to Jo's burgers. While they ate, she tried to convince him of her theory that the O-Bar-Z was where the baddies were headquartered. He was turning out to be annoyingly skeptical.

"Twenty miles or so that way." Cass took another bite of the green-chili cheeseburger while she pointed in a southerly direction. "There's a ranch called the O-Bar-Z. It's infamous for being a headquarters for drug trafficking. It changes hands pretty regular and I'm willin' to bet good money that the newest residents are our baddies."

Wallace was busy eating his own burger, minus any green-chili. He took a long drink of diet coke before speaking. "That's all you've got? A hunch?"

Cass shrugged. "Yep. I reckon you can call it that. But if I weren't pretty dang sure, I'd let you know." She drank a little iced tea, washing down the last of her food. "Fact is, I'm not opposed to a little more confirmation my own self and since ya'll ain't cool enough to do some of that satellite voodoo and check it out, I'm gonna do a little walking and see what the locals have to say." She didn't want to tell him that she'd already done all the talking. It was dark now, and scouting trips were better done alone. Wallace just had to stay out of the way a little longer.

"How is that supposed to help? The locals?"

Cass chose not to take offense and pretend he was just stupid. She knew better now, but he could still be ignorant. He knew his stuff, but he didn't know this part of the world. "I know you're from back east, Wallace. Just trust me. This is my kinda place. You stay outta the way for a bit. I'm native enough to make it past the smell test. You, on the other hand," she shrugged, gesturing towards him.

"What?" he asked. "I'm dressed western. I'm even driving a pickup truck. The Cowboy gave me direct orders not to let you go off on your own again. The Archodore thing was not exactly in the plan."

Explaining exactly how obvious it was that he was a yankee would take all day. His clothes were awful and that pickup he brought, it was more like a car; what Cass's sister always called a girly-man pickup. There was no way Wallace was gonna fool anybody. He was surprisingly useful for an easterner, but he was still from the other side of the Mississippi, and that wasn't the best way to gain the trust of a rural New Mexican.

"Fine, you sit here in the café and listen for something useful. This is the local's favorite joint and most of 'em will pass through. And they'll all want to share the latest news with their friends. You just stay here, drink some coffee, and you'll be fine. Might even hook a conversation with someone curious about why you're here."

"No, I'm going with you and that is the end of the story."

She sighed, flipping a fork around in her fingers. "You're not getting' it, Wallace. It ain't up for a vote. You stay here like a good boy or I'm gonna tell the waitress that you work for the BLM."

He just stared, confused. "Huh?"

Cass rolled her eyes. "You just proved my point. If you don't know what kind of trouble runs around in a green pickup, you clearly ain't from anywhere near here. All you need to know is that with a few short words, I could have you run outta town with fifteen shotguns ready to pepper your backside if you turned to look back. That is why you are staying here until I get back."

"Whatever." An unhappy affirmative, but an affirmative nonetheless.

She could tell that he wasn't at all pleased with the situation, but she had made her point. It was always easier to buck the voice on the phone that the person standing in front of you.

"Hang tight. I'll be back in a little while." She grabbed the ticket and took it up to the counter. After standing there for a few moments, Jo noticed and came around to check her out. Cass sat the ticket and a twenty dollar bill on the counter and leaned against the well-worn wood while the cash register chinked.

After a few moments and a few buttons pushed, Jo proffered a handful of change and a receipt. Cass nodded, busy getting a toothpick out of the cranky dispenser, and said, "Keep the change and keep my buddy over there in coffee." Cass nodded to where Wallace was sitting. Cass almost felt sorry for him, but found it more amusing than anything else. He'd made fun of her in the city. Too much fun now that the tables were turned.

She laughed and leaned over the counter, "He ain't from around here or anywhere this side of the river. I got some runnin' around to do. Figured here would be a good place to leave 'em for a while. That alright?"

Jo looked appreciatively at Wallace and nodded. "He's fine. It'll give me something nice to look at this afternoon."

"Great. Thanks," said Cass, taking the receipt.

Once again, Cass looked for a ranch pickup that was too fancy. She figured that the O-Bar-Z would have nicer equipment than the other places--having an alternative source of income and all that. Ranching wasn't exactly prone to making people wealthy. She checked all the usual places: the feed store, the café, the vet, and the bar, but to no avail. All the rigs were the standard beat-up, out-of-date pickups that tended to populate places like Ebbson. She wasn't surprised that the O-Bar-Z boys weren't in town. But it sure would've made it easy.

She got in her own rig and waited. She'd noted which pickup belonged to Andy Jimenez, and at the moment it was parked outside the feed store. After a few minutes of listening to the radio and wishing for a better air-conditioner, Cass saw Jimenez get in his rig and drive off. She waited a short while and then followed. Between the limited choices of road and the huge cloud of dust that every vehicle stirred up, it was easy enough to stay back and follow him to his ranch.

She almost forgot about ditching Wallace, but when she did remember, it was with a laugh. The boot was on the other foot.

56

New Mexico

HER SUSPICIONS about the O-Bar-Z's illegitimate history were reinforced when Cass saw the gate. It was gaudy and expensive and exactly what she would have expected from some rich, citified, cartel boss. Tailing Jimenez had led her right to it.

It was locked, but that wasn't the problem. It was electric. Her brother would know how to trick it, she figured, but she was less skilled at that sort of thing. She drove up the road away from the gate and got ready to walk.

It was dark by the time she made it to the hill that blocked her view of the ranch beyond. She hoped that the headquarters would be just on the other side. She was hurting in way too many directions. The cuts and the walk had just about worn her down. The burger seemed a long time ago.

She'd brought the rifle that her brother had given her last Christmas, a Ruger Gunsite Scout, slung over her back and she had started noticing how heavy the dang thing was. She rested for a couple of minutes and then headed up the hill.

It took half an hour to get to the top. Navigating the rocky terrain in the dark, was not exactly easy. She found a bit of scrub to use as cover and unslung the rifle before lying down beside a sagebrush. Just as she'd hoped, the ranch headquarters was situated there on the other side of the hill.

There was a ridiculous amount of lights. It looked like there were at least six large buildings. A main house, an old house, a bunkhouse, two barns, and a hanger, she guessed. The hanger would make sense considering the long, lighted piece of tarmac that lay between her hill and the barns. Cass judged it to be long enough to accommodate aircraft up to and including small private jets. She shouldered the rifle and looked through the scope. Like she'd told Wallace, good money.

Through the scope, she could make out all the buildings and the people guarding them. The barn was dark except for a single floodlight, the main house was well lit and at least two guys were walking around it in what looked like a patrol, if she'd ever heard of one. The boss bad guy was probably staying inside and keeping to the main house. It was adobe, with few windows. A good choice, easy to defend.

The bunkhouse was busy too, but in a different way. There were lights on and she could make out several figures moving around inside. The bunkhouse was probably being used just like it was designed, as a place to quarter the many people it took to man an operation, be it a drug setup or whatever.

The last thing of interest was the hanger. Cass muttered "Bingo," under her breath when she got the scope focused on the last building. It was a large structure, metal, well-made. There were no windows other than the two vents just under the eaves on each side. She assumed there were some on the other side that she couldn't see.

The doors were all closed and armed men were standing

guard and patrolling around the hanger. Five gets ten, that anything important was happening in that building. She put the rifle away and started working back down the hill. She decided that a little help would be nice, even if it was Wallace.

With that in mind, she dialed the number he had given her. Before the second ring, he picked up.

"Hello"

"Wallace. I got a sight more than a hunch now. You ready to get out here?"

"Where is 'here'? I've been looking for you for the last two hours."

He sounded a little irate. Cass tried not to laugh at the image that came to her mind of him wandering around Ebbson, trying to find her or find out where she was. The word, 'stonewalled' came to mind. "Forget about it. I want you to meet me at the O-Bar-Z. I'll be waiting outside the gate. It's hard to miss."

She gave him simple directions. Twenty miles south, two miles west, and then another two or so miles south until he reached the big gate. There was only one road south out of Ebbson. Wallace could figure it out.

It was a lot faster going back down the hill. She stumbled back to her parking spot, fell into the pick-up seat, and drove back towards the gate. Wallace wasn't there yet, so she kept driving back towards town. She met the girly-man pickup that was coming south and sure enough, it was Wallace. Best to make sure, she didn't want the bad guys finding her snooping at their gate.

She spun a one-eighty and drove back by the gate. She slowed down and leaned out the window. "Follow me."

She continued on down the road for a mile, near where she'd parked earlier, before she pulled into the barditch and stopped.

Wallace pulled in, the small vehicle scraping its underbelly on rocks as he pulled into the ditch. Cass tried not to laugh.

"Okay," said Wallace, crossing his arms and wrinkling his forehead as soon as he made it out of the car. "What have you got?" Cass could tell that he wanted to say a few more things to her, mostly unflattering, but he restrained himself. Good boy.

Cass quickly explained the layout of the ranch headquarters, and drew a simple diagram with her finger in the dry dirt. Wallace stayed pretty quiet until Cass finished. Then he snapped a picture with his phone of the diagram in the dirt.

"I'll send this back, see what they want to do. Good work, Miss Elkins." He fiddled with the phone, no doubt sending the message back to Virginia.

Cass patted him on the back, maybe a little harder than necessary and started walking back to the pickup.

"Where are you going?"

"Back to town."

Cass waited to make sure he made it out of the ditch and then threw a little gravel his way and left him in the dust.

57

New Mexico

IT WAS JUST A HOUSE, but the owner had two rooms to rent. Wallace had secured it earlier and Cass was thankful. She felt like she'd been---well, mauled by a pointy-toed cat. Cass locked the door behind her and fell onto the bed. She closed her eyes and saw nothing but ideas. She knew that sleep would be hard to get until she had everything figured, but she also knew that she would plan better after some rest that she dearly needed. Luckily, it was not a new problem. She carefully tuned out her racing thoughts, one by one, and replaced them with a simple blackness. She focused on the blank void, diving deeper anytime a thought broke through. It only took a few minutes of her vigilance for sleep to break through the lines and win the battle with consciousness.

She slept, more soundly than she'd expected, and woke up as refreshed and ready to face the day as she could have hoped. She did feel better, but everything still hurt. She dusted off her pants and rummaged in her bag for a clean shirt and socks. She found a dry-tumbleweed-camo shirt and untangled it from the menagerie of ammo, knives, and other tools that filled the bag.

Her granddad used to tease her about being paranoid, but her go-bag had come in handy more than once. A worn, but still very durable duffle bag, stuffed full of handy stuff. She kept a Glock, a magnum revolver and a few hundred rounds for each, extra shirts and socks, a useful assortment of knives, a rope, some leather straps, two pairs of pliers, and rolls of both duct tape and baling wire. There were also a few other, less useful, luxuries like a couple of paperback books and a harmonica.

It weighed more than was handy, but that was the price of preparedness. Just in case, some of the stuff was contained in two smaller bags, light and ready to go. Critical kits. A gun, a hundred rounds of appropriate ammo, already in magazines or moon clips, a knife and sharpening stone, duct tape, and a pair of pliers. In a fix, she could grab one of the smaller bags and move in a real hurry. She'd never had to abandon the rest of her kit before, but there were plenty of possibilities that would favor speed over stuff--and she was ready for that too. She sat down in the worn recliner that served as the room's only chair and pulled out her phone.

It rang before she could dial a number.

"Yeah," she answered, putting it to her ear, already guessing that it was the Cowboy by the lack of identification on the caller ID. She didn't get many blocked numbers.

"Are you ready?"

"Guess so." She leaned forward in the chair and rested her elbows on her thighs. "What for?"

"Does it matter?"

"Don't know. What is it?"

"The next challenge, of course. You've found the base of operations by now, I'm sure. What are you planning now?"

"I was planning on calling you and relating what I found, but that's been changed. Looks like somebody beat me to it." She glanced towards his room, unsurprised. She'd figured on it. Saved her the trouble. "Now, I'm gonna go down to the cafe, have me a burrito for breakfast and see what the weather's going to do. Might even see about buying a horse. Heard there was some good'uns on a place around here."

"And after you waste all morning?" He sounded a little peeved. Cass enjoyed hearing it.

"Gonna take a closer look at that place. Get a good bead on where the girls are and see what it's gonna take to get Anne out of there."

"Sounds like you have a plan, then. Keep me informed."

"I'll let Wallace do that, he might get bored otherwise."

"I see." The line went dead and Cass put the phone back in her pocket before getting up and doing just what she'd told the man on the phone.

As expected, Jo's breakfast burritos were good and after one of each, a brisket, and a steak and tater, Cass went out and took a seat on the porch next to the trash can and the newspaper box.

She leaned back on the bench and looked at the sky. It was blue and a little hazy. The wind was blowing lightly, about twenty to twenty-five miles per hour, and the dust was just starting. She knew without trying that it was about to get worse. For once in her life, that knowledge made her smile.

Well before noon, it had turned into a full-on sandstorm, a real yankee-chaser. Cass ate her extra burrito and got dressed for the rest of the day. She pulled her hair back and braided it tight, covered her head with a leather doo-rag, and her face with a dark brown bandana. Her dark, wrap-around sunglasses covered what little remained and she went out to meet Wallace.

He was waiting in the front room of the little inn, pacing in front of the door.

"That's a new look," he said. "Desert-ninja."

All that mattered was that it would protect her from the sand, allow her to breathe and see outside. "Let's go."

58

Virginia

THERE WAS NOTHING quite like watching a new one grow. No matter how many innocents he introduced to the game, it was still exciting to see what they would do. The Cowboy had never found two to be exactly alike, but there were commonalities. After all, he had picked them.

Each and every recruit was something special, a member of an elite subset of the human race with the potential for great and terrible things. Society scorned such individuals in their true form, and most were doomed to living a socially acceptable lie or becoming part of the criminal class. A few played along in the military, somehow surviving the onslaught of structure and hierarchy that they would otherwise abhor. They have a chance to excel, but only rarely, and so much of their lives are still a façade.

Shrinks and doctors called them all sorts of names and di- agnose a slew of so-called disorders in a futile and misguided attempt to bring them back into the fold of society. Some even try to label all such rebels as evil. But in truth, the men and women that the Cowboy sought were not evil. They were just without the unconscious limitations of their brethren.

Normal people have limits, lines that they don't cross, thoughts they don't think, places they won't go. They fear what lies beyond their own limitations--and even more, they fear those who can go where they cannot. The limitless.

They don't respect the rules of the world because they don't need them. The only rules they follow are the ones they make themselves.

The Cowboy knew all this because he was one of the same breed. He'd been brought into the game a long time ago, and now he was the one doing the recruiting--and he was good at it.

Scary good. Like his newest one.

Elkins was turning out to be quite a handful. Less than two weeks out of the pack and she'd already stopped listening to him or anybody else. She was leaving a trail of discarded human refuse in her wake, moving fast and hard towards her perceived goal--and closer to an ultimate confrontation with much more than she had ever faced before. The Cowboy had great expectations. She was moving fast and in the right direction. One way or the other, she'd serve her purpose soon--and he even hoped she'd see it his way.

59

New Mexico

WHEN WALLACE LEFT HER, it was blowing hard enough that the iron arc over the gate was swaying. Visibility was already less than a hundred yards and Cass had to lean into the wind to stay standing and turn her head away in order to breathe. Facing the wind, it was as if the air rushed by too fast to inhale.

The world was one swirling mess of brown grit that wanted to scrape the flesh off your face and tear the air from your lungs.

Cass had seen worse--and worked outside through the majority.

It was part of the world she had been raised in, part of the geography, and a leading reason for the lack of overpopulation and the preference for long, low building designs.

Sandstorms meant no skyscrapers, and no yankees.

Cass didn't even try to be sneaky, she just followed the road until she crossed the cattle guard into the little, fenced-off trap that isolated the headquarters of the O-Bar-Z. She remembered the layout well enough from her first scout to know where the main features lay. Keeping as near to the perimeter fence as possible, just out of sight of any building, she eased around until she was behind the hanger. She focused and moved closer. The tin-covered building became visible and so did the men who were guarding it. Two at the walk-in door and two more circling around.

After watching for a few minutes, Cass waited for the patrol to pass before running up and pressing her eye to the cold galvanized skin of the structure.

Just like any such building on a ranch, or otherwise remote locale, there were more than a few bullet holes in the tin. Cass looked inside.

The girls were there. Wearing dirty lab coats, hair greasy and matted, and expressions of fear. They moved slow, deliberate, as if they had to force themselves to keep going. They kept their eyes lowered and didn't speak much as they went about their work. Cass knew she was short on time, so she tried to memorize as much about the makeshift lab's contents and layout as she could. She recognized one of the girls from pictures that Dobbs had shown her. The other was from Colorado. But no Anne.

A glance at her watch reminded her that she only had a few more seconds before the patrol came back around and even in the fog of sand, she'd be easy to spot if they got too close. She took one more peek, looking for Anne, but to no avail. With moments to spare, she sprinted back into the dust and out of sight.

Careful to keep her bearings, she moved on to the next barn. It was empty and unguarded so she went inside. It was a horse barn, divided into several stalls, stocked with hay, and featuring a very nice, insulated, and lit tack room in the back. She opened the door and found a mattress and what was supposed to look like someone had been sleeping here. But the rumpled blanket was covered in more than a day's worth of dust. Even the relatively well-built tack room couldn't keep the dirt out.

Turning the light back out, she braved the storm once more. The final barn was older, and probably what had been replaced by the newer horse barn. It was less-sealed and more of what a real ranch would have. Stalls down one side and what had been a sort of basic repair shop along the other. The tools were mostly gone, just a few templates and a couple of outdated implements hung on the wall behind the poorly stacked hay that now dominated the space. It was good hay, small squares of alfalfa. Horse feed. But where were said horses? Hopefully, they'd just been turned out. No reason for stock to suffer for human idiots.

The door to the old tack room was barely functional, hanging by a thread--literally. Some old orange bale twine was all that kept the door from falling. With a certain lift and shove, Cass got it open without bringing any debris down on her head, but it was a close thing. She winced at the noise it made. Only in the middle of a shrieking sandstorm would such a grating racket be irrelevant. She felt for a switch and flipped it, hoping for light, but no. Instead, she pulled a small tac-light out of her pocket.

Someone had been sleeping in the small room. There were no amenities, but the dirt floor worked fine so long as you weren't too squeamish. Clearly, the man was not. He'd been camping in this spot for a while. The dirt was too messed up to worry about disturbing it during a search and Cass didn't waste any time being careful. She found a bag of clothes, sized for a medium guy. That was about it except for a gold-plated 1911 and a handful of peppermint candy.

The door screeched open and she turned around.

60

New Mexico

MAKSIM LOOKED DOWN at the gun. It was a revolver, large caliber, maybe a forty-five or a forty-four. He passed his glance over the demon holding it and decided it was probably the latter. He also decided against trying anything. Usually, a revolver meant a short delay, the time it takes to cycle the action. In that time, a hand could be clamped around the cylinder and beneath the hammer, stopping the action and saving himself from a lead breakfast. It was good info and handy just as long as the person holding the gun didn't know it too. This one did.

The hammer was already halfway back, the slack taken out of the trigger and the action just a twitch away from completing its cycle and blowing his insides out.

"Forty-four?" He gestured to the gun with his eyes, careful not to move his body in anything that might be perceived as threatening. All the standard plays had already been ruled out. Only talking was left--at least until something changed. Like that trigger finger.

"Hello," he said, slowly raising his hands. "Can I help you?"

"By putting your hands up on top of your head and taking a knee or two."

Maksim nodded and complied. The voice was muffled and of a range that he couldn't tell if it was a man or a woman. Not that it mattered. The important thing was that there was no gesturing or waving with the gun. Very professional.

"There's no reason to shoot me. Who are you?"

The demon snorted a short laugh and said, "How 'bout a reason not to?"

"Your life. There are men outside who would love to kill you. You don't want them to hear."

"It's a real sandstorm out there. Ain't nobody gonna know where or what the sound was."

"Fine. You're in charge. What do you want?"

"Those girls. Out of here. Can you help with that?"

Maksim shrugged. He had no plans on dying for the project. It was always better to be alive. Not a lot of opportunities came up at the morgue. "Probably."

"Good. Then we have something to talk about."

Maksim's phone vibrated. He gestured with his eyes towards his pocket. "Phone call. Want to answer? It's in that pocket there, on the left side."

"No. I'm good right where I'm at. You go ahead and answer. Move slow and put it on speaker. Try anything and you'll be dead."

He nodded. He glanced at the number and was relieved to see that it was blocked. That usually meant one thing. Maksim hid his hope. If anyone might be of help at the moment, it was him. "Hello?"

"Maks, are you alone?"

The demon nodded.

"Yeah. On my break."

"Good. It's time."

"When can I expect you?"

"I won't be coming. You should get out. Good luck."

"Wait." Maksim sighed as the line went dead. So much for luck.

The line went dead and Maksim smiled at the demon. "What can I help you with?

61

New Mexico

CASS DIDN'T CARE how helpful the guy seemed, she didn't have the luxury of trust. Her gun stayed right on target and she kept her eyes on the nape of his neck. Sights were distracting and entirely unnecessary at this range. Her eyes could pick the target and easily keep watching for any sudden or suspicious movement of his body. A twitch too quick and she'd be one bullet down and he'd be dead. Not a bad idea, but she had him mostly caught and he was sure to know something useful.

"Listen close," she said. "I'm gonna tell you real specific what to do. Do it and live."

He nodded and seemed to relax a little. That worried her, but he didn't make a move. He just waited for her instructions.

She made sure not to get distracted, keeping her eyes on target as she spoke. "Turn your toes out as far to the sides as they'll go." He did. That would make it a whole lot harder to move in any direction without losing his balance. "Now slowly look to your left. There's a hook with some leather straps. Take the best looking one and tie your feet together. Do it good and don't let them toes come in. I'm watching." As he bent over, she shifted her focus a little to adjust for the new angle and position of his body. Still on target, the new angle allowed her to see him work as well. He tied a decent knot.

"Now, grab another strap and do it again, knee high."

He almost lost his balance, but caught himself admirably and finished the knot. He stood up and said, "Is that enough? I'm not going very far. You're impressively thorough."

"Take two of the longer ones. Tie a slip knot in either end and make sure the center is what pulls the loops tight. Give it about a foot between the loops, no more." She watched his throat. He swallowed twice before he finished. Before she could explain what to do next, he figured it out. He put one loop from each strap over his head and pulled them snug around his neck. "Like this, yes?"

Cass nodded ever so slightly, concentrating on keeping the gun steady. It was not much, but her arms were beginning to tire. Much longer and she'd have to shoot him to be safe--or her finger would twitch.

He put each hand behind his back and through an open loop. "I would've asked if you wanted them in front, but I don't want to waste the time." He pulled down and tightened the loops.

Cass relaxed a hair. "Turn around slow and let me see." He did and she was pleased with the result. His hands hung midway down his back, elbows bent and a very limited range of motion. He could move his elbows out to the sides a few inches, but too far or too hard and the loops around his neck would tighten. She made a mental note about the potential for short elbows and deemed it acceptable. "Alright. On your knees and we can pow wow."

He was obviously unhappy about the last command. The way his legs were tied made it impossible to kneel with any grace. He lowered himself as far as possible and then was forced to just plop the rest of the way. He instinctively tried to help his balance, but his hands were tied. He grimaced as the loops tightened. The target was still his throat and Cass could tell that he was still breathing, just more uncomfortable, and highly restrained. She lowered her gun. But she still had a target.

62

New Mexico

"RUN ME DOWN on this place," the demon said. "Who's where? How many? And what in the name of crying out loud are ya'll working on?"

All Maksim had concluded about the demon was that it was American--the dialect was too odd to be anything else--and that it was impressively paranoid. The bindings were very effective. If he moved his arms, the strap got very tight around his throat. It was already going to make talking difficult. He could raise his hands a little father up his back, but it was an awkward position and his muscles would start shaking after a short time. He was really tied up. Damn if he hadn't gotten caught by someone with some brains. It was kind of refreshing--if inconvenient.

He decided to start with the last question. "A weapon of mass destruction."

It didn't seem all that surprised. It nodded slightly and said, "That's interesting. But tell me about the people first. That's a little more practical at the moment."

Interesting--and smart. The demon was more concerned about stuff that was an immediate threat. Maksim had already decided to talk, and he did. "Twenty-one, including me. Four inside the hanger, two pairs on patrol. The rest are usually cheating on Allah in the bunkhouse with a bottle of whiskey and a stack of videos."

"Nobody in the main house?"

"Mr. John. The guy in charge. He's there."

"Alone?"

"Sometimes. I try to avoid him."

"What's your job, then? You don't strike me as a fanatic."

"That's my job. I'm the level head who knows how to buy supplies without getting shot by a redneck." Maksim smiled, but the expression pushed against the noose and devolved rapidly into a grimace. A very honest grimace that would help distract from the omission. It was true that he served as a glorified gopher at times and it was better if that was all he appeared to be.

"Hmm." The demon started popping the knuckles on its left hand. "Tell me about the girls. How many are there? What's the routine?"

"Two. Alternating shifts. They never leave the hanger and there are always two men outside the door and usually four inside."

"That's a few." The demon grew silent except for the knuckle popping. Maksim wished he could see its eyes, but the dark glasses revealed nothing.

"I've got to ask. What are you doing here? Are you alone? What do you expect to accomplish?"

"The girls are always in the hanger. That what you said?"

Maksim nodded.

"Okay. Thanks. Close your eyes and count to a hundred--

and thank the Lord that I'm giving you tomorrow and pray we don't meet again."

Seeing no other choice, Maksim closed his eyes. He heard the sound of a holster being filled, then a snap, and a ripping sound. He realized what it was, just before it was stuck on his face. Duct tape. Over his eyes, across his mouth before he could protest, and then the demon reinforced his bindings. Maksim concentrated on his breathing. He heard the door close and he allowed the anger to come. Pray? That demon had better be the one praying that they never meet again. He imagined what he would do to it. Pain was a skill and he'd had no shortage of instruction in prison. He was smarter now, smart enough to not go back, but the temper that had always landed him there was still just as hot as ever. Being smart just meant picking the time and place to let it out.

He pulled himself back together and concentrated on the most crushing concern. Escape. He tensed his neck to resist the strap and rolled onto his side. He was able to shrimp around on the floor. It was slow and painful, but it was something. He was unsurprised to find that the demon had gotten to his gun, but he'd had plenty of time to stash weapons and hide shivs. That was another lesson he'd learned well. One could never have too many weapons hidden and ready. He found a sharp one and started on the tape. He would get loose and then he would get in the plane and be gone. There was always a time to leave and this was it. He'd be short on money, reputation, and friends, but he'd be alive. Survival was the only true victory.

63

New Mexico

IT WAS A BROWN OUT. There was nothing else to call it. The black Lambo was cruising along anyway. It was Bobby's favorite sort of road. Long, straight and empty. The lack of visibility just made it more exciting. The coordinates that the Cowboy had sent were close. A couple of miles. He sent a quick text to Cass and told her to wait up. He'd been sending them for hours and still hadn't gotten a response. This one ended with the fact that he was only a mile away. That did the trick. The phone buzzed and he mashed the accelerator when he read the reply.

Just in time. He slowed as he approached the turn off and tried to spot the ornate gate he was supposed to be looking for. He finally saw it, open, and spun onto the ranch's driveway. He spared a moment to read the directions from Cass. As per, he slowed when he reached the last hill and carefully rolled across the cattle-guard. He hugged the fence to the right, lucky that the ground was hard and bare, and followed it around until he reached the corner. He turned it so that it pointed back towards the way he'd come. He stepped out and remembered that his phone was on the console. He leaned back in to get it and was hit from behind. He spun, reaching for his gun, but there was nothing to be seen.

He closed the door and his phone buzzed. Another text: Got you.

When he looked up, she was there, barely. Head to foot, she was decked out in shades of sand. He looked down at his black clothes and shrugged. She made a twirling motion beside her head and then gestured for him to follow. She led him what he guessed was about a hundred yards to an old barn that looked like the last place he wanted to be in a dust storm. She went inside and with a disapproving shrug for good measure, Bobby followed.

"Uh, is it safe in here?" Bobby couldn't help watching the way the walls moved. Walls should not move that much unless they are part of a tent.

She probably rolled her eyes, then she said, "Of course not, my plan is to get smashed by a barn. Thanks for joining me."

"You said you were crazy. I was just trying to be trusting." Bobby shrugged. "Love the new look."

"Thanks. It works." She put her hands on her hips. "Let's get serious. Here's the plan."

"The plan."

"According to my information, there's at least twenty bad guys." She waved over her shoulder. "The girls are in the hanger. That's where we're going."

"Twenty is a lot."

"Yeah. But there shouldn't be more than eight to mess with at the hanger. We'll get the girls and go from there. That work?"

It wasn't a question, but he answered anyway. "That works."

"Aces. I've got the patrols pretty much figured out. We'll do them first."

"Do them?"

She nodded, very serious, maybe even a little solemn. "They're bad guys and twenty is a lot. You got your knife sharp?"

She was probably right. There was no reason to risk it. Simple was usually best. And knifes were real simple. He nodded, equally serious. He'd just do it and not look too hard at the aftermath. He liked guns, more distance, further from the smell, but he knew how to get close--when he had to. This was probably one of those times. He took a breath, shut down the part of himself that would be uncomfortable, and said, "Yeah."

"Alright." She bent down and drew a map of the compound in the dirt.

"I've got a satellite shot on my phone, if you want to use that?" Bobby proffered the phone.

"Too late," she said and started pointing. "This is the hanger and there's the only door in." She stabbed her finger into the dirt twice. "There's two guys outside the door." She demonstrated a route around and between the hanger and the two barns. "There's a couple unlucky pairs running this and..." She pointed to a spot behind the other barn. "...right there is the spot where even you can sneak up on 'em."

"Okay. The patrol, the doormen and done?"

"Inside. There's probably four guys inside the hanger."

"Probably. That's not a good word."

She stood and dusted herself off--rather uselessly, Bobby observed. "I got a little look inside and saw two, but the info says there's a good chance of four. We'll just expect four and at best, we'll be pleasantly surprised."

"Yeah. Move out?"

"Yeah. Let's go." She pulled her knife, straight out of an old movie, and started towards the door. "Stay close. If you get lost, follow the fence line back to the car and we'll meet there with the girls." She put her hand on the door and glanced back. "Any questions? We won't be able to talk over the wind out there."

Bobby grinned and pulled out his knife. "Let's ride!"

It was impossible to tell if she laughed or not, but Bobby thought she relaxed a little. She opened the door and he followed her outside into the storm.

64

New Mexico

THE WIND WAS HOWLING, sand hurtling through the air. The sandstorm had worsened while she'd been inside talking. It was awful.

Hell on earth.

Perfect.

Bobby was beside her, not so comfortable, but willing.

The plan was simple enough. The patrols would be coming around soon. Cass glanced at Bobby and he nodded. She nodded back briefly. Ready. Two knives, two throats, easy as pie. The men came around and then passed by, not looking too hard. Three quick steps forward, pull head back, cut. Cass thought it through once more and then it was time to move. It went just like it was supposed to. Two down.

They drug the bodies a few yards so that they wouldn't be seen by the next patrol and waited. There were two exterior patrols guarding the captives. They came around and were taken the same way.

Bobby gestured towards the barn door and Cass nodded. Next came the two standing outside the walkthrough door. They would be harder because they would have their backs to the wall. Total surprise was unlikely. Cass ripped the scarf from one of the dead men and motioned for Bobby to follow. She led them upwind of the door and hoped that he understood. She counted to three by pumping her arm and then let the rag go. It blew past the men and she followed. They couldn't help but glance at it as it went by and in that split second when their focus was away, they died. Time was becoming a factor, so the bodies were left where they lay. They needed to be in and gone before the dead men were missed.

She pointed at herself and then swept her arm to the left, indicating her plan. Then Bobby mirrored her and nodded. That was the plan. The door was unlocked and guarded on the inside as well. Cass firmed up her mind, brought her gun up to a low ready, and opened the door. She took in everything to the left, not thinking about the right. Hard as it was, she had to trust that Bobby would handle it. After the door opened she forgot about everything but her responsibility.

One just inside the door along the wall, close, easy shot, no sights required. One to the upper chest and done. Eyes already moving to the next one, seated, a little farther away. Eyes moving past to the one turning, raising a weapon. Front sight, two shots, center of mass. Down to one, back to the chair, halfway up, gun drawn but not aimed. No time to aim, just shoot. Not a good hit, but enough of a distraction. Gets time to aim, no more misses.

Cass swept her eyes over her targets and made sure they were down for good. Satisfied, she turned her attention to the other side. There were two bodies, both down. The world seemed to broaden and sounds came back. Bobby was saying something, she'd remember what it was in a moment. The calm was receding and her brain was beginning to catch up to what had happened. The first real thought was that there was only one bullet left. She reloaded, pocketing the partially fired moon clip. Gun in her right hand, she looked around for Anne.

"Where's Anne?" she said, concerned. There were two girls, moving very slowly, not answering. One was Jessica Brighton, the other was a face from a vaguely remembered list of missing women Dobbs had shown her. It didn't matter. Neither was Anne.

Cass repeated the question, louder, and she still didn't answer. What was the matter? They were crying, not speaking.

Cass pulled back as Bobby tried to touch her arm. "What?"

"We need to get out of here."

"But I don't see Anne. I have to get her out of here."

"If she's not here, then we have a problem. We don't have time to find her. We have to leave, right now."

Cass growled, but nodded. He was right. First thing first. They gathered the girls and herded them out the door. They balked at the blowing sand, but were too dazed to do much more. Little nutrition and less sleep, if Cass had to guess. They'd never make the hike to the gate, not with the wind blowing against them, and maybe not even if it was at their backs. It would mean trouble, but they had to get the car closer. Cass leaned up to Bobby's ear and spoke in his ear, letting him know what she was thinking. He nodded and motioned for her to take the girls and meet him behind the hanger, along the fence. He picked up his pace and quickly disappeared from sight, but not before she noticed the limp. A quick look at the ground revealed the rapidly clotting drops of blood. That was what he'd been telling her. She remembered now. He was hurt.

A few minutes later, a black blob coasted through the sand.

She pulled up her gun, just in case, then relaxed. It was indeed who she was expecting. It was Bobby's Lambo.

"Get in," he said, reaching across to open the passenger door. "Quick, before the door blows off."

She loaded the girls. It was cramped, but there was room. The door was whipping, but it survived. Cass leaned in and said. "Where would she be?"

Bobby was clutching his leg, which was pretty red. "We can come back."

"No, they'll be gone. 'Sides, that lab has to be sterilized. Way it sounds, they were awful close to a real nasty weapon. Can't let 'em get away with it."

"Sterilize?"

Cass grinned. "Sure. Easiest thing in the world."

"Sounds fun," he said. "Wait here, then. I'll be right back. Faster than you can say Bobby Blade."

Her face had switched back to serious and she looked hard at Bobby. "No. No more time. You're hurt pretty bad. Skedaddle."

"You're coming too. I'm not leaving you here."

"I texted Wallace. He can wait at the gate until I call. Now git." She didn't stick around to argue. She closed the door and disappeared into the sand. As long as she kept moving and kept to the plan, she figured she had a decent chance of success. Not that it mattered, it wasn't impossible and it needed to be done. Simple as that.

The Lambo disappeared into the storm and she started walking. First thing was the lab. She'd seen what they were growing. Wheat. Food. That plus the phrase "weapon of mass destruction" was more than just a little bad. It had to be destroyed. That was important--and easy. She worried only for a moment about starting a grassfire, but remembered the state of the surrounding pasture. The O-Bar-Z was severely overgrazed.

There wasn't enough to burn outside the fence that contained the headquarters. She'd seen it before. Worst case, the fire would get all the buildings, but it would stop.

She reached the old barn, went inside, and picked up a bale of hay.

65

New Mexico

CASS'S BACK WAS BEGINNING TO HURT, in addition to everything else. Maybe it was better to say that her back was taking a spot at the forefront of the pain hierarchy. She ignored it enough to keep going, grabbed the last bale of hay, and carried it out. There was more hay, but this would have to be enough. All she had to do was get the fire going. The bale slipped a little and she grunted with effort as she got a better hold. The wind made it hard, pushing against the bale and making her stumble and weave on her way to the lab. This was the last load, then she could leave. She dropped the bale on what appeared to be a hydroponic setup of some sort, and cut the twine. The square of straw fell apart and did a good job covering the growths. The rest of the barn lab was already covered in dry hay. Cass poured all the oil, solvent, and other flammables she had found in the barns over the dried straw and ignited the one burner she'd left intact. The hay lit up and she lit out, leaving the door open behind her. The wind would oxygenate the blaze quite well. Or it would have if it hadn't decided at that moment to subside. Cass knew as well as anyone how temperamental the weather could be, and until now she had never wished that the wind would keep blowing. A still moment had always been a blessing.

But today, the wind had been her ally, her cover. It didn't stop completely, but it calmed enough that in moments, what had been a few feet of visibility turned into a quarter mile or more. She could see all the buildings and that meant that they could see her.

Hopefully, the blaze would bring them out, but then they would be looking for the culprit. She had to move.

Her phone vibrated and she answered.

It was Wallace. "Where are you?"

"Busy."

"I need to talk to you. There's something you need to know. The Cowboy just called. Maksim Derchev. He asked for you not to kill him."

"Too late."

"What?"

"Cool it. Done and done. Bobby's headed out with one of the girls. I'm finishing up out here. That one's tied up in the barn. Lucky fellow."

"You're alone?"

"Yes."

"I'll come help, just wait."

"No. Listen. The nefarious plan, whatever it was, is toast. The job's done, the world is safe and all that. No need to worry."

"Then get out of there."

"Thought about it, but no. Anne is still here somewhere. I don't have time to chat. I've got to get her now."

"Maksim has information."

"Then come get him."

Cass started towards the bunkhouse. She'd made up her mind, but they needed to know that the big danger was over. She had business to take care of and she'd rather not get bombed or bothered before it was over. "I'll talk to you later. Supposedly, there ain't but a few left. I should be able to handle it."

"How many does that make?" Wallace sounded worried.

"Twelve." The yard fence was now visible through the sand and Cass took her gun, the 5-inch Smith, out of her pocket.

"That's a lot."

"Maybe." Cass gritted her teeth and her lips curved up just a little. Everybody was a skeptic. That was why they never got anything done. It might be a little crazy, she'd be the first to admit it, but it wouldn't be the first time she'd pulled off something that, after closer inspection, seemed improbable. "But if it ain't impossible, it can be done. Heck, I've even practiced for this sort of thing. That's more than I usually get."

"It's suicide."

"Now if I thought that, I wouldn't be doing it. I'm not stupid, I'm stubborn. Huge difference."

"How's that? Still ends the same. Still dead."

"Not at all." Cass checked that the gold-plated 1911 was ready to come out of her pocket and walked down the path to the front door of the bunkhouse. "Stubborn works. Later." She hung up.

She checked her breathing. It was coming slow and steady despite the thrill of her heart getting ready. Her mind emptied, and thinking, in the traditional sense, stopped. There was no more to think about until something new happened. The decision had been made. It was as simple as that. She was ready because she chose to be. It needed done, therefore it would be. As far as Cass was concerned, it was already over. There was nothing left to do but what came next. Worrying never did anything but slow her down. When it came time to get down to business, there was nothing that worked better than knuckling down and diving in. She was as ready as she was going to get. She went in. The whole building was one room except for the bathroom. Bunks along the walls, a huge TV, and a couple of good tables to play cards on--but no people. She cleared the entire building within a handful of seconds and realized what it meant. They'd regrouped, dug in, probably in the main house. All twelve, in one place.

She headed towards the big house.

There were three entrances. One was facing the barns, one was facing the bunkhouse, and the other led to a garage on the side nearest the entry road. She had no good way to pick. If they were smart, they'd be watching all three. She looked at the black smoke that obscured the hanger. It was thick and blowing towards the house. That was her only way to get close. She exited out the far side of the bunkhouse. The smoke was getting thicker and the wind was picking back up. She grinned. A whirlwind was moving in. It looked like it was on the right path. All it had to do was grab the smoke and hit the house. For the first time in her life, she thanked the Lord for the wind and prayed for it to blow like the dickens--and for that dust-devil to keep moving straight. She switched to her revolver and waited. The devil did it. When it hit, the smoke and dirt cut the visibility. Cass ran inside the maelstrom. She had to run to stay inside of it, and it didn't quite hit the house. But it got her close enough. Twelve targets, one hostage, no time to waste. Cass moved. She turned the knob and kicked in the door, careful not to kick so hard that it came back on her.

The door was open and there were targets. Close. One. Two.

Through the door, and the room was clear. Shots were good,

moving on.

Another room. Three. Four. Only two left in the gun, Switch. Safety off, eight ready. Another door, empty.

Moving. Movement, target, target, clear. Pairs are nice. Moving on. Next room. Noisy, targets moving. They know. Will be ready.

Open door, keep low, keep moving. Hit, hit, miss, hit.

Out.

Ditch 1911, forty-four back out. Two bullets, one target. Target small, obscured. Can't miss. Don't miss. One shot is good and he's down, but not done. Last bullet. He's dead. Didn't hit Anne. Good. Put last bullet in.

Check the room.

Check the house.

All clear

She checked the bodies--dead or close enough. She went back to the room where Anne was. Her friend was shaken, but not totally out of it. She smiled her thanks and Cass said, "Hola, Amiga."

Anne's smile widened just a little and Cass started thinking again. She helped Anne up, seeing that she was a little weak, probably from adrenaline let down and shock. Anne got to her feet and started to speak, but she fell, slowly, reaching out as the impact blew her back and then down.

Cass should have ducked, should have taken cover, but she didn't. Anger makes everyone stupid.

Cass turned and shot. From the hip, no thought, just instinct and rage. Her eyes were locked on the man as the left side of his chest exploded. One shot, one devastating impact. That was why a forty-four was the best. She'd paid minimal attention to the other men she'd shot. There had been no time, no reason. All she'd needed to know was her hits and any good shooter knows her hits as soon as she presses the trigger. She didn't miss a thing this time. He fell and was dead and she was happy about it. There was no doubt.

Her gun was empty, so she put it back in its holster while she looked over her friend.

She knelt down. There was nothing to do. No farewell, no drama, no desperate CPR. Cass knew dead and that's all there was.

She took a Sig off the nearest body, stood up, and left, taking a last look at the shotgun man on the way out. He was different than the others. Dressed like a local rancher, but filthy. Beyond the smell of fresh carnage, he stunk of feces and urine and all the other smells that make people stink. His eyes were open and in death, they looked normal, not like before. She inspected her memory and decided that the only way to describe his expression would have been mad. His eyes had been crazed, unaware even. It was strange, semmed stranger the longer she thought about it. Where had he come from? Why? It didn't make sense. Cass's head was beginning to hurt, too much had just happened. She held it off as best she could and tried to make things make sense. It had to make sense.

She examined the man. There was straw, hay, on his clothes. There was no good reason to care, she knew that. It was over. Everybody was dead, no need to play detective. But curiosity was better than the alternative. She needed to think about something else for a while.

Outside, the hanger was still burning, sending up billowing black plumes of acrid black smoke into the air. The wind had calmed down and she could see the entire headquarters. There was little to be done. The fire would burn down eventually or it would spread, but not far. The O-Bar-Z had been overstocked and the grass was so short and scarce in the pasture surrounding the HQ that it wouldn't burn worth a damn. The fire was contained. There was no worry. She'd seen to that.

The hay had come from the barn, so that's where she went, walking slow. Concentrating on not thinking. The barn door was open, swinging a little in the wind, but not too bad. She went in and there it was, a hole in the floor, beneath where she'd taken the hay to start the fire. She knelt beside it and shined her taclight down. The stench was awful, concentrated human filth, but she was too out of it to care. It was a small pit, eight by eight, she guessed, maybe six tall, concrete walled and stocked- -or at least it had been. The remnants of food containers were everywhere and there were several empty water containers. The cot was torn and the floor was covered in nastiness that she preferred not to dwell on. A hidey-hole, some drug lord or other must've been a little extra paranoid--and somebody had gotten stuck, gone crazy, and shot her friend.

After everything, it was the revelation that pushed Cass to tears. It was so stupid. Random. No reason in the world, but her friend was dead and so was the fool who'd marinated in that pit of madness. No reason at all. It only took a minute for Cass to pull herself back together. She wiped her eyes with the back of her hand and sat down, thinking. If she had a bunker, there would be four things. Water, weapons, food, and cash.

She leaned back down and looked once more, this time for something in particular--and there it was. A duffel under the cot, and one on top of one of the shelves. She looked around and found an old hoe. It was splintery, but a heck of a lot better than going down. She hated small spaces as it was, minus the nastiness. Carefully, she managed to haul both of the bags out. Setting them down, she looked inside, trying not to be too hopeful, but excited nonetheless.

Just as she'd expected, there was money, and plenty of it.

She closed them back up.

The tack room door moved and she pulled out her knife. It was the man she'd tied up earlier. He'd got loose. She realized that she probably should have checked on him sooner--and thought about making sure he was safe from the fire. It looked like it was going to stay contained to the hanger, but she'd had no way of knowing that. Well, it didn't matter now. What mattered was the guy with a knife standing in front of her. He could burn later.

"Morning," she said.

"I'm pretty sure it's afternoon."

"Meh." Cass shrugged. "Whatever."

"What's that burning I can smell?"

"The hanger."

"The lab? The specimens?"

"I reckon."

"You?"

"S'it matter?"

"No." He looked thoughtful. "Can I call for help?"

"If you feel like it."

"I see."

"Okay."

"Can I leave?"

"I don't know." If he didn't attack her, she had no reason to kill him, but she hated to let him run loose either. "I don't think you should. You're still a bad guy."

His eyes glazed over and made him look kinda scary for a moment as he said, "I don't like prison."

Cass realized that she was tired and out of bullets. A knife fight was not a sure thing. "Let me make a call."

"Who?" He edged forward.

Cass instinctively squared off with him. "A Cowboy."

He lowered his knife a hair and his posture relaxed. "That wouldn't be *the* Cowboy, would it?"

"You're Maksim Derchev."

"Yeah."

"Well, lucky you."

"Hello?" Wallace peered in the door.

"Got a gun?" Cass asked. "Come hold it on this fella. If he runs, just slow him down. Cowboy said not to kill 'im." She turned to Maksim. "He probably wants to recruit you. You gonna drop that knife?"

He did and she tied him back up, though not quite so thoroughly as before. "Load him up, Wallace. I'll be right along."

Cass stashed the bags back in the pit and covered it up before following. His little pickup was still amusing, but Cass didn't feel like laughing yet. She was too tired. There was nothing left to distract her. The sounds came back. She started remembering the details. It was interesting, only the sights and the smells had seemed important. The screams, the shots, all of the noise she didn't hear was coming back. It was gone when it had happened, but she could remember it now. And the other bullets, the ones that they had fired. She reached up and felt of her left arm. The ones that had come mighty close. She checked herself and realized that there were numerous minor wounds and it looked like some of the claw wounds were bleeding again too. Grazes, splatter, or other shrapnel she supposed, it was hard to say and she didn't care. It was over. It was done.

Those few seconds continued to get clearer as she stood there. The sounds kept getting louder, clearer. Besides the people and the bullets, there were the hits. Their misses that splintered walls and the hits that made that special thwack sound and the flesh splattering. There were voices too. The man holding Anne had said something. Something to stall her, in a thick accent, but it had been irrelevant. The only silent man had been the one with the shotgun. Too quiet. He'd caught her by surprise.

Cass's heart twisted as Anne's death sunk into her a little deeper. Every time she thought of it, it was more real. She remembered more of her friend and thought of more things that would never happen.

Wallace, wisely, didn't touch her. He just opened the passenger door and let her get in. She sat down and leaned back and let him close the door. He couldn't help looking at her, his face a mix of worry and something she didn't understand.

Cass was busy putting it back together. The outside. By the time they turned onto the highway and headed back towards town, her face was a mask, hiding the pain. The phone buzzed. She pressed the proper button and said, "Eh?" into the mouthpiece.

"Well?" asked the Cowboy, his voice inscrutable.

"I'm not dead."

"That's good to hear."

"Anne's dead, and so are all the targets."

"I'm sorry."

"No point in it. It's too late now. But, the civilized world is safe from another nefarious plot, yeah? That's good."

"Cass..." he started, but she cut him off, "later," and hung up.

Her head against the back window, she turned a little towards Wallace and said, "I'm hungry. I want one of Jo's green-chili cheeseburgers and a lot of iced tea."

66

New Mexico

THERE WAS A KNOCK ON THE DOOR.

"Drew, honey, get that, would you please." His wife's voice came from the kitchen, plenty loud enough to be heard over the television. Andrew Jimenez would have rather stayed put, but he knew better. Supper was in the works, no reason to interrupt it for something like answering the door.

He got up, pulled the loop off the hammer of his Vaquero, walked across the room and opened the door. He wasn't expecting anybody in particular, but he sure wasn't expecting what he saw. It was the girl he'd met at Jo's the day before. Didn't remember her name, from somewhere on the east side was all he could recall. She looked dog-tired and then some, leaning on the porch post like it was all that was holding her up.

Jimenez nodded politely and said, "How do, Miss? Can I get you something? Come on inside." She nodded in thanks and followed his gesture inside.

"Have a seat. You want some coffee?" He shrugged. "It's

decaffeinated, damn those doctors, but it's pretty good all the same."

She nodded again. "Thank you."

When he returned with the coffee, she hadn't moved hardly at all, but her eyes seemed a little clearer, more focused. Before he could ask what she was looking for, or figure out how to ask, she made it unnecessary.

"Heard you had a couple of horses for sale?" She smiled a little, like she knew too much.

"Don't think so."

Her smile widened. "I won't tell nobody so long as you sell me two or three. That's good stock and there ain't nobody that owns 'em anymore. No point in not getting some good outta all this. Can't help it if they jumped the fence, now can you?""

Jimenez frowned. "Who are you?"

"I like rain, guns, and fast horses."

She sat down the half empty mug and stood. "I'll give you ten thousand for my pick of three and halters for all of 'em." She tossed something at him and he caught it, barely. It was money. Ten thousand. He gave it to his wife, promised an unneeded explanation and followed the girl outside.

By the time he found her, she had two ponies caught and one more on the run. He watched, noting with some relief that she knew her stuff. Unfortunately, he realized, she was doing a very good job of picking three horses.

"This'll do. Thanks," she said, letting him open the gate and let her out of the corral. She led her horses out and handed two of the lead ropes to him. "Hold these a sec," she said, and started messing with the other. As he watched, she looped the lead rope over and tied it back under the halter, making reins of a sort. She put a foot on one of the fence rails and threw her other leg up and over the horse's back. She put her hand out for the other leads.

"Okay, then. Good luck." He handed her the other horses and she left without another word. He watched her go until he couldn't see her anymore. When she was good and gone, he checked the gate and went back inside. Supper was waiting.

67

New Mexico

CASS WALKED the horses a distance, getting the feel for them, but she needed to move faster. It was dangerous, running unknown horses in relatively unknown ground, but it needed to be done. She clicked her tongue and tightened her calves and made the horse break into a trot. The other two did the same, wanting to stay together, as horses always do.

She made it back to the O-Bar-Z in good time and was pleased to see that everything was as she left it. The hanger was still burning, but it hadn't spread to her stash. Slipping off the horse, she started saddling. There was more than enough tack to be found and she came up with three good sets of what she needed.

The horse she rode in was a big blue roan with a straight, strong back and powerful-build, good for carting her weight a good ways without getting too tired. Handled decent too. A little cold to start off, but he hadn't tried to buck and that was about all that mattered. She brushed him, checked for burrs, and put on the saddle she'd found. It was a pretty standard western rig, black leather, and not overly tooled. She didn't care for the ones that were tooled all over, they tended to rub worse.

Her main mount all set, she turned her attention to the other two. A well-proportioned, but smaller grey, and a beautiful buckskin. She set them up with pack saddles loaded with the cash and some food she'd robbed from the kitchen. The grey acted good, but the buck was a little flighty. It took a couple of tries to get everything cinched down on him. Cass knew she should've picked a calmer one, but she had a weakness for good-looking buckskins.

She fitted a headstall for each horse, tied the pack horses to the main saddle, checked all the cinches again, and mounted. With a single glance back at the house--the house where Anne died, she pointed her ponies east and a little north and hit the trail. There was a crunch as her cell phone met the underside of a hoof, and then another, softer sound as the battery met a similar fate.

68

Idaho

THE GIRL'S NAME was Opel and Bobby took her home. The silent stage didn't last. She talked the entire way and not a bit of it was banter. He realized, disturbingly, that he'd rather talk to Cass. Despite how irritating she seemed to be. One way or the other, he was very glad when he dropped her off.

He realized he was in Idaho. That was new. He saw a sign for the Clearwater State Highway. That sounded good. He took the turn and hit the gas.

69

New Mexico

THE COWBOY OPENED THE DOOR of his rented pickup, a real one, and stepped out into the hard, dry heat of the High Plains. It was hot. That was all there was to say.

He had not been in contact with Cass Elkins in over a month. After she leveled the O-Bar-Z terror plot, there'd been nothing. No trace of her in any system that could be hacked or tracked. She'd ridden back into town with Wallace, ate a big meal at the local café, and then disappeared. He'd put a tracker on her pickup, but it was still in Ebbson, parked behind the diner.

It wasn't surprising that she'd cut him off, but it was impressive how fast and how thoroughly she'd managed it. She was even better than he'd hoped.

Her intervention had kept whatever they had been developing in that barn out of the world for the time being. Maksim had not believed that the danger was real, but the potential was too great to take any chances. The idea of breeding and infecting the food supply with a strain of wheat, genetically-engineered to produce a toxic protein... Even the slightest chance of success was too much. It had been the perfect first mission for his newest fish. Consequences of failure had been minimal, but it had been real. Not even Maksim had known she was coming until she was there. He had not foreseen the death of the Chavez girl, and although he could not say that unseen factors were not expected, he could say that this particular outcome was dangerous.

Had the girl lived, keeping his involvement in her kidnapping a secret from Cass would have been important, but not critical. Eventually, she would have been so far into the life that she would understand, perhaps not forgive, but forgiveness was not a thing that he needed.

Now, Cass would consider him responsible---and she would be correct. He'd seen that her determination was as unrelenting as he'd desired, but that very weapon would be turned against him. He would have to stop her, and that would be a waste.

But, only one man knew he was involved and that would soon be remedied.

Cass needed a target for her vengeance. The Cowboy needed a man dead. It was tidy and convenient. Now all he had to do was get her moving again.

He left the keys in the ignition and surveyed the ranch that had been the bait. It was dry, but looked like it had gotten a decent shower in the last week or so, judging by the texture of the ground and the hint of green color. What few cows remained were gathered around the windmill, poor and waiting to be fed. The Elkins Family, sans Cass, had weaned and sold the calves the week before. Alan had been monitoring her accounts and it registered when the check was put against the loan. It had been a sad crop of calves and the market was down. There was no way she would be able to keep the ranch. Not without some sort of outside income. Her yearly evaluation with the accountant was scheduled for today. She had to show reasonable progress towards the loan or she would lose her chance. There was no doubt that she would show up and even less that she would be ready to take what he had to offer. He smiled. It was all about the timing.

He went up to the house and let himself in. The lock was easy. He started a pot of coffee and found enough stuff to make breakfast. The appointment was at 9am, and according to his watch, which was rarely wrong, it was a quarter 'till. He sat down with a plate and a cup of coffee and waited.

Nine came and went and he began to doubt. Just after, a small British convertible pulled into the drive. The accountant, he assumed. He was surprised to see a young woman, late teens, he guessed, get out and stomp up the steps. He watched through the window. The girl looked out of place. She wore a bright orange bikini top, denim cutoffs, a beret, and looked good doing it. Only the beat-up cowboy boots belonged on a working ranch.

She opened the door with a key and came in. He leaned back at the kitchen table and tried to act like he belonged. It should have worked. That's when he noticed the resemblance. Cass had a certain look to her eyes when she meant business. Not a glare like some people, no, a flatness, a cold look that made one think of steel or granite.

Her sister had that same look as she pointed a large revolver at his heart, if he had to guess her target. The hammer was already back and her finger hovered over the trigger. Very professional.

"What are you doing here?" She kept the gun steady. Definitely a family resemblance. "Are you from the bank?"

"No, I'm not from the bank."

"Are you a fed?"

"No."

"Then who are you and what are you doing here?"

"I'm a friend of your sister. I was here to see her."

"She ain't here. Can I help you?"

"Do you know when she'll be back? Or where I might find her?"

"She's not here."

"It's about the ranch. Business. I owe her some money."

"I'll tell her you stopped by."

"I'm certain that she needs the money right away. As she told it, the ranch's finances are pretty tight right now."

"That banker came out a week early. I set him straight."

"He'll be back."

The girl grinned and shook her head and she stopped reminding him of Cass. The older Elkins was dangerous, but this one was even better, and smarter. Too smart. He wondered why she thought the banker wouldn't be back. She seemed very sure.

He kept his hands on the table.

"I took the liberty of making a pot of coffee, can I get you some?"

She took a deep whiff of the air and cocked her head to the side. "Smells decent. Go ahead."

She tracked him with her gun, not as stiff as Cass, not as focused, but he got the impression that this kid was more of a natural. He did not take her relaxed posture as a sign of weakness. He put the mug on the table and sat back down. She sat down across from him and took a sip.

"Not bad," she said.

"Well, if you'll allow me to, I'll leave you. Just give your sister a message for me." He started to stand up and she leaned forward and shook her head once. He got the message.

"Tell her yourself."

"Carlos," Cass Elkins said from behind him. "Meet my little sister."

"There's definitely a resemblance," he said. "It's a pleasure."

"Sure." The kid didn't relax a bit.

"If I wanted to talk to you, I would've," said Cass, still behind him.

"I have something you need."

"That a fact?" She stepped around into view, arms crossed, eyes flat.

"I believe I owe you some money."

"Well that's nice, but it'd wait."

"Your loan is up for review today, is it not? And I can see you got a little rain, but those cows are mighty thin. I thought you'd want the money now."

"That's mighty thoughtful, but I'm doing just fine. I took care of it yesterday. I'm sure you could've got in touch with my banker if all you wanted was to pay up. What's the real score?"

"I have a name for you. Pyotr Derchev."

"And?" She hid it well, but he knew he'd finally broken through. He could sense the wounds, still raw, that rose to the surface. "That the guy who did it?"

"Yes."

"You got more than a name?"

He, slowly, pulled an opaque plastic tube from his pocket and handed it to her. "In there. Read fast."

"Or what, it'll self-destruct?" The kid giggled.

The Cowboy nodded. "Exactly."

"Cool," she said.

Cass was looking hard at the tube, but hadn't opened it yet. She looked at him. "What am I supposed to do with this?"

"Whatever you think needs done."

She started popping the knuckles of her left hand and nodded. "Can the system get him?"

"No. He's too connected. He's dangerous."

She put the tube in her pocket and crossed her arms again. "Thanks. Now you can leave."

She nodded at her sister. "Make sure he makes it to the highway."

The girl said, "Yep," and followed him out. She watched him until he headed out and then followed him several miles until he reached the highway. She was still watching when he finally went over a little hill and lost sight of her.

He relaxed and smiled.

The hook was set.

ABOUT THE AUTHOR

Brown, a proud resident of the Texas-Arizona Border, is a world-champion martial artist, a competitive shooter, a lifelong cattleman, and an avid collector of hobbies.

For more, check out:
www.al-brown.com
and
www.facebook.com/ToughTarget

www.ingramcontent.com/pod-product-compliance
Lightning Source LLC
Chambersburg PA
CBHW050559260626
47157CB00002B/624